LIPSTICK
IN THE BASEMENT

B. Bernard Ferguson

Desert Rocks Publishing

10170 W. Tropicana Avenue #156148, Las Vegas, Nevada, 89147-8465

This novel is a work of fiction. The characters, names, incidents, dialogue, and plot are the products of the author's imagination or are used fictitiously. Any resemblance to actual persons, companies, or events is purely coincidental.

Book Cover Design by WordSugar Designs

ISBN: 978-0-9978651-1-0

To the memory of

Narsis Reese Ferguson

(1925-2009)

Table of Contents

Acknowledgements

I am indebted to my childhood friends and beta readers, Alan and Kim Zinsmeister of Los Angeles, California, for your unyielding support and for the input both of you provided throughout the writing of this novel. Thank you so much!

Thanks also to Jeannine Martin of San Jose, California for not only serving as one of my beta readers, but for being my sounding board throughout this writing journey. Your steadfast encouragement has always meant the world to me.

Special thanks to my wife, Diane, not only for your continued love and support, but for sacrificing a portion of our precious time together just so that I can sit in front of my computer, imagining life through the minds of my fictional characters. I love you more than my words can ever express!

LIPSTICK
IN THE BASEMENT

CHAPTER 1

Saturday, December 13
Reese Valley Lighthouse Park
11:48 a.m.

In his former life, Braxton Steele had been a second lieutenant in the United States Army, where, following in the footsteps of his father, Colonel Frank Steele, he'd requested assignment to the army base in Stuttgart, Germany. The same base where not only his father had served, but where he'd spent nearly equal time living between Poland and Germany, so much so that he had been able to learn both Polish and German as second languages. Stuttgart was also where psychological counselling revealed that years of childhood abuse had taken its toll, implanting invisible scars so severe Steele had yet to separate from.

During his deployment in Germany, part of his assignment had entailed flying military-grade drones to monitor troop movements. He had also been responsible for interrogating enemy combatants, skills he'd hoped would be adaptable for civilian use once he left the service, an event that unfortunately happened much sooner than expected when his and Madison's lives had turned upside down following the loss of their first child during the eighth month of pregnancy. Within weeks of the baby's death,

Steele had resigned his officer commission and requested a return to the States.

Following his discharge, he and Madi had moved to Reese Valley, a little suburb with a population of twenty-two thousand located on the Puget Sound, between Edmonds and Everett, approximately twenty-five miles north of Seattle. Thirteen months after moving to their new home, the Steeles had been blessed with a son they named Grant. Eager for employment, Steele accepted a position at Edward Jones Investments while, at the same time, resuming his collegiate studies in pursuit of a master's degree in criminal psychology. After three years on the job and not finding the work fulfilling, he quit and joined the ranks of the RVPD where, on just his second day on the job, he was first on scene at a homicide that turned out to be the first of many that would occur in the little seaside town.

Fast forward. On a gloomy Saturday afternoon in Reese Valley, the usual crowd had gathered at Lighthouse Park. Most of them stopping what they were doing to watch Steele launch the SLX Phantom R3-Standard Quadcopter and maneuver the drone high above their heads. Flying the drone was all he could do these days to recreate to the extent possible, the adrenalin rush he experienced during his military days.

At first, the SLX performed a barrage of aerial acrobatics over the parking lot before darting far out over the Puget Sound disappearing into the fog. Suddenly, it reappeared and sped along the breakwater to the delight of the crowd that clapped and cheered as the drone came to an abrupt stop and hovered just above their heads. The SLX was a beast. Capable of flying at speeds of up to 50 MPH for about twenty-five minutes on a single charge and came equipped with a 3.5K HD video camera allowing it to livestream images from up to a half mile away.

After a quick ten-minute flight, Steele was ready to pack it in for the day when he gave in to chants from the crowd for an encore. He still had some juice left, so without hesitation, he pulled back on the lever, and the SLX took off like a rocket. Onlookers again cheered as they watched the drone descend from the sky and speed straight toward the lighthouse before coming to a blunt stop within feet of passersby who were walking along the white picket fence.

Soon thereafter, the SLX could be seen hovering over the rocks at the water's edge. Steele saw something on the controller panel that caught his attention. He maneuvered the SLX in for a closer look and realized that the object he'd spotted in the water was a deceased body floating face down. Even on the small panel, the bruising around the left ankle was as plain as day. His heart started racing, and all he could think about was how history seemed to be repeating itself. This time, however, instead of being that rookie cop when the Reese Valley murder investigation was first opened, he was now the lead detective on the case.

Scene 1

10 Marine View Drive
Reese Valley, Washington
12:30 p.m.

Professor Atticus Dobson peered through a pair of high-powered binoculars from the distant hills overlooking the lighthouse as police officers and crime scene analysts methodically paced along the shoreline just beyond the seawall, looking for evidence. He grinned at what he considered to be a spectacle, knowing that regardless of how long or hard they searched, it would be nearly impossible to link any evidence they might find to him. Shortly after they'd arrived, officers had pulled the woman's bloated body from the water. He figured it wouldn't be long before RVPD notified the public of her name, although that really wasn't of much concern to him. He already knew who she was.

Atticus was tired of the charade, and for whatever reason, he suddenly became agitated and stormed downstairs where he started pacing back and forth across the dimly lit basement of his quaint little coastal home bequeathed to him by his late grandfather, Eugene Hilborn. With every pass, he kicked his foot violently toward the shackles affixed to the end of the thick chains. After the first abduction, he'd purchased a concrete saw from the Home Depot on Highway 99 and cut square-foot openings in the basement floor before cementing the four bolt-hold anchors in place. On occasion, up to two women would be shackled in the basement at the same time, none of them ever lasting more than three days.

Atticus had managed to deal with the headaches for the past five years but after his most recent murder, the pounding in his head just wouldn't let up. He tried to calm himself, to put his mind somewhere else. Anywhere else. But the pain continued to intensify, a sure sign that the itch had returned where scratching meant killing again.

He walked over to the workbench and began staring intently at the ultraviolet light, something he did often, but substantially more during the winter months when his seasonal affective disorder zapped his spirits. Shortly after moving to the northwest and not being able to shake what he thought was just a severe case of the blahs, he'd started seeing a clinical psychologist and had learned that the lack of sunlight was behind his chronic depression.

After sitting in front of the UV light for a while, Atticus scraped his hand across the top of the workbench, clearing away a few scattered dust-size pieces of metal left over from the last end cap he'd drilled into. Then he opened the drawer where he kept his knives and began gazing at his "little babies," as he affectionately referred to them. He loved them equally, but the two that got most of his attention were the breaking knife, because of its ability to cut through carcasses, and the boning knife, because of how easy it made slicing and trimming.

There was a skinning knife in the drawer, but the last time he had used it was when he was seven during the time he and his parents had briefly lived in Nevada. He'd trapped a small bunny behind his home, and rather than kill the animal first, he'd used two large rusty nails to stake the animal's hind legs to the hardened ground before removing its fur while the bunny whined and squirmed until its heart beat no more. When he was done, Atticus ripped the bloodied animal from the nails and flung it deep into the desert brush. Still, even though he hadn't killed in several years, he had never stopped wondering what it would be like to remove the skin of a human.

The last of his babies was his cleaver, the only knife in the drawer he had yet to use. Just looking at the knife was enough to cause his heart to skip a beat, and when he felt the sweat beads starting to gather on his forehead, he slammed the drawer shut. Atticus reached down and tugged on the handle of the cabinet below, and as soon as he opened the door, he saw the decomposed rodent that had obviously gotten into the rat poison before slipping through one of the small gaps in the cabinet several years earlier.

He kicked the dead rodent aside and then got on his knees to take inventory of the contents. Everything was covered with dust. But it was all accounted for. The rope, saw, stun gun, flashlight, batteries, tackle box, double-sided zip ties, duct tape, latex gloves, drill, several meat hooks, and five little brown bottles labeled CHCl3, better known as chloroform, which although banned as a consumer product in the United States since 1976, Atticus knew exactly where to get more of, should his on-hand supply ever run dry. It was all there, just as he'd left it.

He closed the cabinet doors, stood up, and opened the knife drawer for one last look. There was just something about that cleaver that made him want to touch it. Atticus wanted to close the drawer and just walk away, but the attraction was too great, and when he couldn't take it any longer, he snatched the cleaver from the drawer and immediately began walking—actually, running—toward the large, stainless steel double doors.

He pulled one open, stuck his hand inside, and flicked on the light to illuminate the temperature-controlled meat freezer. In his psychotic state, he hoped that he had left at least one of the women in there. But it was not to be, as both the metal shelving along the walls of the freezer and the meat hooks that ran along the ceiling were desolate.

Still holding the cleaver in his hand, he stepped inside and stood on the bloodstained metal grate that covered the drain pan. It had been years since he'd given the grates a good scrubbing, and over time, a good number of the one-inch square openings had become clogged with dried blood and flesh from animals he had hunted and skinned in the freezer. He suddenly noticed what appeared to be fingers sticking out from under the pile of burlap sacks at the rear of the freezer.

His heart raced as he stepped toward the rear of the cold compartment where, one by one, he began removing the burlap sacks from the pile and tossing them aside, first slowly, then progressively faster as the bottom of the pile began to draw nearer. Nothing. All that remained was a limb from one of the women he'd dismembered years earlier.

After laying the cleaver atop the pile of burlap sacks, he reached his hand to the top shelf of the freezer, grabbed one of the six small plastic trays, and peeled back the lid, exposing a set of human eyeballs frozen in the blood of the victim they had been removed from. He stared at the contents and rubbed his hand slowly across the reddish-colored frozen matter. All signs of life had vanished from the eyes a long time ago. Still, Atticus knew exactly which of the women they had come from. He could see their faces, including the similarity in the fear that registered in their eyes just before he slit their throats.

"Why are you looking at me!" His voice echoed through the freezer loud enough to cause the metal walls to shake. He continued staring into the plastic tray and, in his rage, grabbed hold of one of the S-shaped meat hooks and flung it violently along the top rail of the meat freezer, crashing into the hooks nearest the door.

Atticus slammed the tray down hard on the shelf, then picked up the cleaver. He ran out of the freezer and straight over to the workbench, where he leaned over and blew the dust off the Smith-Corona Classic 12. About five years had passed since he'd last used his old typewriter. But now that he had killed again, it was time to update the manuscript.

CHAPTER 2

As he stood in his office and looked across the parking lot into the forest of evergreens, the only thing the detective could see clearly on this supposed day of rest was the reflection of himself in the window. Not only a good investigator, Steele also topped the list when it came to Reese Valley's finest officers, and while his demeanor was always as solid as his name implied, he never let on to his colleagues just how difficult it was for him to deal with these types of investigations. The murders seemed to reawaken horrid memories of when he'd lost his daughter, and with each one, it was as if he was losing his little girl all over again. So here he was, forced to once again reflect upon the day he'd pushed his way through the heavy double-doors at the rear of Zagan Poland Military Hospital only to be immediately sickened by the sound of little heartbeats echoing throughout the hallway.

Thump-thump, thump-thump, thump-thump. The sound had seemed to grow louder the closer he got to Madi's room. She had been rushed to the maternity ward, and there must have been at least ten expecting moms on the floor preparing to give birth, each of them hooked to fetal monitors that emitted the joyous sound of happy little heartbeats. Except for the monitor strapped to Madi's stomach. Their baby had died.

Steele had opened the door to the examination room, and the sight of despair on Madi's face was all he needed to see in order to corral his emotions. He knew that for the time being, the most important thing for him to do was to mask his true feelings and be strong for her. He walked over to Madi and placed his arms around her, inadvertently laying his arm across her stomach. His heart had ached, knowing that although he and Madi would follow through with the normal childbirth process, their baby would not be breathing when they entered the world.

The two of them had spent the next twenty minutes crying in each other's arms until both had completely emptied the tears from their bodies. They knew this sudden shock to their psyches would affect them for years to come and that they would likely never fully get over it. They also knew it was time to summon Dr. Wells to the room to induce labor. The outcome was inevitable with no way of getting around it, and at a few minutes before three the next morning, after only four pushes, Madi had given birth to a beautiful baby girl they named Ania. It was a Polish name that means "grace."

Steele had sat stoically in the chair next to the bed, staring at the back of Madi's head for several hours as she lay facing the wall. He knew his wife was awake. He could hear her sniffling as she tried to choke back sobs. Siting there in the subdued lighting, many of the questions one would normally expect from someone who had just lost their child raced through his mind. *How could something such as this happen to us?* followed by, *what in the world could we have ever done to deserve this? We have tried our very best to live a decent life, not bothering anyone, and always respecting others, so why is God punishing us?* Steele had sat there telling himself to pull it together, but the questions just wouldn't stop coming.

At seven fifty-five and with Madi still lying with her back toward him, Steele had gotten up and leaned over into the bed.

"It's time for that meeting, sweetheart."

"I know," she'd responded. "I just can't pull myself to go through that right now. Would you mind going down there by yourself?"

In the midst of their grieving, Steele and Madi had made the decision to have Ania's little body cremated and her ashes scattered off the coast of the Baltic Sea.

"I'll take care of it," he'd replied, before kneeling next to the bed as he had done at home on numerous occasions. He placed his hand on Madi's shoulder and began praying.

"Father God, I know that you make no mistakes. Be with me and Madi as we journey on together without Ania. Comfort us as we mourn and help us to remember that we are not alone. Grant us the light of Your love in the darkness of grief. Amen."

"Amen," Madi had responded in a soft voice. She opened her eyes, turned toward Steele and extended her arms toward his as he held her tightly.

Steele was so caught up in his thoughts that he never heard Randy Polk walk up. Randy wasn't just a good friend, he was the one analyst in the lab who Steele knew he could always count on for a quick turnaround.

"Excuse me, Detective. Sorry to bother you," Randy said from the doorway.

"No need to apologize. You have something for me?"

"I figured you'd want to see this right away. The medical examiner's report is in, and it looks like the same person who killed those other women is at it again," Randy responded, handing the report to Steele.

"Thanks, Randy," Steele replied, taking hold of the report and walking toward his desk.

The medical examiner confirmed the identity of the deceased woman to be Sylvia Larson, a twenty-year-old Caucasian woman who was reported missing two days ago. According to the report, her throat had been slashed with what appeared to be a large serrated knife, and both of her eyes were missing. There were also skin abrasions on her left leg near the ankle. The coroner estimated she had been murdered approximately twenty-four hours prior to her body being discovered, and it appeared she'd been killed at some other location before her body was dumped in the water.

Steele searched through the DMV database and pulled a copy of Sylvia's drivers license. He learned she lived at the same address as her aunt, the individual who had called RVPD to report that Sylvia had never come home after work.

CHAPTER 3

Monday, December 15
RVPD Headquarters
2:00 p.m.

Media kits had been distributed earlier in the day, and at two o'clock, several news trucks lined the narrow street in front of RVPD Headquarters as Steele walked out and took to the podium to brief the crowd.

"Good afternoon, everyone. At this time, all I have is preliminary information, but I wanted to at least update you on our investigation surrounding the body of the individual pulled from the Puget Sound yesterday afternoon. The name of the deceased is Sylvia Larson, a twenty-year-old Reese Valley resident. The official cause of death was a knife cut to the throat. With that, I'll try to answer as many of your questions as possible."

There was movement in the crowd as a man's voice rang out.

"Do you believe this murder is any way connected to the murder of those other five women, Detective?"

Preferring to know who he was speaking to, Steele tried in vain to associate the voice with a person, and when he couldn't, he decided to answer the question anyway.

"Again, it's way too early in our investigation to make definitive conclusions. That said, because of similarities in the manner in which this victim died when compared to prior victims, that is certainly one investigative track we're following."

"Detective Steele, am I hearing you correctly that you believe the same killer has resurfaced and is now lose in our community?" a female reporter he had never seen before asked.

"No. I'm not saying that. And you are?"

"Jolynn Rider. With the *Reese Valley Herald*," she responded. "So you're saying this murder has nothing to do with the deaths of all of those women way back when?"

"I'm not saying that either. Again, it's way too early to rule out anything. We're exploring every angle, including a possible connection to those past murders, and when I have additional information, I'll hold another press conference."

"Okay, I'll accept that, Detective. But can you at least give us a typical profile of who we should be looking out for on the chance we do have a serial killer in our community?" Jolynn asked.

Steele thought long and hard about the question before answering.

"A typical serial killer may have been a victim of childhood abuse, either mental or physical, or even sexual. They may be a loner, but could also be your average Joe, someone who blends into the community without bringing much attention to themselves. They are likely a white male in their midtwenties or possibly thirties. They have a real affinity with power, and they're able to easily manipulate others. They're egotistical, but at the same time, they're charmers, knowing exactly how to tap into another person's weakness, getting them to do things they normally wouldn't."

There was some noticeable shuffling back and forth among the reporters, but when no questions came his way, Steele resumed speaking.

"I would also like to get the word out to the public that, just this morning, RVPD put up a ten-thousand-dollar reward for information leading to the identification and arrest of the person responsible for this crime. Any information, no matter how insignificant it may seem, should be called into our tip line."

After lobbing the first question, Atticus opted to linger at the back of the crowd. He had gotten exponentially more from the press conference than he'd anticipated. The new reporter in town, Jolynn Rider, made it all worthwhile. She had caught his attention the moment she started speaking. Not only was she assertive, but also she didn't try to hide her skepticism. Atticus watched Jolynn as she approached the detective and exchanged business cards. She was perfectly suited for what he had in mind.

Scene 1

Reese Valley State University
5:00 p.m.

It was five o'clock straight up, and with the exception of the usual few stragglers, everyone was seated. As he always did, Professor Atticus Dobson adjusted his wire-rim glasses as he stepped away from the table at the front of the room to face his students. Like clockwork, he cleared his throat while, at the same time, adjusting his bow tie.

"Well, everyone, you made it to the last class, and for those of you brave enough to have allowed me to torment you over the past months, I applaud you. Please give yourselves a hand."

There was immediate cheers throughout the classroom.

Atticus smiled as he looked out across the room, before abruptly closing his binder and returning it to his briefcase.

"I tell you what," he said. "Rather than putting you through one final lecture, I would like to switch things up a bit this evening. You've indulged me for the past several weeks by sitting in here taking notes, listening to my lectures, and muddling through pop quizzes, so I think it's only fair to allow you to ask those pressing questions about me that I know are on your minds."

Again, the students cheered as they clapped their hands and banged on the desktops.

"So who wants to start?"

Diane Howard raised her hand.

"Yes, Ms. Howard," Atticus said, acknowledging the student.

"Professor, when did you first know that you wanted to be a psychologist?"

"Great question. I would have to say that it was during my sophomore year of college when I needed one additional course to be considered full-time and psychology was the only course that seemed to fit into both my work and academic schedule. But then, I got this harebrained idea that if I learned enough about how humans think, I could then use that knowledge to get over on my parents. So I kept taking psychology courses, and before long, it only made sense to stick with the program if I wanted to graduate on time."

The class erupted in laughter, a bit surprised that the always serious professor had a playful side he'd kept hidden from his students all semester.

"Wow, I didn't expect that answer, but I have to admit I like it," Diane responded.

"Yep. It may have started out for all the wrong reasons, but I actually became fascinated with the field of psychology, and to this day, I can't think of another discipline I'd rather focus my attention. Great question. Who else has a question for me?"

Roger Grimes raised his hand from the back of the classroom.

"Yes, sir. What would you like to ask me?"

"I have a question, Professor, but not for you. All semester long, I've been wanting to ask the detective something."

"That's not at all what I had in mind when I suggested we do this, but I will leave it up to the detective as to whether or not he wishes to take questions from his fellow classmates."

Steele stood and faced the back of the room.

"Sure, no problem. What's on your mind?"

"Well, Detective, at the beginning of class when we all introduced ourselves, you mentioned that the most important aspect of psychology for you is that it allowed you to control your emotions."

"Yeah, what about it?"

"Well, with all the stuff in the news about police officers these days, I was just wondering how was that working for you?"

Laughter immediately filled the room as several students turned in their seats toward Roger, not surprised in the least that he would come up with such a below-the-belt question, but just as quickly, other students began chiming in on how awful and inappropriate such a question was, and while Atticus was on the verge of stepping in, he decided to just allow things to carry on for a while longer primarily for his own amusement, but also so that he could see the detective in action.

Steele continued looking toward Roger without immediately responding.

"Most of the time," he finally said in a stern voice, causing the laughter in the classroom to come to an abrupt halt. After another short pause, he said, "I still seem to struggle when I'm being provoked, though."

Roger was not quite finished with his joking and decided to keep pushing.

"Well, I guess I'd better not provoke you if we ever encounter one another outside of class, Detective."

"That would be quite wise on your part, Mr. Grimes," Steele replied.

The vibe in the room had taken a turn for the worse, and the laughter was gone. More than his response, it was the way the detective said it that immediately put everyone on notice that he was not one to be played with.

Although Steele never raised his voice during the entire time Roger had been attempting to make him the butt of his little joke, there was no doubt that he meant every word about it being best that he not be provoked.

Steele calmly sat back down but continued looking toward Roger, who tried his best to focus on anything other than the detective's gaze. You could hear a pin drop, and for the next fifteen seconds or so, time seemed to stand still in the classroom with the only sound being the occasional student shifting in their chair.

Taking note of the overwhelming sense of discomfort within the room and wanting to get things back on track, Atticus stepped in to break the tension.

"Okay, that seemed to get a bit off track, but still, I'm hoping each of you noticed how psychology played into that little exchange. For those of you planning a future in psychology, its vitally important that you are able to recognize both verbal and nonverbal cues individuals are projecting and then adjust accordingly. That's all I'll say about that for now."

Everyone continued to look straight ahead toward the front of the room, not wanting to lock eyes with Steele who continued glancing around the room every fifteen seconds or so, even though Atticus had attempted to restore order. Two things were for certain. As much as the detective tried to blend in by giving that spiel about just being another student, he was still a cop at heart. Secondly, there was no way he was going to just sit back and allow some young punk half his age who reeked of privilege get away with talking shit to him. Time flew by and before long, the clock made a loud ticking sound as the hands shifted over to the eight o'clock hour. Class was over, and for most students—Roger Grimes, in particular—it couldn't have come soon enough.

"Well, class, looks like this semester has officially come to an end, and with that, I wish each of you a very joyous holiday. Please enjoy your winter break, and I hope to see several of you next semester in my criminal behavior course."

Atticus pretended to be busy with his paperwork, but more than anything else, his attention was squarely on the detective. He had seen enough. More, in fact. His objective in allowing the banter to continue longer than necessary was merely so that he could get a read on the detective's tolerance level as well as how he would respond if pushed. For years, he watched Steele during press conferences and often wondered if the detective was really as cool under pressure as he appeared or if that was just some facade being portrayed before the camera for public consumption. He asked the detective about his plans for next semester and was thrilled to learn that he would again have him in class.

For as long as he could remember, Atticus wanted to get inside the detective's head. He was tired of twisting the minds of impressionable teenage students and needed a challenge, someone who would push back and wasn't so gullible as to believe anything he'd throw their way just because of his status within the university. Steele was perfect, and now Atticus had the detective right where he wanted him.

CHAPTER 4

Tuesday, December 16
RVPD Headquarters
10:30 a.m.

It was standing room only when Detective Steele entered the briefing room, holding a manila folder in one hand and carrying a box under the other arm marked with a large sticker that read EVIDENCE. With the last murder occurring about five years ago in the case that drew national attention to the little Reese Valley suburb for all the wrong reasons, everyone anxiously awaited the detective's briefing on the recent death of Sylvia Larson, particularly after word began to spread around the department about a possible connection between the current investigation and several unsolved murders. The envelope containing $160 with the word *slut* written across the front of the currency had arrived at RVPD within the past hour.

"Let's go ahead and get started," Steele opened. "Because the initial murders in this case occurred years before the majority of you in this room today were even on the force, I thought it would be beneficial if I take some time and lay out the entire chain of events, including why I think we may be dealing with the same person."

Steele opened the folder and removed five photographs of women and pinned them to the large corkboard at the front of the room. The photos were obtained from the Department of Motor Vehicles, or in some cases, the victim's social media profile. Looking at the photographs five years after they had been filed away, the same thing that stood out then stood out now. They were all beautiful but different in every way from their ages to their races. Their hairstyles ranged from ponytails to dreadlocks. The tallest woman was six foot two while the shortest was just shy of five feet. The one commonality among the photographs, however, was that, aside from wearing heavy makeup, the lips of each of the women were covered with bright red lipstick.

Steele pointed to the photograph on the far left side of the board.

"The first victim, Belinda O'Connell, a twenty-three-year-old Caucasian woman. Her naked body washed ashore behind Reese Valley Lighthouse Park. Her throat was cut using a large serrated knife, and both of her eyes were removed. There were also skin abrasions on her left leg just above the ankle, leading us to believe a shackle was likely used to restrain her mobility."

Steele pointed toward the second photograph on the board.

"About thirty days later, Gretchen Sullivan, a thirty-seven-year-old Caucasian woman, was killed in the same fashion—a deep cut to the throat, both eyes removed, and skin abrasions just above the left ankle. A hiker came across her naked body while walking their dog through Lower Reese Gulch Park Trail Head when the dog broke loose and ran deep into the woods and started barking incessantly, resulting in the hiker eventually following the trail to determine the cause of the dog's refusal to heed the command to return."

Steele tapped his finger on the third and fourth photographs on the board.

"Continuing on, our next two victims, Amanda Johnson, a nineteen-year-old African American, and Christina Perez, an eighteen-year-old Hispanic, were killed using what we believe was the same serrated knife, but in both instances, the victims were nearly decapitated. Like the others, their eyes were removed, and skin abrasions were present on the left leg. Their naked bodies were discovered in an abandoned van parked on Front Street near Reese Valley Lighthouse Park after the vehicle was cited for parking violations. Responding to a report of a suspicious van in the area, a police officer arrived on scene, where, in addition to noticing the pungent odor coming from the van, the officer spotted a swarm of flies making their way into and out of the partially cracked driver-side window. When the officer got close enough to peer through the front windshield, she saw what appeared to be a foot sticking out from under a gray wool blanket in the rear compartment. Based on parking citations, the bodies appear to have been there for at least two days before being discovered."

Steele tapped his finger on the final photograph at the far-right end of the board.

"Victim number five. Seoyeon Kim, a twenty-one-year-old Korean. Just like the other women, her eyes were removed. However, rather than her throat being slashed, it appears she was strangled to death. Additionally, her left hand was cut off and was never recovered. She too had skin abrasions on her left leg just above the ankle. A jogger found her naked body propped behind the steering wheel of her car parked near the overpass next to the railroad tracks that run alongside Reese Gulch, which marked a change in the killer's routine. In addition to the missing limb and the ligature marks around her neck, during the autopsy, it was also discovered that a purple orchid flower was inserted deep into her throat."

Steele paused for a moment before speaking again.

"But were it not for the quick thinking of the officer first on scene, this could have been much, much worse. It was after dark when they located the vehicle, and noticing the driver side window was rolled down, rather than just opening the car door, the officer used their flashlight to inspect the interior. That's when they noticed a trip wire attached to the bottom portion of the driver side door and running along the carpet toward the back seat. As it turned out, the suspect had secreted a pipe bomb in the trunk of the vehicle next to the gas tank. Lucky for us, the vehicle was parked in a remote area that allowed us to deploy our bomb disposal robot to open the trunk without fear of causing harm to nearby residents should the bomb happen to explode in the process. Once we got the trunk open, we used a water cannon to disarm the device before removing the body."

Steele pulled one of the small plastic bags from the box and held it up for a moment for the officers to see.

"About a week after the first murder, an envelope with three twenty-dollar bills with bright red lipstick spelling out the word *slut* written across the front arrived at the front desk, but because it didn't contain a note of any kind, the envelope was just plopped in the eccentric file. A week after the second murder, we received another envelope, this time with two one-hundred and three twenty-dollar bills with the word *slut* written on them, again using bright red lipstick. Remembering the first cash envelope sitting in the file cabinet, both were sent to the lab for comparison to DNA samples taken from both victims, and just as we suspected, tests confirmed that the lipstick on the currency belong to Belinda and Gretchen."

Steele acknowledged an officer raising his hand.

"Officer Reynolds."

"Sir, do you think the women had the lipstick on them when they were abducted, or do you believe the perpetrator got into their homes at some point?"

"That remains an unknown. What we do know is that about a week after each murder, an envelope containing varying amounts of currency with the word *slut* written across the front arrived at our front desk."

Steele paused to again look around the briefing room.

"But it gets worse. In each instance, when the bodies were discovered, the faces were cleansed of any trace of cosmetics, and the lips of each victim was burned using some sort of acid that took off the top layer of skin leaving severe scarring around the edges of the mouth. Finally, it's important to note that, in each of the cases, it appears the women were killed somewhere other than where their bodies were discovered."

The briefing room was quiet as police officers mulled over what they had just heard, grateful that the photographs of the women pinned to the corkboard looked like glamor shots depicting women with perfectly styled hair, warm eyes, and bright smiles as opposed to how their mutilated bodies must have looked at the time they were discovered.

Steele pulled Sylvia's photograph from the manila folder and pinned it to the board next to the five women.

"The medical examiner's report showed a deep, oblique, long, incised injury on the front of the victim's neck. There were no defensive injuries and findings were compatible with a homicidal cut throat by a right-handed person from behind after the head was restrained firmly."

The detective pulled the autopsy photo from the folder and handed it to one of the officers on the front row to start passing around.

"I want each of you to take a good look at the cut to Ms. Larson's neck so that there is no misunderstanding as to what we are dealing with here. This person is extremely dangerous, and we have to pull out all the stops if we're going to catch them."

Steele began walking around the briefing room, looking into the eyes of each officer as they glanced at the autopsy photo before passing it along. Some of the officers made it known that they were disgusted at what the perpetrator had done to the young woman and vowed to make an arrest while others were visibly shaken by what they saw in the photograph, with one officer asking to be excused to compose himself.

Steele walked to the back of the room and retrieved the photo.

"Okay. I think I can safely say that everyone in here understands the gravity of this situation. Are there any questions I can answer for anyone before I take off?"

Seeing none, Steele resumed speaking.

"Very well. We have a few leads that need to be run down associated with the Larson murder. Stay put for a minute while Detective Lomax hands out assignments."

As soon as Steele left the briefing room, his cell phone started vibrating. He pulled it from his pocket.

"Steele."

"Nice job, Detective," the distorted voice on the other end of the phone said. "I'm a bit perplexed as to why, during your little talk yesterday, you didn't mention anything about the girl's eyes missing or the marks around her ankles. That said, I do appreciate the part about me being charming, although I don't view myself as egotistical in the least bit. A more accurate description would be that I'm a person who is just extremely sure of himself."

"So you were there."

"By the way, it sounded to me like the two of us have something in common."

"And what could that be?"

"Our parents, Detective. We both had parents who screwed up our heads."

Steele started thinking about the strained relationship he had with his father and, in the process, forgot he was on the phone, which delayed his response. After a much longer pause than he would've liked, he resumed speaking.

"We have nothing in common!"

But the damage was done. Atticus was actually just throwing mud on the wall hoping something would stick. And stick it did. Steele fumbled instead of answering and, in doing so, provided the professor with just the opening he needed.

"So, tell me, Detective. Was it your mommy or your daddy who did you wrong?"

"You think this is some sort of game?"

"I know it is," Atticus responded.

"I don't know who you are, but I don't play games."

"Oh, you'll play along. And each time you refuse to answer my question, a woman dies."

"Like I said, I don't play games."

"You don't have a choice, Detective"

"Or what?"

"I already told you what," Atticus responded. Then disconnected the call.

Scene 1

Reese Valley Chocolate Company
4077 Lincoln Avenue
Reese Valley, Washington
1:00 p.m.

Craving some chocolate mint fudge following his phone conversation with the detective, Atticus hopped in his SUV and drove over to the Reese Valley Chocolate Company. After making his purchase and returning to his car, just as he was about to pull away from the curb, he noticed the middle-aged woman walking down Lincoln Avenue. She was the spitting image of his mother, Judith, which caused the hair on the back of his neck to immediately stand up. The woman had an exaggerated hip sway just like his mother, who always looked around when she walked, hoping someone was watching. She even wore her hair the same way, pinned high up on her head, and even from thirty yards away, Atticus could clearly see the thick layer of bright red lipstick on the woman's lips.

He turned the engine off and watched through teary eyes as the woman disappeared into the little chocolate shop. His heart began to pound as the horrors of his childhood came roaring back. He recalled all of the times he would kick and scream, then kick some more, then scream some more, until he would finally give in to Judith's death grip as she squeezed his cheeks together and smeared bright red lipstick all over his face while he peed his pants.

He thought about the times he struggled under her weight as she pinned him to the ground and would slap him until he relented.

Why can't you just be normal? She'd scream as loud as she possibly could, her face no more than an inch away from his. *The way you always stand in front of the mirror and pull on your collar like some freak. And then for whatever the hell reason, you like playing with my frigging lipstick. You know what I think, Atticus? I think you're an effing sicko!*

He remembered trying to disappear whenever Judith was around figuring if she couldn't see him, perhaps the physical abuse would somehow stop. But it never did. Atticus looked into the rearview mirror and slightly raised his chin to expose his childhood burn marks, a reminder of the countless times Judith would heat a butter knife on the stove and then press the red-hot metal against his neck before ripping both it and the skin away.

He remembered it all. Perhaps a bit too well. Judith chasing him around the house when he had done wrong, and how he would run upstairs and wedge himself under the bed. He could still hear her voice. *You stay under there until I tell you to come out, and you had better not make a sound,* resulting in the quiet time under the bed sometimes lasting for several hours. Spending so much time under the bed staring through the worn fabric, Atticus had counted the box springs more than a thousand times, and each time, they numbered four hundred. He looked toward the entrance to the chocolate shop, and suddenly, the woman walked out.

"I hate you! I hate you! I hate you!" he yelled, banging his fist on the steering wheel before regaining his composure and breaking into a loud laugh, recalling the beyond-brilliant act he'd put on for the police officers who showed up to inform him that Judith was dead.

Atticus had been twenty-two years old at the time when he'd answered the knock on the front door and found the two RVPD officers standing there. After telling the officers that only he and his mother lived at the residence, the officers relayed the somber news that Judith had been killed in a motor vehicle accident on Highway 167 earlier that morning. According to the officers, her car appeared to have veered across all lanes of the highway and, after clipping a tree, rolled several times before coming to a stop near 212th Street. Once Atticus had composed himself, the officers advised that, unfortunately, they were treating the incident as a homicide because of the bullet wound in the side of Judith's temple, which of course resulted in more crying on Atticus's part and the officers trying to console him as best they could. After expressing their condolences, the officers told Atticus they would be in touch with any further developments in the case and walked away as he stood in the doorway with tears streaming down his face while biting down as hard as he could on the inside of his lip to keep from laughing. He'd known Judith was dead. It had been he who'd murdered her.

Scene 2

83001 7th Street
Reese Valley, Washington
2:00 p.m.

Detective Steele spent the next couple of hours trying to shake his mind away from what he'd gone through on the telephone. The call had come out of nowhere, and be it sheer luck or otherwise, the person on the other end had succeeded in unnerving him. Nonetheless, he would have to deal with that later. Right now, the detective had a murder case to solve.

He opened the desk drawer and began searching through the files until he came across the contact information for Belinda O'Connell's parents. Because he was new to the force and assigned other duties at the time of the murder, this would be his first time speaking with Belinda's parents. Steele picked up the phone and dialed the number. Patrick O'Connell answered on the first ring.

"Hello?"

"Hello. Is this Mr. O'Connell?"

"Yes, it is. Who's calling?"

"Sir, my name is Detective Braxton Steele. I'm the lead detective on the case involving your daughter's murder, and if you wouldn't mind, I'd like to stop by and ask you some additional questions."

"Sure, Detective. I'll assist in any way possible to help bring the coward who killed my daughter to justice. When would you like to stop by?"

"Would two o'clock today work for you, sir?"

"That's fine. I'll see you when you get here."

At a little past two, Steele parked in front of the O'Connell residence, and within minutes, he and Patrick were sitting across from one another at the tiny kitchen table engaging in small talk. Patrick had placed a carafe filled with steaming hot coffee at the center of the table next to a large scrapbook opened to a page with photos of Belinda and his late wife, Evelyn. Belinda had been the O'Connell's only child, and Evelyn had died unexpectedly twenty-three months ago.

Patrick took a sip of coffee from his cup.

"You know, Detective, Evelyn never really recovered from Belinda's death, and while the official cause of her death on her death certificate says a heart attack, I just know my Evelyn died of a broken heart. Our Belinda was her everything. They talked every day, sometimes as many as four or five times."

"I'm so sorry for both of your losses, Mr. O'Connell," Steele responded.

"Thank you, Detective, but you know, every day I seem to get a little stronger, especially since I pass by the cemetery during my afternoon walks, which gives me a chance to just sit on the lawn for a while and talk to my girls. Wish I had them here with me, but I imagine it wasn't in the Lord's plan. Anyway, what is it you wanted to talk to me about?"

"I need to ask you some sensitive questions, sir, and hope you don't find them offensive."

"Let's just see where this goes. Ask away."

"Do you recall whether or not your daughter wore red lipstick often?"

"No more than any other girl her age. Belinda wore several colors of lipstick, although red seemed to be her favorite and the one she wore most of the time. Not really sure what that has to do with anything."

Steele began flipping through the case file.

"That's what I'm trying to determine, sir. Also, I don't see any mention in the investigative notes about your daughter having a companion at the time. Did she have a boyfriend or ever mention that she was serious about anyone in particular?"

"Not that I'm aware of, Detective. My daughter always claimed she was too busy to settle down, you know, with her work and all. She was one of those Youber drivers."

"You mean, Uber?"

"Yeah, I guess. I always thought she was saying Youber. Anyway, she drove people around town anytime she wasn't working at some office building. Belinda worked for some temporary service agency that sent her all over the place. I never really liked all that moving around and would tell her how I wished she'd just stop jumping from job to job and put down some roots."

"I understand."

Steele annotated the case file, then spent the next forty-five minutes or so carefully going over the investigative summary and verifying that everything else noted in the file from the initial interview with Patrick and Evelyn was accurate. He verified that Belinda's parents first reported her missing when she failed to return home on Sunday evening following a weekend of touring the city with out-of-town guests. Three of her high school friends had flown into town and were staying at the McClendon House Bed and Breakfast on 47th.

Investigative notes showed that all three of the friends had been interviewed after they'd left Seattle, but none had been aware that Belinda was missing until they were contacted by police officers days later. In separate interviews, each of the women confirmed that the last time they saw Belinda was when they'd said their goodbyes before leaving Pike Place Market around 6:00 p.m. on Sunday. Investigators had determined that the women were forthcoming, and none had ever been considered persons of interest.

When recalling the events of that evening, Patrick said that Belinda had called him around seven o'clock to say that she was on her way home but was stopping by the Space Pin to see if her hand-painted silk scarf was at the lost and found. Belinda had gone to the Space Pin the week prior, which was the last day she recalled wearing the misplaced garment. When Steele let Patrick know that nowhere in the case file did it mention anything about Belinda being at the Space Pin, Patrick said that he had been so distraught over his daughter's disappearance he may have forgotten to tell that to the investigator who took his statement. Once satisfied that he had gotten all he could from Patrick, Steele stood up.

"Thanks for your time, Mr. O'Connell. You have my word that I'll do all within my power to identify the person responsible for your daughter's death."

"I appreciate you saying that, Detective. Please feel free to stop by anytime. To be honest, it gets a bit lonely these days, and I enjoy the company. I always have fresh coffee."

Steele smiled and nodded his head. "Thank you again, sir. We'll be in touch."

After getting back in his car, Steele took a moment to make a quick note in the case file about Belinda possibly stopping by the Space Pin on the evening she'd gone missing.

Scene 3

87790 53rd Street W
Reese Valley, Washington
5:30 p.m.

Steele arrived home around five thirty, drove his car into the garage, then rushed into the house and into Madi's welcoming arms. The moment he stepped through the door, he was met with the aroma of garlic and onion and fresh shrimp, letting him know that Madi had once again come home early from the office so that she could surprise him with his favorite dish: linguine with shrimp scampi. Unfortunately, the detective's current mental state was ill-equipped to fully appreciate his wife's little surprise. And she could tell immediately.

One look at his face was all it took for Madi to know that her husband was in trouble. She was accustomed to seeing Steele withdraw from the world from time to time and figured that by just letting his emotions run its course, in time, he would fill her in on what was bothering him.

The drive home from the O'Connell residence was grueling, and there were more than a couple of times along the way when Steele had thought he was going to have to pull off the highway just to compose himself. He sensed the onset of his depression creeping in well before he got off the phone with the unexpected caller, and while preparing for the interview with Belinda's father served as a momentary deterrent, he was under no illusion regarding how long he would be able to hold the despair at bay he knew was lingering and waiting for just the right time to rear its ugly head.

Steele's ears became flooded with pain as the ringing grew louder with each passing moment and the horrid images of his abusive father, retired army Colonel Frank Steele, hijacked his brain. He pictured the colonel's hardened face and how, for as long as he could remember, the man was the prototypical drill sergeant who demanded everyone, including his family, address him by his military rank. He thought about how the colonel only respected those who demonstrated strength, and because the colonel consistently reiterated just how weak of a person he believed him to be, nearly every conversation between the two of them seemed to be used merely to highlight Steele's inadequacies.

Although he was merely trying to jerk the detective's chain, Atticus was right on point regarding Steele having parental issues. Steele and the colonel had always shared a somewhat tepid relationship that seemed to only become more fractured with time, and through it all, the colonel never tried to hide the fact that although Steele was his oldest son by five minutes, Brice was his favorite, something that had always pained Steele, causing him to question if the difference in the way he and his brother had been treated was because Brice was nearly a carbon copy of the colonel, while Steele's skin tone and hair texture paralleled the physical characteristics of his African American mother.

Trying to follow in the colonel's footsteps, the twins enlisted in the army under the buddy program, and like the colonel, Brice was a career soldier, spending nineteen years in the service and achieving the rank of captain. Steele, however, although achieving the rank of lieutenant, resigned his commission after only serving ten years when the grief experienced by his family following

Madi's miscarriage made it impossible for the two of them to continue their deployment.

To this day, in spite of Steele excelling within the law enforcement profession and rising through the ranks of the Reese Valley Police Department, the colonel had yet to forgive his son for not being able to, as he put it, "hack it" in the army. Nor did he ever pass on an opportunity to let others know just how proud he was of what Brice was doing in the military, even though his twin brother had unfortunately been killed in an off-duty motor vehicle accident three years ago.

With the ringing in his ears not backing off, Steele pulled his cell phone from his pocket and dialed the number for Dr. Beale. But after only two rings, he hung up. He stood in the middle of the bedroom for a moment before deciding to change out of his work clothes and crawl under the covers, figuring the best way to deal with what he was going through was to take his prescribed medication and just try to sleep it off.

More than two hours had passed since Steele had first hopped into bed, and he was wide awake. The ringing was still there, and the pain in his ears was excruciating. About a thirteen on a ten scale. He pulled two more pills from the drawer and tossed them in his mouth, using only saliva to chase the painkillers down. He gripped his ears, inadvertently digging his fingernails into his skin as he attempted to dampen the pain, and when the detective finally fell asleep, his last mindful thought was an image of the colonel in all his glory, frowning and spewing those hurtful words from his lips he seemed to utter so effortlessly.

It should have been you who died in that car crash instead of Brice.

CHAPTER 5

Wednesday, December 17
87790 53rd Street W
Reese Valley, Washington
4:00 a.m.

The moonlight sneaked its way into the bedroom through the razor-thin opening at the bottom of the shades. It wasn't much, but enough to partially illuminate the detective as he leaned against the door facing staring lovingly at Madi as she lay sound asleep just three feet away. There was a note on the nightstand that read, "I don't expect for you to understand, so, all I'll say is that I just can't take it any longer. The colonel's voice has reached a feverish pitch and the pain in my head has become unbearable. I guess the old man was right after all. Although I gave it my best, it turns out that I'm not as strong a man as I thought I was. My prayer is that one day you will forgive me for what I have done."

Steele left the last words he would ever write in plain view next to the alarm clock, ensuring Madi would find them once she awakened. The yellow sticky note he placed on the nightstand was very specific: "Do not allow Grant into the garage under any circumstances."

He turned and walked down the hallway toward his son's bedroom and noticed that a little stuffed animal had fallen to the floor. He stepped into the room, picked up the toy, and held it close to his chest for a long time as he stood motionless staring at Grant. He prayed that one day when he was old enough to understand, he would forgive him for the hurt and anguish he was about to cause Grant and his mother. After using the furry creature to wipe away his tears, Steele gently tucked the little toy under the blanket next to his son and quietly made his way downstairs and into the garage out back.

He opened the car trunk and removed the freshly laundered police uniform and shiny black shoes, and while he knew the Fraternal Order of Police would support his family in their grief, there was one final detail far too important to leave to anyone else. Steele pulled the life insurance policy from the manila envelope for one final look. He wanted to be certain he had read it correctly. The suicide clause stated that no death benefit would be paid if the insured committed suicide within two years of taking out the policy, but with it being more than ten years old, the detective was confident collecting on the insurance wouldn't be an issue. He returned it to the envelope along with other documents listing account balances with the name and address of various financial institutions, and placed the envelope on the roof of the car so that it would be discovered by investigators.

He also placed an old five-by-five photograph on top of the police cruiser, a feel-good moment showing Steele as a young child, smiling, dressed in a straw hat, printed T-shirt, and cutoff jeans rolled up to his knees to keep his pant legs from getting wet while he stood next to the colonel at the water's edge. For anyone looking at the photo, it would surely conjure up memories of the good old days when fathers and sons spent Sunday afternoons fishing. But for Steele, the photo was bittersweet. While it memorialized the first time he had ever gone fishing, the image also depicted a boy who'd spent his entire life struggling to shed the stigma of being an utter disappointment to his father.

Steele removed his pajamas and donned his police uniform, then slid his wedding band from his finger, and placed it atop the car next to the five-by-five photo. He reached into the trunk and retrieved his service weapon and gun clip then sat on the concrete floor. He leaned back against the rear driver side tire holding the Glock 27 in one hand and the metal clip with a single forty-caliber round in the other. He was at total peace as he shoved the clip into the bottom of the firearm, tapped it twice with the palm of his hand to ensure it had seated properly, then chambered the only round he would need. He tasted vomit in his mouth after he gagged while trying to position the firearm far back in his mouth at just the right angle to ensure that, once fired, the bullet would shatter his spinal column at the base of his skull.

Knowing that there was no turning back, Detective Steele began the countdown exactly as he had worked out in his mind. Five, he readied himself by clearing his mind one final time. Four, he slid his finger from outside the guard to just over the trigger. Three, he closed his eyes. Two, Steele took a deep breath, sucking in as much air through his mouth his lungs would allow. One.

***

Startled by the loud noise, Madi sat straight up and immediately reached her arm toward Steele's side of the mattress.

But he wasn't there. The detective had also heard the sound, and thinking it was a gunshot from outside their home, he jumped out of bed and was already standing at the window looking outside.

"It's okay. Must have been backfire from a car passing by. Try to go back to sleep, sweetheart."

"That just about scared me to death. How are you doing? Did your headache finally go away?" she asked.

"I'm fine. Close your eyes, sweetheart. Get some rest."

Madi quickly fell asleep without a clue that the loud popping sound from just outside their bedroom window had awakened Steele from one of the worst nightmares he had ever experienced. This one seemed much more real than the others, and although the darkness that blanketed the room shielded his sweaty face from his wife, his heart was still pounding as he continued looking out the bedroom window, trying to gather his thoughts. The nightmares and sleepless nights were nothing new for the detective. The result of years of being tormented.

Although the abuse at home had started when he'd been around three, Braxton was five years old when he first experienced bullying from someone other than the colonel. The kid who first started picking on him was named Helmut Krause, and the bullying occurred during the time the family was stationed in Germany. Braxton and Brice attended Stuttgart Elementary School, located about 150 kilometers to the east of the French border and 150 kilometers north of Switzerland. First, the taunting was limited to name-calling, before escalating to Helmut taking Braxton's lunch. After about a week, Helmut started shoving Braxton in the back and tripping him from behind by sideswiping his heels together, which would usually cause Braxton to lose his balance and stumble forward. What Helmut didn't know, however, was that Braxton had started taking martial arts lessons a couple of years earlier, and although he was quite adept, from the very beginning, it had been pounded into his head that he was to never resort to using his fighting skills unless it became a life-or-death situation due to the potential harm he could inadvertently cause to another kid.

It didn't take long for his mother, Kandace, to notice that something was happening at school. Instead of the normally happy-go-lucky kid who was always eager to discuss with his mother all he had learned in school that day, Braxton became noticeably withdrawn, clinging to Kandace more than normal, which was the first clue that something was amiss. Brice was fully aware of what his brother was going through, but the boys were under a mandate of sorts from the colonel that they each had to fend for themselves. So Brice continued to stand back and watch as Helmut tormented his twin brother, not because he couldn't step in and put an end to it, but out of fear of how the colonel might react if his orders were disobeyed.

One evening when Braxton and Brice had been sitting on their bedroom floor, rolling a rubber ball back and forth, the door had suddenly swung open, and the colonel was standing there. Startled, the boys immediately hopped up and stood at attention. They had known that they hadn't done anything wrong, but their hearts were racing all the same, knowing that it didn't take much to piss the colonel off.

"I understand you're having some problems with a bully at school."

"Yes, Colonel," Braxton responded.

The colonel turned and left the bedroom, and a little over fourteen hours later, he was standing in the school principal's office explaining his son's sudden mood change and how he suspected it was due to him being bullied at school. But his attempt at soliciting the school's assistance in the matter fell woefully flat when, within minutes, it became apparently clear that the principal wasn't overly concerned about involving himself in the situation, and in that moment, the colonel made up his mind that he would handle things in his own way.

"Thank you for your time."

Without saying another word, the colonel stood up and left the principal's office. He began making his way toward the parking lot, his eyes staring at nothing but what was directly ahead while those who happened to be close by looked on as the military man strutted proudly down the hallway. Forty-five minutes later, the colonel was on base where his first order of business was to pay a visit to his good friend, Ethan Warwick, aka Wick, the man who taught defensive tactics to military personnel. Wick was a notable black belt in German jujitsu, a type of martial art related to traditional Japanese jujutsu developed in Germany in the 1960s using techniques from jujutsu, judo, karate, and various other traditional and modern martial arts. After explaining what was taking place with his son, Wick agreed to teach Braxton the art of jujitsu.

After work, the colonel had swung by the house and picked Braxton up to bring him back to the base. When they walked into the gym, Wick was in the far corner going through some stretching exercises. After a quick intro, the colonel had retreated to a chair on the side of the mat, turning his son over to Wick.

Braxton faced Wick and placed his hands at this side. As if on cue, both he and Wick bowed toward one another as a sign of mutual respect.

"Okay, young man, show me what you got. I need to know where we should pick up from your last set of lessons. We'll start out with some basic moves. Show me a front snap punch."

Braxton immediately went into his fighting stance and then made a small jab with his left fist. As he brought his arm back, he twisted his hips and then thrust his right fist forward.

"Okay, not bad. Now, let me see a one-step snap front kick."

Again, Braxton went into his fighting stance and brought his knee up to the height of his hips. He quickly snapped his foot out toward Wick, stopping just short of landing a blow before placing his foot back on the ground.

Wick smiled. "That's pretty good. Can you perform a hip throw with a shoulder arm lock?"

"Yes, sir."

Wick moved closer to Braxton and, without warning, threw a straight punch toward his face.

Braxton brushed off the punch using a basic inside forearm block, then stepped forward toward Wick with his left foot and twisted his body while placing his right arm in the small of Wick's back. Then he folded his body and slammed Wick to the mat. Once he released his hold, both jumped up from the mat, placed their hands at their sides and bowed toward one another.

Wick patted Braxton on the shoulder and asked him to go stand over near the free weights while he spoke with his dad in private.

"Sir, I don't know what to tell you. I have no idea why your son is allowing himself to be bullied. He's more than capable of defending himself."

"Told you my kid could fight. He just won't!"

"Tell you what, sir. There's a martial arts tournament coming up a few months from now for kids Braxton's age. If you agree, I'll coach him and get him ready. Perhaps he just needs a couple of fights under his belt to build his confidence."

"Fine, if you think that's all it'll take."

"There's no guarantee, but it's certainly worth a try."

"Well, let's give it a go and see what happens."

Over the next three months, Braxton was dropped off at the base gym, where he and Wick practiced for two hours a day, four days a week, up until the day before the tournament, and on that morning, the colonel and Braxton arrived at seven forty-five. Wick had arrived moments before. Sensing someone's presence, he turned around and saw Braxton standing there.

"You ready young man?"

"Yes, sir," Braxton responded.

"Bring all your gear?" Wick asked, pointing to the duffle bag.

"Yes, sir," Braxton responded while opening the bag to expose its contents.

"Let's see. You've got your white belt, mouthpiece, hand gear, foot gear, groin cup, head gear, a bottle of water, and a breakfast bar. Nice. Looks like you have it all. Now I'm about to tell you something that I want you to always remember."

Wick bent over and placed his hands on Braxton's shoulders.

"When it comes to competing, your attitude, regardless of whether you win or lose, will always be what people will remember most about you. Sure, we all want to win trophies, medals, and patches, but the fact that you're competing in the first place means you've already won. So, when you go out there, I want you to think about one thing and one thing only. Do your best. If you do that, then you'll be a winner. Fair enough?"

"Fair enough," Braxton responded.

Thirty minutes later, Braxton was standing on the mat, face to face with Finn Becker, a kid about the same size he was. While this would be Braxton's first competition, Finn had competed for the past two years, and was not only good but had never lost a match. As soon as the referee gave the signal for the ninety-second match to begin, Braxton and Finn immediately started circling one another around the mat. Finn tried to strike first by attempting to land a front snap kick that Braxton easily blocked. Finn immediately followed with a quick front snap punch that caught Braxton off guard, striking him in the chest.

Shaken up a bit, Braxton did his best to stay away from his opponent by backpedaling, zig-zagging across the mat without ever attempting to throw a punch of his own. He looked around and happened to catch eyes with Wick, who just smiled and mouthed the words *It's okay. You are doing fine*, and while Wick thought that Braxton was just experiencing first-tournament jitters, he had no idea that when Finn successfully landed his punch, for a brief moment, Braxton literally froze as his mind flashed back to times he had been tormented both at home and at school.

Figuring Braxton would simply continue to run around the ring, Finn came straight at him and attempted to throw another front snap punch. After all, landing his first punch was as simple as it gets. This time, however, Braxton was ready. Using a straight-arm-lock technique, he knocked Finn's strike downward with his left hand. Then Braxton grabbed Finn's wrist and twisted so that he now stood side by side with Finn. Without hesitation, Braxton used his left elbow to strike Finn on the side of his head, and although he was careful not to really unleash on his opponent, it was a good thing that the kids wore head gear during tournaments. Otherwise, the blow likely would have done some damage.

After a brief pause, Braxton went in again. He interlocked his left arm with Finn's right arm just under his armpit and, after grabbing hold of his wrist, began applying pressure and twisting Finn's wrist clockwise, causing him to go to the mat. The ring judge stepped in immediately and tapped Braxton on the shoulder, signaling for him to release his grip and let Finn up.

Both Braxton and Finn backed away to their respective corners, neither taking their eyes off the other. When the ring judge signaled for the round to start, the opponents squared in their respective fighting stance. Out of nowhere, Finn bought his right knee up and twisted his body so that he was standing sideways in front of Braxton before extending his right leg, striking Braxton below the belt and causing him to fall to the mat in harrowing pain.

The ring judge rushed in and sent Finn to a corner of the mat while squatting down to check on Braxton's condition. After about fifteen seconds and receiving assurances from Braxton that he was ready to continue, the ring judge assessed Finn with a one-point deduction and cautioned him about low blows. Braxton and

Finn bowed toward one another, and while the opponents were backing away to resume the round, Finn caught Braxton off guard when, out of nowhere, he attempted to punch him in the face. An obvious dirty move.

Braxton stepped forward and deflected the strike with a basic inside forearm block then immediately landed a blow to Finn's bicep with a hammer fist so powerful that it caused Finn's arm to go limp. When the ring judge saw Braxton draw his hand back, he knew exactly what he was about to do.

"Don't!" he yelled, but before he could rush in to protect the defenseless Finn, Braxton struck his opponent on the side of his neck with a scissor hand, causing him to crumple to the ground.

The uneasy hush was deafening when compared to the energy and excitement that had filled the room just moments before. All three judges were on the mat attending to Finn but keeping him stationary until paramedics arrived. He wiggled his fingers on command, but there was no visible movement from his lower extremities. This was unchartered territory for the martial arts studio. Cautioning fighters for pushing the envelope was fairly common during competition, but never had the judges encountered a situation where one competitor had gone after a fellow competitor so aggressively.

When emergency medical personnel arrived, Finn had just started moving his toes. Still, they secured his neck with a cervical neck brace before placing him on a spinal board for transport to the local hospital as a precaution. The noise level in the room began to progressively rise with most of the talk among spectators centered on poor sportsmanship. The colonel saw everything but remained in his seat, while Wick stood up and walked over to where Braxton was standing in the corner by himself.

"What happened to you in there?" he asked.

"I don't know. He wasn't fighting fairly. He tried to hurt me, and I wanted him to stop."

Wick was just about to say something when he looked up and saw one of the judges walking toward the colonel. After a while, the colonel made his way over to where Braxton and Wick had huddled in the corner.

"Grab your bag, Braxton. Let's go!"

Although there was no way of knowing exactly what the judge said to the colonel, Wick had a pretty good idea. When the three were outside, the colonel placed Braxton in the car and walked over to speak with Wick.

"They disqualified my son from the tournament on the grounds of malicious intent to inflict injury on a fellow competitor. They said his conduct violated the rules and spirit of the tournament."

"Well, Colonel, if I'm being honest, I would have to agree with their decision. The thing is, I had Braxton ahead on points until he went after that kid. Has he ever exhibited loss of control like that before?"

"You know, I think we'll hold off on the lessons for a while. I need to assess some things."

"Understood, sir. You know where to find me when you're ready to get going again."

The colonel got in his car and drove off the lot. As soon as he and Braxton were clear of the martial arts studio, he looked over and began lavishing him with praise.

"You did good in there, son. Hell, I knew you could fight. That's exactly how I want you to defend yourself. You hear me?"

"Yes, Colonel," Braxton responded, shocked beyond belief that not only was he apparently not in trouble for being tossed out of the tournament, but for whatever reason, the colonel actually seemed to approve of something he had done. Which was a first.

Three weeks later, Helmut blindsided Braxton by shoving him in the back so violently that it caused him to stumble forward, dropping his lunch tray and spilling spaghetti, green beans, apple sauce, and milk all over the cafeteria floor. Helmut stood there, laughing loudly, while the other kids backed away as fast as they could, not wanting to become his next victims.

Braxton's initial instinct was to get up off the floor and show Helmut a thing or two, but instead, he spent the next several minutes on his knees collecting his thoughts and doing his best to clean up his spilled food while Helmut stood over him, shouting verbal abuses.

"Look at him on his knees, everybody. I bet he wants to cry. What's wrong? You want your mommy? Clean that mess up! You're nothing but a little sissy!"

After shoving Braxton in the back of the head for good measure, Helmut walked to a table located at the rear of the cafeteria where two boys had sat down moments before, preparing to eat their lunch. Helmut only had to look in their direction for them to know what was expected of them. They quickly hopped up from the bench and walked away, leaving behind their untouched meals.

After wiping up as much food and liquid as possible with napkins he pulled from the dispenser, Braxton got to his feet and sat his lunch tray on a nearby table before leaving the cafeteria. He had lost his appetite. Not because of fear, but because he had made up his mind. Today would be the day he finally retaliated.

The end of the lunch period was getting close, and Braxton could be seen in the distance, standing by himself over near the jungle gym. Within seconds, Helmut started heading toward the play area, followed closely by several other children who somehow always seemed to be close by anytime the bully felt the need to exert his will. Helmut thrived on all the attention.

Braxton pretended not to see Helmut walking toward him. Truth is, he'd spotted him as soon as he stepped out of the cafeteria and was actually hoping Helmut would try picking on him again. So he waited, all the while keeping his gaze straight ahead and rhythmically pushing the empty swing seat back and forth, something he had been doing for at least fifteen minutes as he eagerly awaited the bully's next move.

Helmut walked up to Braxton and stood directly in front of him.

"What are you doing over here, you little sissy?"

Braxton was never given an opportunity to respond before Helmut drew his arm back and took a swipe at him. But he missed. Braxton had easily dodged the enormous hand without moving an inch from where he stood. There was a sudden gasp from the crowd of onlookers who were just as surprised as Helmut that he failed to find his target. Helmut swung again, this time much harder and with a closed fist, and again, he missed.

"I'm warning you, Helmut. You need to turn and walk away."

"Shut up, you little sissy!"

"Just leave me alone!"

Not wanting to somehow become entangled in what was surely to come next, the crowd of students backed away but continued to focus their eyes on the two classmates facing one another on the blacktop. Without saying a word, Helmut lunged at Braxton in an attempt to take him to the ground, which proved to be a big mistake. With one hand still resting on the jungle gym, Braxton sidestepped the bully and, in one motion, hit him in the neck with the back of his left hand, causing Helmut to bend at the waist.

Both embarrassed and irritated, Helmut regrouped and charged again. This time, Braxton kicked him below the belt, causing him to shriek as he grabbed at his groin in agonizing pain. Helmut was gasping as he folded at the waist, and for the first time, Braxton was able to look the bully straight in the eyes. The martial arts lessons had worked. This was far easier than Braxton could have ever anticipated and better than he had hoped for. He had sent the message loud and clear that he was no longer to be messed with.

But then something happened. Perhaps the compilation of months of being antagonized by the bully or just getting caught up in the moment, but while Helmut was still bent over in pain, Braxton reached for the swing, and once he felt the chain in his hand, he wrapped it twice around Helmut's neck. Without hesitation, he pulled violently, causing Helmut to gasp for air as he instinctively moved his hands from the crotch to his neck in an attempt to slide his fingers under the chain so that he could breath.

Braxton started pulling harder on the chain, and Helmut fell to the ground. He was now on his knees, helpless and retching between uncontrollable coughing. It seemed as if Braxton had snapped, if only for a moment.

Suddenly, the skirmish was over. Braxton released his grip on the chain and continued standing over the bully as he fell the rest of the way to the ground, landing next to Braxton's feet. He knew that the point had been made. What he didn't know, however, was that movement in the window shade of the administration building in the distance was not caused by the wind. Principal Warren had witnessed the near strangulation.

When the colonel came home later that evening, Kandace filled him in on the call she had received from the school principal advising that Braxton had been expelled for being involved in a fight where he nearly killed another student, and as usual, the colonel began walking toward the door. He was headed to the spot where he always administered discipline.

"I'll be out back. Send him to me."

"Yes, Colonel," she responded meekly, already fearing what was about to happen to her little boy. But in her mind, she had no choice but to do as she was told.

Braxton hated being summoned knowing what was about to take place. But he wasn't surprised. He knew he was in trouble for getting expelled from school. He walked into the garage, and even before his eyes could focus on the colonel, the large hand came crashing against his face, knocking him to the ground. His jaw felt as if it were on fire.

"Get up!"

"Yes, Colonel," Braxton responded, pulling himself up off the ground and standing at attention.

"I understand you were kicked out of school."

"Yes, Colonel."

"The next time that son of a bitch puts his hand on you, you better kill him! Is that clear?"

"Yes, Colonel."

The colonel grunted something inaudible as the brushed past Braxton, who continued staring straight ahead at the clock on the wall. He knew the drill. The colonel was very specific. Braxton was to stand there without moving for ten minutes exactly after the colonel left the garage. Which he did. And later that night when he finally fell asleep, he dreamed of the colonel and him catching rainbow trout while the two stood at the water's edge for the first and unfortunately the last time they would ever fish together.

Scene 1

10 Marine View Drive
Reese Valley, Washington
1:15 p.m.

The RVPD press conference two days ago marked her first day with the *Reese Valley Herald*, and Jolynn Rider more than lived up to her reputation. Not only did she display elements of persistence while attempting to clarify points with Detective Steele, but anyone watching her pepper the detective with questions knew immediately that she was not intimidated by the police. Steele took note of the new reporter's tenacity immediately. But he wasn't the only one.

It was late in the afternoon when Atticus accessed the *RV Herald*'s website on his computer and began scrolling through the company's directory. Jolynn's photograph, email address, and phone numbers were midway down the page. He pulled a burner phone from the cabinet drawer and dialed the office number.

"Jolynn Rider," she said, answering the phone on the second ring.

"Hello, Ms. Rider," Atticus responded, speaking through the voice distorter.

"Who is this?"

"I'm the person you were asking all the brilliant questions about at the press conference the other day."

Jolynn didn't say anything for a long while, but Atticus knew she was still on the phone. He wanted to allow a little time for things to set in.

"First, let me welcome you to our fine city. Oh, and that little house you purchased over on Loveland is to die for. Real close to the office, I see."

"What?" Jolynn responded, her voice cracking as she nervously spoke.

"Don't worry, Ms. Rider. All I want from you is your expertise, and as long as you do as I say, I won't kill you like I did the other women. So here's the deal. Under no circumstances are you to contact the RVPD. Do you understand?"

Jolynn didn't respond. Instead, she sat quietly, staring at Detective Steele's business card that was poking out from under her desk phone.

"I'm sorry, Ms. Rider. I forgot to mention what a touching moment that was between you and Quinn this morning when you dropped the little tyke off at the daycare. Nearly brought tears to my eyes. I must say he looks quite tall for his age. What is he? About four? Must take after your ex-husband. Oh, and that 1969 red Mustang in your father's garage. What a beauty. Love that car! Shall I go on?"

"What do you want?"

"I told you, Ms. Rider. Do I have your attention now?"

"Yes," Jolynn answered.

"Good. And do you understand?"

"Yes."

"Here's what you're gonna do. Pick up Quinn from daycare at your usual time and take him to your babysitter. Leave him there. At seven this evening, you'll drive over to the parking lot across from Varley's and pull into a stall near the back, away from the street. I'll be watching. And make sure your cell phone is fully charged and turned on. You'll be needing it."

Click! He disconnected the call.

Scene 2

7:00 p.m.

Atticus stood near the railroad tracks and watched as Jolynn pulled into the lot. She parked in an empty stall near the back and began looking around nervously. After about a minute, he dialed her number.

"Hello?"

"Quinn really looked happy when you handed him off to that young lady in the blue dress. I'm sure she'll take very good care of him."

"Why are you doing this? Please don't—"

"Listen up, Jolynn," Atticus calmly interrupted. "I want you to roll down all of your car windows."

He could see that she had started crying and was shaking uncontrollably as she began rolling down the windows. At one point, she looked in his direction, but he knew that was just by chance as there was no way for her to see him from his vantage point.

"Now, I want you to get out and start walking toward the lighthouse. Take your cell phone with you and don't look back for any reason."

Click! He disconnected the call and watched through his night-vision binoculars as Jolynn opened the car door and stepped out. She walked at a nervous pace, and in less than two minutes, she was at the corner. Just as she was about to cross Second Street, her cell phone started ringing. She picked up immediately.

"That's far enough. You have ninety seconds to get back to your car. Go!"

Click! The phone went dead the moment Atticus disconnected the call.

Jolynn sprinted back to her car, and as she began reaching for the door handle, her cell phone started ringing. She was both out of breath and crying uncontrollably when she climbed into the driver's seat and answered.

"Place your cell phone on speaker, Jolynn, and lay it on the dashboard. Then I want you to reach under your seat and pull out that bottle of water."

"What?" she managed to say between sobs.

"Just do it."

He watched as Jolynn grabbed hold of the water bottle. Her hands were trembling.

"Now remove the cap and start drinking. Don't stop until the bottle is completely empty, and you had better not spill a drop."

But Jolynn didn't move. She wanted to, but there was a sudden disconnect between her body and her brain. So she sat there motionless, staring at the blue liquid, shaking wildly in her hands. From following sex crimes, she knew that roofies mixed with water would turn the water blue. Prior to relocating to the northwest, Jolynn had written several news articles about women being slipped the date-rape drug and later waking up to discover they had been physically assaulted. She was terrified.

"Remove the cap and drink the water, Jolynn. It would be a shame for anything to happen to little Quinn."

Jolynn screamed loudly as she ripped the plastic cap off and brought the water bottle to her lips. Forty seconds later, she swallowed the last of the bitter blue water before tossing the empty bottle aside.

"Why are you doing this?" she yelled, slapping both hands hard against the dashboard.

As the sun was slowly replaced by darkness, Atticus kept a careful eye on Jolynn. Not only did he have a clear view into the Honda, but he was also able to hear her voice through the cell phone. She was starting to slur her words, which meant it wouldn't be too much longer. The Rohypnol was starting to take hold.

Twenty minutes had passed since Jolynn finished off the water, and it was becoming a struggle for her to keep her head from slamming against the steering wheel. Atticus watched as her body began to weave back and forth and then sideways before suddenly slumping across the center console toward the passenger seat. And when he was certain she was no longer moving, he drove into the lot and pulled up next to her vehicle.

Scene 3

10 Marine View Drive
Reese Valley, Washington
11:00 p.m.

Jolynn woke up in a panic, finding her arms and legs were bound. She couldn't move. Nor could she see through the canvas hood that Atticus had placed over her head. The wicked stillness in the room was nothing like she had ever experienced, and as her senses began to liven, she could feel the icy-cold floor beneath her body, letting her know that her clothing had been removed.

Her mind was racing out of control, unsure whether it should try to fight back or just surrender to the fear that was at that very moment waging an all-out assault against her will. Thinking the worse, Jolynn screamed as she pulled and pulled and pulled, trying her best to break free, stopping only when it became evident that the harder she pulled, the deeper the sharp edges of the plastic restraints cut into her skin.

The narcotic was starting to wear off, but her words were still slurred. Just not as much as on the ride from the parking lot. Atticus scooted his chair closer, and suddenly sensing his presence, she gasped.

"Congratulations, Jolynn. You're still alive, which means you passed your first test." Atticus got out of the chair and kneeled next to her. "Hopefully, your good fortune will continue," he said in a measured voice, placing a hand on the back of her neck.

Jolynn jerked her body and tried her best to pull away, but her movements were restricted. She was still groggy, but that didn't stop her from noticing the heaviness of her left leg. She also noticed that each time she moved, there was an odd sound. Like a chain being pulled across cement.

"Relax," Atticus said, pressing down hard on the back of her neck. "If your body isn't positioned just correctly, none of this will make sense."

He grabbed hold of Jolynn's shoulders and swung her around so that her head was pointed toward the staircase. Then he got to his feet and stood about two feet from her head and started tapping his finger on the video camera.

"Now listen to me carefully. While that chain shackled to your leg will limit your mobility to six feet, you'll have no problem getting to everything you'll be needing. Also, there are motion-sensing video cameras throughout this room, all pointing at you from every angle you can possibly imagine. I'm tapping my finger against one of them at this very moment. I want you to imagine the face on a clock, Jolynn. This particular camera is positioned at twelve o'clock."

Atticus took a few steps to his left and picked up the bucket. He began banging it against the cement floor. Startled, Jolynn rolled her body away from the sound.

"This is a metal bucket. You'll be needing it when the time comes to relieve yourself. I've placed it at three o'clock."

"Please don't do this."

"It's already done, Jolynn. It's already done. Now listen up and please don't interrupt me again. I need to explain this second test to you."

Atticus took a few more steps to his left and started tapping his foot on the floor.

"I'm now standing at six o'clock. Here is where I've placed several burlap sacks. As cold as it gets down here at night, you'll be glad I left them for you."

He stepped to the left again and started tapping his foot on the floor.

"Do you hear me tapping my foot on the ground, Jolynn?"

"Yes."

"Good. Where am I standing?"

"You're behind me," she responded, starting to cry softly.

"Wrong! I'm standing at nine o'clock, Jolynn. This is where you'll find your daily food rations."

Atticus bent over and grabbed hold of Jolynn's leg. She screamed, and her body tensed up in response to his touch.

"Don't move."

He leaned in and used his knife to cut the zip ties off her ankles.

"Now listen up. This is important. Remember those video cameras I told you about earlier? Well, they don't miss a thing."

He reached over and cut the zip ties off her wrists, and although her arms and legs were no longer bound, Jolynn knew that even without him saying so, she was expected to remain perfectly still.

Atticus stood up and backed away a few steps.

"Stand up."

Jolynn tried her best to stand, but partway up, she lost her balance and fell back to the floor. She raised her hands to the hood covering her face.

"Why are you doing this?" she screamed.

"I need for you to stand up, Jolynn," Atticus repeated in a slow, measured voice. But she continued lying on the floor. Whimpering.

He stepped forward and, using his left hand, grabbed a fistful of the hood along with her hair and yanked her up, causing the chain to rattle loudly as it rubbed against the floor. Once she was on her feet, Atticus slid his right hand under her armpit and pulled her close to his chest, inadvertently brushing along the side of her breast. Jolynn felt violated. They were so close that she could taste his cologne, and while she stood there totally at his mercy, the muffled cries began to find their way through the canvas hood.

Atticus loosened his grip and turned Jolynn around to face him.

"In a moment, I'm going to remove the hood from over your head, but there's one rule you must adhere to. You must not open your eyes under any circumstances, not now, not tomorrow, not ever. Remember: there are several cameras pointing directly at you that will pick up your every move. I'll be checking the tape every day, and if you disobey my orders, or even forget and inadvertently open your eyes, I'll know, and I'll kill you. Any questions?"

Jolynn didn't respond. Instead, she stood there shaking like a leaf in the wind.

"Well, all righty then. Seeing that there are no questions, your second test begins...now."

Atticus reached toward Jolynn and removed the canvas hood. He looked her over from head to toe, taking in all of her nakedness. He could see her straining to keep her eyes shut as she desperately fought against the urge to sneak a peek at this thing standing before her.

"Good luck, Jolynn," he said before turning and walking up the steps.

CHAPTER 6

Thursday, December 18
10 Marine View Drive
Reese Valley, Washington
1:15 a.m.

Atticus checked the tape and saw that for the past two hours, Jolynn hadn't moved an inch; in fact, she was standing in the exact location she had been in when he'd left her. She had also managed to keep her eyes tightly closed the entire time. She was the person he truly wanted to tell his story, and in a weird sense, he considered her somewhat of a chosen one.

The moment he opened the door, Atticus heard the metal chain briefly rattle as it slid across the floor. He saw that Jolynn had turned toward the sound and was facing the staircase by the time he reached the bottom step. Her eyes were still closed.

He walked passed Jolynn, making his way over to the metal cabinet. After picking up one of the little brown bottles, he removed the cap and began pouring the contents onto a cloth.

"How are you doing, Jolynn?" he asked, tucking the cloth in his back pocket.

Jolynn didn't respond. She continued standing with her body facing the staircase, trembling as she used every ounce of her energy to keep her eyes closed.

Atticus opened the knife drawer and removed the boning knife. He started walking toward her and noticed her trembling was becoming even more pronounced.

He walked up from behind and swung his left arm violently around her shoulder. He pulled her close to his chest.

She gasped.

"I reviewed the tape, Jolynn, and saw where you opened your eyes."

"Please don't hurt me! I swear I didn't open my eyes."

Jolynn's heart was racing, and her knees buckled, causing Atticus to tighten his grip around her shoulders in order to keep her from falling to the ground.

"I know you didn't, Jolynn. Actually, you're doing quite nicely. But now, I feel it's important that you really get a taste of what the other women went through."

He held the knife in his right hand as he began running the dull edge lightly from left to right across her neck.

"I cut 'em, Jolynn. I cut 'em real good."

Jolynn winced and was just about to squirm before suddenly remembering the knife was pressing against her neck.

"I bet you didn't know I kept all of their eyes. Naw, you couldn't have known that. They're right over there in that meat freezer, say about five feet from where you're standing. You just can't open your eyes to see. Tell me, Jolynn: What do you think was going through the minds of all those women right before I used this very knife to cut their throats?"

She didn't answer as she continued standing as still as humanly possible while tears streamed down her cheeks.

"I asked you a question, Jolynn. What last thoughts do you think were running through the minds of those other women right before I murdered them?"

Jolynn felt the sudden jolt of pain in her neck from the back of the knife being pressed deep into her skin before Atticus loosened his grip to relieve the pressure.

"I don't know," she responded, her soft voice quivering, barely louder than a whisper.

"Fair enough. Then tell me your thoughts. What are you thinking about, Jolynn?"

"Please. I don't want to die," she pleaded.

"I'm not going to kill you. That is, as long as you do exactly as I say. You should feel special, Jolynn. Do you feel special?"

Before she could say anything, Atticus resumed speaking.

"You don't have to answer that. So here's the deal. I've been writing a manuscript that sort of tracks my work. Rather than a novel, it's more like a short story. In any event, I want to make sure it gets out there. That's where you come in. At the appropriate time, you'll receive my manuscript in the mail. I'll send it to your office. Once you receive it, your job will be to publish it in the local newspaper. You do that, and you won't suffer the same fate as the other women I've murdered. Until then, just continue doing your job as usual."

Atticus lowered the knife from her neck and stuck it in his back pocket. Handle down.

"You really should feel special, Jolynn. No other woman has ever gotten out of this basement alive. But I digress."

Atticus stood there for a long while, deep in thought and with Jolynn still pinned tightly against his chest.

"I'm going to kill again, Jolynn, and there's nothing you or anyone else can do to change that. Just remember what I said about not going to the police. I can get to you or your family anytime I want, but as long as you do as you've been told, nothing will happen to either of you. Watch your mail for the manuscript. When you receive it, you publish it. Immediately!"

Atticus reached into his back pocket, removed the cloth, and held it tightly over Jolynn's nose and mouth until she passed out. Several hours later, she woke up to discover that not only was she seated back behind the steering wheel of her car, but she was fully clothed.

CHAPTER 7

Saturday, December 20
Langley, Washington
3:00 p.m.

The ferry transporting commuters over to Whidbey Island pulled dockside at Clinton Terminal just after two o'clock, and within minutes, Jennifer Rollins and her entourage walked off the shuttle, piled into four awaiting Ubers, and headed northwest on WA-525. Ten minutes later, the ladies stepped out of the vehicles in front of the Spoiled Kitten Winery on Maxwelton Road for their first wine tasting of the afternoon. Two years had passed since the engagement party, and now, Jennifer and Craig were finally getting hitched. Figuring the curtain was falling on her spur of the moment getaways with her girls, Jennifer wanted to ensure today was one for the ages. And so did her girls. The ladies had a full day of festivities planned that would both start and end with drinking wine.

They walked into the tasting room, and almost immediately, Melinda, the maid of honor, tossed her credit card on the glass counter and ordered a case of the Estate Pinot Noir. The ladies had recently began venturing outside of the typical sweet white wines they usually ordered whenever they were out for a night on the town, and each had accepted the challenge to only drink red wine for this special occasion. Jennifer made the transition to drinking reds a little over three months ago and, during that time, had grown to appreciate them. Pinot Noir was her favorite. After collecting the wines from the counter, the ladies made their way outside to the lawn area where tables and chairs were reserved for them.

Although a mere eleven months into the wine game, Jennifer considered herself somewhat of a connoisseur and spent several hours updating her social media followers on her varietal pick of the week.

Jennifer picked up her glass, swirled the wine around several times, and raised the glass to her nose. She inhaled the aroma, then took a sip.

"Wow! Now that's yummy. I really love the rich, spicy oak flavor of this wine. It sorta reminds me of that cinnamon smell in my grandma's kitchen."

"Yeah, I was just about to say my wine kinda taste like a cinnamon cookie with a hint of oak," Melinda responded, breaking out in laughter.

"Well, Melinda, do you even understand what oakiness means?"

"Can't say I do, Jennifer."

"Well, I'll tell you. It's when wine has been aged in an oak barrel and wood chips have been added during the process. How about tannin? Do you know what tannin means?"

"No, Jennifer. I've never heard that term associated with wine."

"Well, I'll tell you. Tannin refers to the structure of wine. How about complexity? Do you know what it means for wines to be complex?"

"Don't get your panties in a knot, Jennifer. I was just kidding."

"No, you wanted to go there, Melinda. When someone says a wine is complex, they don't mean the wine is difficult or anything like that. What they're referring to are the various layers one happens to unravel when they are either sipping or sniffing the wine. Like when I said I loved the rich spicy oak flavor. What I didn't say was that I also tasted black cherries when I sipped it. Think of it like when you meet someone. I know you would rather hang around someone who you found intriguing rather than someone who is boring. That's exactly how wine is, Melinda. Some are boring, and some are intriguing, hence the word complex."

"All right already. I said I didn't mean anything by my comment."

"Well, in that case, I accept your apology. You know I take my wine drinking seriously, Melinda."

Everyone was looking at someone else within the group, hoping the other person would be the first to speak. After several tense seconds, Melinda decided to break the ice. She stood up and began thumping the side of her wine glass with her fingernail.

"Now that that's settled, it's time to really get this party started. Right, ladies?"

"Damn straight!" Gail shouted. "Now pour me some more of that spicy oak. My glass is dry."

Everyone laughed, including Jennifer, and with the tension now a thing of the past, the ladies were finally able to chill and take in all of the beauty the winery had to offer. A working farm, the vineyard was breathtaking, featuring picturesque views of tall trees and mountains in the distance. The true attention-grabbers, however, were the two oversized Manx cats for which the vineyard was named after. During the entire time the ladies were there, the cats could be seen patrolling the grounds, ensuring birds who would love nothing more than to have their way with the grapes, clearly understood that they were not welcome anywhere near the expansive rows of vines.

A little more than two hours later, the last of the empty wine bottles was returned to the box, and with four new Ubers arriving at the winery about the same time, the entourage promptly finished off whatever wine remained in their glasses, before hopping into the vehicles for the short ride over to Ott & Smurfy's on First Street. Overlooking the water, the little upscale tasting room was known for providing near-nightly entertainment featuring local artists, not to mention, delicious food and chocolates that complemented their extensive wine offerings, making it the perfect vibe for the island community. At about five twenty, the sixteen ladies moseyed into O & S for Jennifer's bachelorette party with seemingly not a care in the world. Any inhibitions that may have existed earlier were now long gone, having dissipated on the ride across the water or after the ladies consumed their twelfth bottle of wine at the Spoiled Kitten.

Jennifer was first through the door and the one in the group who spotted the handsome gentleman sitting by himself. After using her arms and legs to block the doorway, she looked back over her shoulder toward her girlfriends.

"Watch me work, ladies."

Atticus, dressed in blue jeans, a white, long-sleeve shirt, gray tweed jacket, and black Salvatore Ferragamo loafers was seated in one of the two large leather chairs near the entrance when the women walked in. They arrived just in time to watch him swirl his glass to agitate his 2013 Boushey Vineyard Syrah. No doubt the man was in his element, and even from behind the dark sunshades, he could be seen closing his eyes. Atticus lifted the wine glass to his nose and inhaled deeply, immediately rewarding his senses with the fragrant aroma of dried herb and plum. But when he opened his mouth to explore the contents of the glass, his wonderful experience came to an abrupt halt. Jennifer had flopped down hard in the adjacent chair nearly causing him to spill his wine.

"So what's your name, cutie, and why are you wearing those sunglasses indoors?" she asked, half laughing.

Jennifer picked up the wine bottle from the table and began looking over the label.

"Oh, I see you like syrah. I absolutely love this wine. Did you know the word *syrah* likely came from Syracuse, a city in Sicily? Oh, and nice shoes, by the way. Let me guess: when you take a sip, you're greeted with a punch of flavor that tapers off after a while and leaves you with a spicy peppery aftertaste. I'm right, aren't I?"

Unamused, Atticus didn't respond. Instead, he took another sip and then resumed swirling the wine around in the glass. Some of the women standing in the back near the entrance started snickering, finding it comical that the man seemed to be a thousand times more interested in his wine than the bride-to-be.

Visibly embarrassed, Jennifer leaped from the leather chair. Her face was beet red.

"Let's go, ladies! This guy's a douche!"

Not to be outdone, she leaned in. Perhaps a bit too close, as she inadvertently brushed across the man's nose with hers.

"I bet those are fake diamonds in your cufflinks. And another thing, you didn't actually think I was interested in you, did you?"

Atticus didn't bother to respond. Unfortunately for Jennifer, however, he had locked in on the bright red lipstick she was wearing, making any potential interest she may or may not have held for him completely irrelevant. He was now interested in her.

The time for the women to move over to the private room reserved for their party couldn't have come soon enough, but in her scramble to get away from the man, Jennifer left her coin purse in the leather chair, prominently displaying her drivers license from behind the clear plastic protective cover. Like a hawk with a rabbit in its talons, Atticus was all over it. As soon as the women turned their backs, he pulled his cell phone out and snapped a quick photo before finishing the last of his wine and leaving the tasting room.

Jennifer Rollins had picked just about the worst person possible for her amusement, and in doing so, she put the game in motion.

CHAPTER 8

Monday, December 22
40019 Goat Trail Road
Reese Valley, Washington
6:45 a.m.

Atticus already had his cell phone in hand when he pulled onto the block. He glanced at the photo on the drivers license and then parked his Mercedes Benz G-Class a few doors down from Jennifer's home. He was far enough away as to not draw any unwanted attention yet close enough to see anyone coming out of the home, and with high-end vehicles seemingly the norm for the area, he was able to easily hide in plain sight. For a solid hour, neighbors pulled out of their driveways and drove by the white SUV without paying much attention, and just as he was starting to think that he may have missed his opportunity, the front door opened, and Jennifer stepped out cradling a small dog. She wasn't wearing any lipstick, and her hair was combed differently. But he could still tell it was her.

The little dog hurried over to a large brown spot on the lawn to relieve itself before racing back up the steps and into the house. At five past eight, the garage door opened, and Jennifer backed her silver Audi A6 down the driveway and onto the street before heading south on Goat Trail Road, paying no attention to the SUV that had already pulled away from the curb and was now following a few car lengths behind. Fifteen minutes later, she drove into the parking lot of Bounds Accounting & Business Solutions, a brick building with large lettering that read BABS across the front.

Atticus pulled to the side of the road on Reese Valley Speedway in front of the building and from where he was parked, he had a clear view of the parking lot. He could also see both the front and side entrance doors. Once he saw Jennifer walk inside, he pulled off and headed back over to Goat Trail Road.

He parked and got out clutching a handful of advertisements for a real estate company, that of course didn't exist. It took him less than five minutes on the computer to create the flyers, complete with a fake telephone number and address. The ruse gave him the perfect excuse to walk directly up to the porch without raising suspicion as to why he was there, and should any of the neighbors ask him what he was doing, he knew he could always hand them one of the advertisements.

Atticus knocked on the door and immediately heard the small dog barking from within. He had only seen one car parked in the garage when Jennifer had backed out, leading him to believe she lived alone. When there was no answer after several seconds, he walked around to the side door of the garage, slipped on a pair of latex gloves, and pulled the knife from his pocket. He inserted it between the door and the doorjamb strike plate and began moving the latch slightly inward as he pushed his weight against the door. Seconds later the door opened and as he suspected, there was no alarm.

The door leading into the house from the garage was unlocked and as soon as he stepped in, the cute little dog ran to him, wiggling its entire body in a frenzy.

"Hello! Is anybody home?" he shouted.

There was no answer. The only sound that could be heard in the home was the loud ticking from the wall clock next to the kitchen table. Atticus sat the flyers on the counter and then got down on his knees and turned the dog's collar around to expose his name tag. He gently patted the little dog's head.

"That's a good boy, Tye."

After roughhousing with the little dog a bit, Atticus got up and began his quick tour through the two-bedroom one-bath home with Tye following closely behind. He walked into the bathroom and noticed the abundance of flowers. Everything was a floral print. The wallpaper, the photos on the counter, the lid cover, even the toilet paper had little flowers, a dead giveaway that a man didn't share the home. The empty closet in the neat little secondary bedroom that resembled something out of a magazine had guest room written all over it, but it was the master bedroom closet filled to the brim with women's clothing and shoes that confirmed his belief that Jennifer lived alone.

Atticus began looking around her bedroom. He noticed a photograph of Jennifer and a guy on her nightstand. Presumably her fiancé. There was also a photograph of an older couple all hugged up and a young woman standing next to Jennifer with her arms wrapped around her waist.

Nice family photo, Atticus thought, as he left the bedroom and walked back down the hallway toward the bathroom. Jennifer kept all of her cosmetics in the top left drawer of the vanity, and no sooner had Atticus picked up the red lipstick and dropped it in his pocket than he heard the sound of keys jingling, sending him hurrying toward the kitchen to grab the flyers while Tye started barking and running toward the front door.

Jennifer was still on her cell phone when she entered the house, while Atticus had already slid under her bed. After a quick stop by the bathroom, she walked into her bedroom and hopped up on the edge of the bed. She dangled her feet over the side and used her toes to flip off her shoes, and when they hit the floor, they were a short three feet from Atticus's face.

Hiding for long periods of time was a skill he had no choice but to perfect as a child, and to this day, unless someone had prior knowledge of him being close by, his presence would go undetected for as long as he needed it to. Atticus closed his eyes, and he could hear his mother's voice: *You stay under there until I tell you to come out, and you had better not make a sound.* His heart began to race, and while he wanted to scream, he remained quiet, just like Judith had conditioned him to do.

Tye was a bit more animated than usual, and while Jennifer noticed his attention being drawn toward something under the bed, she assumed he was just playing with his toys, so she ended her call and dialed another number. After the fourth ring, the message recorder came on.

"Hey, Liz, it's Jen. I had to return home to get the Mulvaney file, but rather than waste any more time in traffic, I think I'll just work from here today. Call me if you have any questions, and if

I don't hear from you, I'll see you in the morning. See ya." She hopped down off the bed and left the room, not returning for several hours.

At around eight seventeen, Jennifer returned to her bedroom carrying a glass of wine. She placed the glass on the dresser and began removing her clothing, allowing her dress, followed by her floral-printed silk panties, to fall to the carpet next to the bed. She answered her cell phone, and based on the conversation, Atticus surmised her fiancé was on the other end.

After a moment, she began using her foot to sling her discarded clothing from the floor to a nearby chair before picking up her wine and climbing up on the bed. For the next thirty minutes or so, Jennifer sipped from her glass while thanking her fiancé for the wine and letting him know both that she enjoyed the particular varietal and that she had consumed the entire bottle. By nine fifteen, she was fast asleep. Still, Atticus wasn't quite ready to come out from under the bed.

He closed his eyes and visualized Jennifer lying on the mattress. Her chest moving up and down as she breathed. Inhale—exhale—inhale—exhale, and once he figured out the cadence, he synced his breathing with hers. He thought about just how vulnerable she was at that moment, sleeping directly above with only the thickness of a mattress and box spring separating the two of them. At nine thirty, Atticus slithered out from under the bed and leaned against the wall next to the headboard.

The little dog raised his head to investigate the sudden noise in the room, but just as quickly, he snuggled up close to Jennifer's naked body and went back to sleep. Atticus continued to stand there. Staring at her. Knowing that it wouldn't take two seconds to cut her throat. But that's not how the game was played, and he was in no rush. It was Jennifer's move, and he would wait for as long as it took for her to visit one of the locations on the game board, and when she did, it would be his turn.

Making sure not to disturb Jennifer, Atticus reached over into the bed and gently rubbed Tye's little head one last time before quietly tiptoeing out of the house and into the cool night air.

CHAPTER 9

Tuesday, December 23
10 Marine View Drive
Reese Valley, Washington
3:00 a.m.

Somewhat disquieted, Atticus was wide awake and roaming around the house well before sunrise. Jennifer was on his mind. The way he saw it, she had committed the ultimate sin. Not only had she invaded his personal space at the tasting room, but she touched his face, something he swore nobody would ever do again after what he'd suffered through with his abusive mother. He could have easily killed her yesterday, but honoring the rules of the game was more important.

By four thirty he had showered and settled on the perfect outfit for the day. He stepped into his closet and removed a pair of blue dress pants, a gray patterned shirt, gray sport coat, and a pair of brown shoes. After getting dressed, he stood in front of the full-length mirror, admiring himself for a long time.

"Classic never goes out of style," he said aloud, adjusting the blue silk pocket square.

Five minutes later, he was still in front of the mirror, staring at himself. Suddenly, a scowl appeared, replacing the smile across his face. He started pacing back and forth across the bedroom, counting to himself with each pass. When he reached twenty-seven, he stopped and returned to the mirror.

"Something is not right!" he shouted.

After another sixty seconds or so of staring at himself in the mirror, Atticus turned and stormed out of the bedroom toward the door leading to the basement. He flung the door open and flipped on the light as he made his way down the stairway to the lower level. Once there, he stood in the center of the basement with his eyes closed.

"It's not right. It's not right. It's not right," he repeated, scratching his head with both hands.

After several seconds, he opened his eyes and smiled.

"The photo. I forgot the frigging photo. She needs to see what she did."

He walked over to the metal cabinet, removed the photo of his mother from the drawer, and started wiping away the dust with his fingers.

"You sit right here, Mommy, dearest," he said, placing the photo atop the cabinet.

He took a couple of steps back and squatted down a bit in order to be face to face with the photo.

"Why can't you give me the respect that I'm entitled to? Why can't you treat me, like I would be treated by any stranger on the street?" he shouted, reciting one of the many quotes made famous by the Joan Crawford character played by Faye Dunaway in the 1981 film *Mommie Dearest.* Atticus hated the film because of how the relationships between the characters aligned with the way he saw the relationship between his mother and himself. Still, he watched the movie at least twice a month, something he had done without fail for the past twenty years.

Satisfied that he had readied things in the basement, he started walking back up the stairway. When he reached the top, he glanced down one last time.

"Perfect," he mumbled, flicking off the light and walking out.

Once back in the kitchen, Atticus filled his cup with coffee, then picked up the remote, and started surfing through the channels, a morning ritual that always ended at the same place. Local news. As chance would have it, a news reporter was in the middle of a story about a convicted child molester being sentenced to 250 years in prison for abusing girls he'd babysat more than a decade ago.

"Our criminal justice system at its best," he blurted out between sips. "You sentence someone to that many years for nothing more than a sound bite? Two hundred and fifty years? Save the bullshit and just throw that freak in a room with the parents of those little girls for five minutes and see what happens. That's how you get justice."

Atticus looked at his watch.

"About that time," he said.

He finished drinking the last of his coffee and switched off the television. After a speedy stop by the powder room for one last look in the mirror, he headed for the door.

Scene 1

40019 Goat Trail Road
Reese Valley, Washington
6:45 a.m.

It was around six forty when Atticus pulled onto Goat Trail Road, and with the preliminary work done, it was now just a waiting game. Like yesterday, neighbors on the block drove past the white SUV as if it weren't there. Also like yesterday, Jennifer brought little Tye out to do his business before the two raced back up the front steps and into the house. At eight o'clock, the garage door opened, and Jennifer backed out and drove past. This time, however, Atticus remained parked at the curb. Knowing exactly where she worked, there was no need to rush. Today's objective was simply to track her throughout the day and see where she went.

When he drove by BABS at a little past nine, he noticed not only that Jennifer had parked her car in the same general area as yesterday, but also that she'd pulled into the spot at the end of the row, making it much easier to keep tabs on her car from the street. Figuring the chances of her leaving the office over the next several hours were slim to none, Atticus drove over to the Red Cup Café for his usual ham-and-Swiss croissant with coffee and, because he never left home without at least a few *Psychology Today* magazines, occupying his time until Jennifer got off work would be a cinch.

In the mood for a true sushi experience, around eleven thirty, Atticus drove by BABS to make sure Jennifer's car was still in place, then it was off to Sushi Kashiba where he was a regular. When he walked through the front door about an hour later, he nodded to the waiter and headed over to the same table he always sat at in the left-back corner of the restaurant. Within seconds, the waiter walked up to greet him, holding the first of his customary two glasses of pinot gris. There was no need to offer Atticus a menu. For the past two years, without fail, he'd ordered the same thing: *omakase.*

He preferred to just sit back and allow the chef to perform his magic. And the meal was always different. More importantly, it was always perfect. As far as he was concerned, this was dining at its finest. A couple of hours later, he was done eating, and after checking his phone messages, he stood up, dropped two hundred dollars on the table, and left the restaurant. It was time to head back across town. If things played out according to plan, Jennifer would be getting off work soon.

Scene 2

RVPD Headquarters
1:22 p.m.

Steele was anxious as he sat at his desk looking over his case notes. He couldn't think clearly. After several minutes of doing no more than spinning his wheels, he pulled his cell phone from his pocket and dialed the colonel's number. After two rings, the colonel picked up.

"Colonel Steele," the gruff voice on the other end barked into the receiver.

The nightmare from the other night was still fresh in his mind, but for some reason, the detective felt that just hearing his father's voice would help ease the pain. Or in the least, help him with getting his mind back on track. He opened his mouth to speak, but nothing came out. Steele tried once more, and again, his attempt at forming words failed.

"Who the hell is this?" the colonel roared into the phone.

Realizing the mistake he had made, Steele hung up. The harsh tone of the colonel's voice made one thing crystal clear to the detective: the person he needed to be speaking with most at the moment was not the colonel but Dr. Nora Beale, the psychologist he'd first started seeing at age five as a condition of being allowed back in school. Dr. Beale had retired from her practice several years ago but always made herself available to counsel the detective anytime he needed what he jokingly referred to as a "brain reset." He dialed her number, and three rings later, the two were connected.

"Hello?"

"Hello, Doc," Steele responded.

Immediately recognizing his voice, Dr. Beale perked up.

"Well, hello, Braxton. How are you, dear?"

"Not so good, Doc."

"The nightmares?"

"Yes."

"And the sound?"

Several seconds passed, and Steele had yet to respond.

"Why don't you come by?"

"I'm leaving the office now. See you in thirty."

"Okay, dear. I'll see you when you get here."

"Thanks, Doc."

The ringing in his ears was back, but this time at a decibel where the detective knew he was in trouble, and while he had access to Dr. Beale anytime he needed her, he preferred bringing his emotions under control by using the skills she taught him when he was young. Most of the time it worked. Just not today.

Scene 3

104 Beverly Blvd
Everett, Washington
2:00 p.m.

Steele arrived at Dr. Beale's home around two o'clock. He walked up the steps, taking note of the abundance of ivy that had grown out of control since he had last been there. The entire front of the house was covered by the shiny green leaves. He pushed a vine aside and was just about to ring the doorbell when Dr. Beale suddenly opened the door.

"Hello, Braxton," she said, extending both arms to give her favorite client a big hug.

"Hi, Doc," Steele responded, leaning in for their familiar warm embrace.

"Come in, dear. I just put on a fresh pot of coffee. You know where my office is. I'll see you in there shortly."

Steele stepped in and began walking toward the study. A short time later, Dr. Beale walked in holding two steaming cups of coffee.

"Here you are, dear. Just the way you like it, three creams, two sugars. I also placed an almond biscotti on the saucer for you. I sampled them at Trader Joe's yesterday and, you know me, I've never tasted a sample I didn't like. Try it. They're delish!"

"Thanks, Doc."

Dr. Beale sat on the couch across from Steele and crossed her leg as she sipped from her coffee cup.

"When did they return?" She asked.

"About a week ago."

"The same?"

"Worse. This time I actually placed it in my mouth. I woke up right before pulling the trigger."

Dr. Beale didn't respond. Instead, she sat quietly with a watchful eye on the detective. She knew him well. She also knew he had more to say.

"It seemed so real, Doc."

"I see. And the ringing in your ears?"

"There hasn't been a day I haven't heard it at some point."

"Is the ringing there now?"

"No. Not at the moment."

"What do you think is behind it."

"I don't know. I'm just tired of it all, Doc."

"I have to ask you, Braxton. Have you thought about actually acting out on your feelings?"

"No."

"When was the last time you spoke with your father?"

Again, Steele sat quietly without immediately responding.

"It's been a while. I wouldn't know where to start."

"But you've been thinking about him lately."

"Not until..."

Dr. Beale watched intently as Steele tried to gather his thoughts. His hand was a bit shaky. Suddenly, he brought a second hand to the saucer about the same time a small amount of coffee sloshed over the side of the cup.

"Until what?" she prodded, trying to get him to complete his thoughts.

"I received a call from someone I believe is responsible for murdering all those women. Anyway, somehow during the time I had him on the phone, the conversation went south and turned into a discussion about abusive parents. Next thing I know, I'm thinking about the colonel. He really hit a nerve, Doc, and for whatever reason, I can't seem to get him out of my head."

"I see. How about calling the colonel right now?"

"Why would I want to do that?"

"How about we do this? Close your eyes for me, Braxton."

He had gone through these types of drills in the past and figured at some point during their conversation that Dr. Beale was going to run him through at least one of the exercises. Steele closed his eyes.

"Now begin breathing deeply, taking in as much air as your lungs can possibly hold. Hold it for a moment, then exhale slowly, expelling all the air from your lungs."

Dr. Beale studied the detective as his chest began to expand and contract with each breath.

"Now, continue breathing, and with your eyes remaining closed, I want you to focus your attention on your head. Imagine tension across the front of your face. Now it's starting to extend itself, wrapping around both ears and ending up at the back of your head. Feel the tension as your head is being squeezed from all sides. Hold it for a moment."

Steele's facial expression changed. He grimaced as if he were in pain.

"Now release it, Braxton. Release it. Your head should feel as light as a feather. You are at peace."

His face instantly softened.

"Now, making sure you maintain that sense of calmness and peace from the neck up, focus on the part of your body between your waistline and the base of your neck. I want you to feel as if your chest is wedged between a giant vice grip. As the tool is starting to tighten, you are experiencing excruciating pain as your back and your chest are being scrunched together. At the same time, five-hundred-pound dumbbells have been fastened to each of your wrists. You feel as if your arms are being pulled out of their sockets. Feel the tension, Braxton. Hold it for a moment. Hold it. Hold it. Hold it."

Dr. Beale watched as Steele's body began to twitch. His facial expression was unchanged, and she could tell that at least from the neck up, the detective was maintaining an isolated state of relaxation. She could also tell that he was still performing the exaggerated breathing technique.

"Now, release it, Braxton. Both the heavy weight and the pressure are gone. You feel as light as a feather. You are at peace."

Again, Steele visibly relaxed.

"Making sure that you hold onto that sense of calmness you've already socked away, we're going to throw you back in that giant vice grip and turn the crank. The pain is horrendous. You can hardly stand it but from the waist up, you are calm. Nothing can interfere with the peace and serenity you feel from the waist up. We're turning the crank a bit more, and your legs feel as if they're about to shatter. They are burning. The pain is like nothing you've ever experienced. Can you feel it, Braxton? Now hold it right there for a while longer."

Dr. Beale saw his legs starting to jerk, and she knew he was exactly where she needed him to be.

"Now, with your eyes still closed, release the pain, Braxton. Not just from your legs but all of that negative energy you've been storing up. Let it all go. Now welcome the lower half of your body to the peace and harmony you are experiencing from the waist up. Picture yourself floating in the placid waters of a still lake. This is where you want to be. You are now at total peace."

She watched as the detective's shoulders slumped and he began to sink deeper into the couch. His breathing had slowed even more, letting her know that his heart rate had returned to normal.

"Open your eyes, dear."

After a few seconds, Steele opened his eyes and looked at Dr. Beale.

"How are you feeling?"

"You still have that magic touch, Doc."

"I'm glad you're feeling better. Let's say you give me a call in a couple of days just to check in. Will you do that?"

"Yeah, Doc. I can do that."

Steele got up from the couch and walked into the waiting arms of Dr. Beale.

"You're going to be just fine, dear," she whispered in his ear.

"Wish I could believe that, Doc. I really do. I'll call you, though," he said, walking toward the door to leave.

Scene 4

Bounds Accounting & Business Solutions
7:00 p.m.

Jennifer was heavy into her phone conversation, laughing and talking loudly when she walked out a little past seven o'clock. A short time later, she drove out of the parking lot with her face partially illuminated by the soft glow of the cell phone screen. After stopping by the gas pumps at the Shell station down the street, she got back in the Audi and hopped on the 525, not stopping again for another forty-five minutes until she pulled off the highway and parked next to the strip mall on the 300 block of Bellevue Way. Atticus was right there.

Pulling over to the curb about four car lengths behind, he had a visual of both the Audi and the strip mall. He lowered his window and immediately got a whiff of fresh tar in the air. He looked across the dark parking lot, and with the other stores in the mall having closed for the evening at six o'clock, Alex Goldbarb Jewelers, the only business with its lights still on, could be seen from a mile away. His heart started pounding as he pulled the neatly folded sheet of paper from his pocket and began scrolling down the list of businesses. The name sounded familiar, but he needed to make sure. About halfway down, he saw it: Alex Goldbarb Jewelers.

"Well, I'll be," he muttered, raising the binoculars to his eyes and monitoring Jennifer's every step as she took the long way around the parking lot that was taped off to prevent cars from parking on the freshly paved surface. He noticed the well-dressed, middle-aged man come from behind the counter and walk toward the glass door the moment Jennifer reached the top step leading to the business. Based on the warm greeting, it was apparent he was expecting her.

Once Jennifer was inside, Atticus pulled the valve stem tool from his pocket and stepped out of the SUV. It took him less than two minutes to get over to the Audi, deflate the driver-side rear tire, and make it back. He raised the binoculars to his face and trained them on the jewelry store. Jennifer was standing at the counter, and the man appeared to be showing her a variety of rings.

After another minute or so of looking at jewelry, she removed the ring from her finger and placed it on the counter. The man began slipping silver-colored loops over Jennifer's ring finger one at a time. When he was done, he made a notation on a piece of paper before placing her ring in a small white envelope.

At eight fifteen, the man walked from behind the counter and escorted Jennifer to the front door. Based on his hand gestures, it appeared he was offering to walk her to her car. But she apparently refused the man's attempt at performing a good deed. Once she left the store, the man closed the glass door and lowered the blind, and when he turned off the lights, Goldbarb Jewelers vanished into the background.

Almost immediately, Jennifer began to panic as she looked across the parking lot toward the Audi that seemed much further away now. She was alone. Not wanting to take the long route back, she stepped under the boundary tape and started walking briskly across the lot. She was still several yards away from the Audi, and as her black Christian Louboutin leather pumps pressed deep into the freshly poured asphalt with each step, Atticus could tell by her facial expression that she was second-guessing her decision not to allow the man to accompany her back to her car.

He continued watching her. Monitoring her every move. When he knew Jennifer was within range, he opened the glove compartment and pushed the button on the jammer, knocking out all incoming and outgoing service to her cell phone.

It didn't take Jennifer long to realize that something wasn't quite right, and when she allowed her eyes to follow along the lines of her car, she noticed the rear tire was deflated and that there was no more than two inches between the bottom of the rim and the pavement. Atticus watched her through the binoculars as she pulled her cell phone from her purse and attempted to place a call. He could tell she was starting to freak out. After another several seconds of watching her pace frantically around her car as if trying to locate a spot where the reception was better, he drove down the street, pulled alongside the Audi, and lowered the passenger side window.

"Hi there. Looks like somebody has a flat. Do you need any help?" he asked.

Startled, Jennifer began back-pedaling.

"Sorry about that. Didn't mean to scare you."

Jennifer continued holding the phone to her ear as if she was talking to someone on the other end, all the while, carefully studying the SUV as well as the man inside.

"Hold on a second," she said, speaking into the cell phone before turning her attention to the man.

"Yeah, I have a flat tire, but my fiancé is on his way to fix it for me. He should be here soon."

"That's great, but seeing that I'm here now and can have you on the road in about ten minutes, would you like for me to help you? I mean, I'd really hate to drive off and just leave you out here all by yourself. And who knows? Your fiancé could hit traffic on his way, and then you're really screwed. Your call, though."

Jennifer resumed speaking into the phone receiver, again pretending to be in a conversation with someone on the other end.

"Hey, babe, a man driving a white Mercedes Benz SUV is out here. He said he can fix my flat in two secs. What do you think? Okay, I'll have him take care of it. Oh, you're not too far away? Okay, babe, see you soon."

Jenifer pushed the button on the phone as if she was ending the call.

"My fiancé isn't too far away, but he said if you can get it changed out before he gets here, that would be awesome."

"I actually think that's a wise decision," Atticus responded.

Knowing that the two of them were the only ones on that particular section of the darkened street, he didn't bother shutting off his engine as he got out of the SUV and slowly walked to the back of the Audi. He noticed Jennifer was keeping her distance.

"Go ahead and pop the trunk so I can grab your spare."

Jennifer was apprehensive, and rightfully so, as she stared at the man from several feet away. He just looked so familiar. She pressed down on the electronic key fob and immediately, the trunk lid popped open.

"Sorry, miss, but I have no idea where to start looking to find your spare tire. I mean, I'll gladly pull it out of the trunk for you, but you need to show me where it is."

Jennifer approached the back of her car, oblivious that Atticus had pulled a dark-colored cloth from his back pocket and had stepped in behind her. He was no more than two feet away when she leaned over into the trunk.

"The spare tire is—"

Her words were cut short when he reached his arm around and pressed the chloroform-soaked rag tightly against her nose and mouth until her world went black. Jennifer was unconscious. Propping her up with one arm, Atticus opened the door and pushed her limp body onto the back seat before hopping in and quickly shutting the door. He secured her wrists and legs with zip ties, then placed a canvas hood over her head. All of this took less than one hundred twenty seconds, and when he was done, he climbed back behind the steering wheel and slammed the SUV into drive.

CHAPTER 10

Wednesday, December 24
300 Block of Bellevue Way
Bellevue Washington
9:38 a.m.

In her haste to get over to Goldbarb Jewelers last night, Jennifer hadn't realized her car was partially blocking the driveway, nor did she notice the sign indicating that because of scheduled street sweeping, parking on the block was prohibited on Wednesdays for the better part of the day. Towing cars in violation of local parking rules was a common occurrence in the area. However, when the tow truck driver noticed the driver-side door was unlocked and the valve stem was missing from the rear tire, he figured something was amiss. Rather than just tow the vehicle, he alerted Bellevue Police Department regarding his suspicions.

Steele was sitting at his desk when the call was put through around nine forty-five.

"Detective Steele."

"Good morning, Detective. This is Detective Lou Collins with Bellevue PD. We have something over here you folks may want to jump on."

"I'm listening."

"One of our local tow companies was about to hook up a silver Audi for illegal parking when they happened to notice the valve stem was missing from the rear tire, which he thought was a bit odd. But when he said the driver-side door was unlocked and there was a woman's purse sitting in the passenger seat, well, that even got my attention."

"I take it you already ran the plates."

"The car came back to a Jennifer Rollins at 40019 Goat Trail Road in Reese Valley. That name ring a bell?"

"Negative. Tell you what, I'll start heading that way. Where exactly is the Audi now?"

"It's still parked on the three hundred block of Bellevue Way. I sent a unit out there to babysit it until I got hold of somebody in your shop. I'll meet you out there."

"Roger that. Give me about an hour. I'm leaving the office now."

"Ten-four."

Scene 1

10 Marine View Drive
Reese Valley, Washington
10:30 a.m.

Jennifer instantly turned her attention to the sound of creaking wood. Atticus had opened the door to the basement and was standing at the top of the stairs. Jennifer sensed his presence and immediately started screaming as loud as she could.

"Help me! Somebody, please help me!" she yelled.

The effects of the chloroform had worn off sometime around midnight, and that's when Jennifer had first become aware that her clothing had been removed and restraints had been placed around her arms and legs. But as bad as that was, being claustrophobic, regaining consciousness and finding that a sack had been placed over her head was worse than any fate she believed stood before her. Her legs had felt as heavy as logs as she began to sense the cold dampness of the cement beneath the plastic sheathing. The metal ring that had been placed around her left ankle seemed to cut into her skin anytime she pulled outside the limits of the chain. Still, although unable to stand, nor see, Jennifer had continued to roll around from one side to the other, while the sound of the chain rattling along the basement floor echoed loudly in her ear.

She could hear the footsteps getting closer.

"Who are you? Why are you doing this to me?"

"Right now, the only thing you need to be concerned with is what I am about to say," Atticus responded in a calm voice.

Jennifer continued pulling against the chain, jerking her body back and forth, trying her best to break loose.

"Why are you doing this?"

"I really need for you to listen. Your life depends on it," Atticus said, still speaking in a measured voice.

Jennifer began screaming as loud as she possibly could as she rolled around on the ground as far as the chain would allow. After watching her twist and turn for about twenty seconds, Atticus stepped in and planted his foot on the small of her back.

"You're hurting me!" she cried out.

"Be still. I told you that you needed to listen. I'm not going to say it again."

Atticus removed his foot from Jennifer's back and stepped back a few feet.

"There are motion-sensing video cameras throughout this room, all pointing at you from every angle you can possibly imagine."

He moved around and stood near Jennifer's head, and almost immediately, Jennifer could hear a light tapping sound. Like metal. She sensed him standing near, but he didn't say anything for several seconds.

"This is a metal bucket," he finally said. "You'll need this when it comes time to relieve yourself."

Jennifer gasped as she fought back her urge to scream again.

Atticus moved around to where he was now standing on her right side. "Over here, you'll find a stack of burlap sacks. It gets cold down here at night, so these will certainly come in handy."

She heard the man shuffling around and sensed that he was standing near her feet. There was about forty seconds of silence before he spoke again, and though she was virtually blind under the canvas hood, Jennifer could feel his eyes burning a hole straight through her body.

"This is the spot where I'll drop off your food. Some days, I may not be here, but if you manage your consumption correctly, you'll always have something to eat. I put a couple of boxes of crackers and some candy out for you. I'm sure it's not your typical diet, but it's better than nothing."

Atticus stooped to the floor, and the moment she felt his hand on her back, Jennifer let out a loud scream and tried to jerk her body away.

"Hold still," he said, still speaking in a calm voice as he reached in and used the knife to cut through the zip ties around Jennifer's arms and legs. "One more thing, and this part is extremely important, in fact, this is what will determine how long you stay alive. Are you listening?"

When Jennifer didn't immediately respond, Atticus repeated his question, but much louder this time. "I asked, 'Are you listening?'"

"Yes," Jennifer managed to say.

"That's good. I told you earlier that there were six cameras pointing right at you, but I didn't say why. So here goes. I'm going to remove the hood from over your head, but here's the catch. Regardless of whether I'm standing here or not, you had better not open your eyes, not now, not tomorrow, not ever. I'm going to roll through the footage from the video cameras every day, and if at any point along the way you forget and accidentally open your eyes, I guarantee you, you'll regret it. Do you understand?"

"Yes," she managed to say through her muffled cries.

"No, I don't think you do, Jennifer" Atticus responded.

Jennifer remained as still as she could, listening to the footsteps moving away from her. She heard some rattling, and then what appeared to be a metal drawer being opened and closed right away. After a few seconds, the sound of footsteps resumed, becoming louder with every step. Her heart started beating faster, and she could hardly breathe.

Atticus bent over and grabbed hold of Jennifer's shackled leg.

"Don't move and don't you dare touch my hand, or this is going to hurt even more."

Jennifer screamed as she tried to pull away.

"Please don't," she cried.

Atticus pulled the skinning knife slowly across Jennifer's thigh exposing the under tissue and causing blood to flow from the wound, while deafening screams pierced through the canvas hood and ricocheted off every wall of the basement. When he was done, he ripped the hood off Jennifer's head and then got to his feet, still holding onto the bloody knife.

"Stand up," he said, reverting back to using his calm voice.

Jennifer struggled to get to her feet but fell back to the ground on her first attempt. Her leg ached and burned at the point of the laceration. She tried again, and this time, she succeeded, finding herself standing directly in front of her abductor.

Atticus took two paces forward, and just as the two had been during their first encounter at O & S, less than an inch separated their noses. Streaks of dark mascara ran the length of Jennifer's face, the result of her uncontrolled cries, but the red lipstick was still fairly intact. Atticus didn't say a word, nor did he have to. Jennifer was well aware of his presence, and for a moment, she thought she had smelled the fragrance before. But that was impossible. The allure of his cologne and what she was going through at the moment just didn't coincide. She was being turned on by the smell of his cologne and, at the same time, fearing for her life.

Her abductor was right in front of her, but she was all alone. The fear was so great Jennifer was becoming disoriented, and there was nothing she could do but stand still and obey, trembling uncontrollably and praying that she could continue fighting the impulse to open her eyes. After what seemed like an eternity, Atticus turned and walked away, leaving Jennifer standing there in her world of darkness as the wooden planks once again came to life under the weight of his every step as he ascended up the stairway.

Scene 2

300 Block of Bellevue Way
Bellevue, Washington
11:00 a.m.

Steele arrived on scene and pulled alongside the curb across from the strip mall. He immediately noticed the two officers from Bellevue PD parked directly behind the silver Audi. About the same time, a man in a dark-blue suit hopped out of a black Crown Vic and started walking toward him. He assumed it was Detective Collins.

"Welcome to our part of the world, Detective. Hope the traffic didn't treat you too badly," Collins said, extending his hand.

"It wasn't bad. Thanks for the call, Detective. And please call me Steele."

"You got it. Please call me Lou."

"Thanks, Lou. So, what do you have?"

Lou handed Steele a manila folder containing some field notes he had taken along with Jenifer's DVM photo.

"As I told you on the phone, the tow truck driver felt something was out of place, so he called it in. And in case you're wondering, I popped the trunk. She's not in there."

"That's good."

"But there's a cell phone in the there."

"That's not good."

"Not at all."

Steele and Lou turned their attention toward the corner of the block when they heard the roaring engine of a truck turning onto Third Street.

"Looks like your flatbed has arrived. We'll get out of your way, but be sure to call me if you need anything. We're here to assist. Just one more thing..."

"What's that?"

"You'll see in my notes where I interviewed the owner of that convenience store across the street after I noticed those surveillance cameras out front. Unfortunately, the one pointed directly at the Audi isn't working."

"What a shocker! How about that one at the corner of the building? Broken too, I'm assuming."

"Actually, that one does work. I reviewed the footage and noticed a white Mercedes Benz G-Class pulling around the corner a short time after the Audi first came onto the block. The problem is that both vehicles move completely out of frame after making the turn."

"Figures."

"Yeah, I know. Anyway, here's the tape. Check it out and let me know if you need me to run down anything for you. Might save you a trip."

"Will do."

CHAPTER 11

Thursday, December 25
87790 53rd Street W
Reese Valley, Washington
5:00 a.m.

Christmas morning in the Steele home was always the same. Braxton and Madi would lie in bed waiting for the moment Grant would come crashing through the bedroom door. Like clockwork, sometime between the hours of five thirty and six o'clock, the bedroom door would fly open, and their little son would hop onto the bed with one goal in mind: to go open presents. But this morning, six had come and gone, and Grant had yet to invade their space. The tradition had been broken, replaced instead by the sound of Steele's cell phone vibrating wildly on the nightstand.

"Not on Christmas!" Madi exclaimed.

"I know, sweetheart. Hopefully, it's something I can just handle over the phone," Steele responded, reaching for the cell phone.

"Steele."

"Merry Christmas, Detective."

Surprised by the call, he sat up in bed the moment he heard the distorted voice on the other end.

"I understand you found the silver Audi."

"Do you have the missing woman? Is she still alive?"

"It's way too late for her, Detective. In fact, she's already dead. She just doesn't know it."

Click! Atticus disconnected the call.

"What was that about?" Madi asked.

"It was him. He abducted Jennifer Rollins."

"That woman who lives over on Goat Trail?

"Yes."

"Oh my God!"

Suddenly, the doors flung open, and in a flash, Grant jumped up on the bed and started tugging at the covers. His timing was exemplary, and exactly what Steele and Madi needed in order to get their minds off the missing woman, if only for a moment.

"Merry Christmas, Mommy! Merry Christmas, Daddy!"

Madi put on the best happy face she could muster under the circumstances.

"Merry Christmas, my sweet little one," she responded, pulling Grant close to her and rocking him in her arms while Steele closed his eyes and pretended to be sleeping through all of the commotion.

"I know you're awake, Daddy. I can see your eyes moving," Grant said, twisting his body a bit to face his father.

Steele kept his eyes closed tightly for a while longer before suddenly jumping out of bed and reciting those magical words, "What's everyone waiting for? Let's go see what Santa dropped off," prompting Grant to immediately hop off the bed and race downstairs toward the Christmas tree.

Scene 1

7:15 p.m.

Playing Oligopoly with a group of friends was how the detective and Madi first met which was why the game was very dear to them. They purchased an Oligopoly game of their own early in their relationship and had always kept it close by, finding time every Christmas to play for at least an hour. Over the years, the game board had become a bit ragged, and Madi knew the time had come to finally retire the single-most thing, she jokingly told everyone, that had brought the two of them together.

Grant had been first introduced to Oligopoly four Christmases ago, and since that time, playing had transitioned from simple fun and games into a Steele family tradition that he not only enjoyed, but also had come to expect. With the family's original game now safely stored away in the plastic tub along with other little keepsakes, Madi ensured Santa left a brand-new Seattle edition of the popular game under the Christmas tree for Grant. The day was winding down, and after spending the majority of it lounging around the house in pajamas, nibbling on the vast array of baked goods on the kitchen counter, it was game time.

As always, Grant immediately called dibs on serving as the banker, which his parents never objected to, seeing it as a way for their son to learn while still having fun. About ten minutes into the game, Steele landed on the Space Pin and decided to purchase his first piece of real estate of the evening.

"That will be sixty dollars," Grant said, smiling broadly.

"Okay, son," Steele responded, starting to count out the money. "Ten, twenty, thirty, forty, fif—"

"Ten more dollars, Dad. I said sixty."

Steele sat there staring at the game board for a long time without saying a word. His eyes began darting from one spot on the board to the next, studying the names and the associated dollar amounts. Suddenly, he spotted Goldbarb Jewelers, and that's when he leaped from his chair, pulled out his cell phone, and snapped a photo of the entire game board.

"I gotta go to the office!"

"No, Dad!" Grant shouted, disappointment already registering across his little face.

"I'm so sorry, son. I have to leave, but I promise I'll make it up to you."

Steele leaned down and kissed Grant on the forehead before hurrying upstairs to grab his service weapon and credentials. Madi could tell by the look on his face that his mind was already working overtime. She also knew that whatever he was thinking about must be urgent for him to leave his family on Christmas Day. By the time Steele reached the bottom step, Madi was already standing there.

"Be safe and hurry home, sweetheart," she said, wrapping her arms tightly around his neck and planting a kiss on his cheek.

"I'm sorry, honey."

"I know," she said softly, doing her best to be the supportive police wife.

Thirty minutes later, Steele was in his office and standing before the cabinet stuffed with investigative files on the murdered women. Not only had the adrenaline rush not subsided, it seemed to be intensifying as he began pulling the files from the cabinet. He had finally stumbled across something that may actually provide insight as to the money envelopes that kept showing up at RVPD following the murders.

During his follow-up interview with Mr. O'Connell, Steele learned that one of the last places Belinda visited before she was reported missing was the Space Pin, which just so happened to be one of the locations on the Oligopoly game board. Add to that, sixty dollars was sent to RVPD after her murder, which was the exact amount of cash it would cost to purchase that property. And now, Jennifer Rollins appeared to have been abducted after making a stop at Goldbarb Jewelers in Bellevue, Washington. Another location on the game board.

CHAPTER 12

Friday, December 26
10 Marine View Drive
Reese Valley, Washington
8:37 a.m.

The anguish started the moment Jennifer first heard his foot hit the stairway, and the closer Atticus got to the bottom step, the more freely the urine cascaded down her inner thighs. She had awakened during the night, and momentarily forgetting where she was, she'd inadvertently opened her eyes before quickly closing them again. But the damage had been done.

During the brief moment she peeked, Jennifer couldn't help but notice the video camera pointed directly at her. She saw the tiny illuminated red light on the front of the camera, which could only mean one thing—her actions had been recorded. It also meant her abductor would know she had disobeyed his strict orders.

Atticus walked up from behind and wrapped his large arm around Jennifer's shoulders, squeezing her, pinning her close to his chest. Her heart was pounding, and she felt a cold shiver run down the full length of her spine in response to his warm breath on the back of her neck. He began whispering softly in her ear.

"You opened your eyes, Jennifer. And that's a pity. Professor Milgram said there would be days like this."

Jennifer had no idea who Professor Milgram was. Her only instinct was to scream. And that she did. She screamed as loud as her voice would allow. It was ear-splitting. And as she pondered her unthinkable predicament, somehow she had the wherewithal to pick up on a strange familiarity surrounding the man based on nothing more than his scent.

"Please don't hurt me. I didn't mean to open my eyes," she begged.

"It's too late for that. You might as well open them and at least get a look at the man who is about to kill you."

Atticus released his grasp and stepped around to face Jennifer, who was trembling wildly as she strained to keep her eyes shut.

"I said open your eyes, Jennifer."

Begrudgingly, she opened them, but all she could see was a grayish-colored shadow of the man standing there. Eventually, she was able to focus, and when she did, everything came rushing back. His face. His fragrance. Everything. Including sudden recollection of her condescending behavior at the wine-tasting room last weekend.

Atticus smiled as he extended his hand toward Jennifer.

"You remember me, don't you, Jennifer? Here, take the dice and drop them on the floor."

Her anxiety level was running amok as she took hold of the dice and tilted her hand to the side, allowing the little ivory cubes to fall to the ground.

"Let's see…six and two."

Atticus stooped and collected the dice from the floor, then walked over to the workbench, and removed the Oligopoly game board from the drawer. He began tapping his finger as he counted off the spaces.

"One, two, three, four, five, six, seven, eight. All righty then. Nordlum is where the next girl will be taken from," he said, loud enough so that Jennifer could hear him clearly from across the basement.

He picked up a small plastic tray from the corner of the workbench and placed it in his pocket before sliding back the knife drawer and removing two knives. As he turned and started walking back toward Jennifer, he started sliding the knives back and forth across one another.

"Slow or fast?" he asked.

"Please don't!" Jennifer screamed.

"Slow or fast, Jennifer? I'm giving you an opportunity to have a say in how you die."

Atticus held up the cleaver.

"This large one here will certainly do the job, but it will take several chops before pain is no longer an issue for you."

He began twirling the boning knife in a circular motion in the air.

"But if I use this one, you'll likely be dead before pain ever has a chance of registering to your brain."

Jennifer started screaming louder and pulling against the restraint of the chain with all her might.

"Why are you doing this? Please don't!" she pleaded.

Atticus continued walking toward her while the scraping sound of metal on metal grew louder and louder with each step.

"Decide now, Jennifer, or I'll have to decide for you."

Jennifer was crying incessantly while flailing her arms in the air trying to ward him off. But to no avail.

When he was within a foot, Atticus dropped the cleaver to the ground and grabbed a handful of Jennifer's hair. In one smooth motion, he cut a gaping hole across the front of her neck with the boning knife as if he was drawing the bow across the strings of his violin. She was dead before her body flopped to the blood-covered plastic sheathing.

Atticus leaned over and removed the shackle from her ankle. Then using the boning knife, he cut out her eyes and place them neatly in the plastic tray.

"You just couldn't obey, could you? Could you?" he shouted, sensing a sudden burning sensation on his leg but not giving it much thought.

He stood there staring at the body for a long time as if he expected Jennifer to answer. After several seconds, he walked over to the metal cabinet and began dousing a white cloth with hydrofluoric acid before walking back across the basement and using the cloth to wipe away all remaining traces of red lipstick from Jennifer's lips. When he was done, he folded her limp body between the plastic sheathing and secured both ends with duct tape.

Scene 1

RVPD Headquarters
12:18 p.m.

Steele would've been lucky to get two hours sleep last night, and while he was tired as all get-out, all he could think about was how his murder investigation was finally starting to take shape. By noon, not only had he spoken with the relatives of the victims, but he was able to pinpoint the last known place each had gone prior to being reported as missing. As he figured, all of the locations appeared somewhere along the perimeter of the Oligopoly game board, but with a boss only interested in results as opposed to theories, Steele decided to keep this newly developed information close to the vest rather than pass it up the chain.

In the case of the second woman murdered, Gretchen Sullivan, Steele had been able to piece together through speaking with her siblings that Gretchen had driven over to Lynnwood, Washington, to Teddy Lauer's in the Alderwood Mall. He learned that she'd planned on climbing Mount Si and needed a new altimeter. An avid hiker, Gretchen had already climbed several of the local mountains over the past year, and with the 3,150-foot ascent of Mount Si slated for her next endurance test, all the adventurer could think of was the most beautiful view of Puget Sound she believed awaited her once she reached the peak.

Steele's assumption was right on target in terms of far too much time passing for the Teddy Lauer store to still have surveillance footage of the day Gretchen had been in there. But his visit was not a total loss. While skimming through the cash register receipts, the store manager was able to pinpoint the exact day and time Gretchen did her shopping as well as the items she purchased, and once Steele was in receipt of that critical bit of information, the two hundred sixty dollars received by RVPD following her death had made all the sense in the world. It was the exact amount needed to purchase the Teddy Lauer space on the game board.

When he had gotten hold of the parents of both Amanda and Christina, Steele had learned that the girls had been virtually inseparable and would routinely stop for coffee at Starrocks. In fact, they'd gone to Starrocks the day they both had gone missing. According to Mrs. Perez, Christina's mother, the one they'd frequented was located on Reese Valley Speedway.

Unfortunately, there were three Starrocks locations on that street; one in the 1000 block, another in the 1100 block, and a third in the 1200 block, and while Steele had paid a visit to each location, neither had surveillance footage for the day the girls had gone missing. But just as he was in the case with Gretchen, Steele was even more confident about his theory when he was able to associate the three hundred fifty dollars received by RVPD following the murder of the two women to a space on the game board.

Steele had conducted a follow-up interview with Chi-won and Min-hee, the parents of Seoyeon Kim. During that conversation, he had been provided a videotape of the last time Seoyeon's parents would ever see their daughter alive. She was the guest performer for an event held at Benoya Hall, the home of the Seattle Symphony, located not only in downtown Seattle but also on the game board for a purchase price of two hundred forty dollars, the exact amount of money in the envelope sent to RVPD following her murder.

Unbeknownst to the parents, Atticus had been seated in the third row from the front of the auditorium, center stage. Directly behind them. And while Steele had no idea what, if any, value the tape could provide to his investigation, he asked Chi-won if he could borrow it on the chance something might turn up later. After much deliberation with the parents who were understandably reluctant to let the last taped performance of their daughter out of their sight, they'd agreed to loan the recording to the detective on condition he return it promptly once the investigation concluded.

Sylvia Larson had been the sixth woman murdered, and it was her place of employment that played into her being selected. While the Seattle Seafarers organization was what's actually shown on the game board, Sylvia was an employee at the Seafarer's Team Store. Add to that, the one hundred sixty dollars received by RVPD was the exact amount required to purchase the Seattle Seafarers space.

CHAPTER 13

Saturday, December 27
3322 Leslie Lane
Reese Valley, Washington
6:00 a.m.

Sergeant First Class Victor McPhee, service number 416-25-8339, was a six foot seven, two-hundred-fifty-five-pound hunk of a man who'd left the military and taken a position with a local telephone provider more than three decades ago. The thing is, the man had never stopped carrying on as if he was still on active duty. Before his medical discharge, Vic had spent seven years in the military, starting out as an explosive ordnance disposal specialist before becoming an Army Ranger assigned to the Third Battalion, Eighty-Fifth Ranger Regiment, Fort Benning.

These days, Vic hobbled around town on his prosthetic left leg, a little parting gift from the army following the injury. Still, the proud veteran wouldn't hesitate to interrupt the conversation if he believed someone was attempting to shower him with pity. He treasured the time spent in the Rangers and harbored no ill feelings from what had happened to him. In fact, he routinely told people that the true heroes in our society were those who had shed their blood on the battlefield, and if you allowed him to bend your ear long enough, by the end of the conversation, he'd have you convinced that his peg leg was his prized possession.

Since retiring from the phone company fifteen years ago, Vic's daily routine had remained unchanged. Come rain, shine, or snow, at six o'clock in the morning, he threw on some clothes, made a fresh pot of coffee, and after filling his mug, grabbed his hat and made his way over to the door leading to the garage where Clover, his faithful black Lab, was there wagging her tail with her partially chewed-up leash hanging out the side of her mouth. If you didn't know better, you'd swear that old dog could tell time. The strolls had also become her morning routine, and if Vic wasn't up by at least a quarter till, Clover would start pulling at the covers just in case he may have forgotten it was go time.

After his discharge, Vic purchased his little house on Leslie Lane and, on that same day, installed a flag pole in the center of the front yard. When he and Clover returned from their morning walk, Vic hustled to the garage to grab Old Glory from the bin and raised the flag to the top of the pole. Always at the same time. Seven fifteen.

The flag was hoisted briskly in the morning, and at five that evening, Old Glory was lowered ceremoniously. Hand salute and all. Even on days Vic was out of town, the fellas from the VFW performed the honors and ensured the tradition was always carried out.

About two years ago, Vic had started donning his military dress uniform on the second Tuesday of each month and driving over to 1010 SE Everette Mall Way. The site of the Department of Veterans Affairs. Once there, he snapped to attention near the front entrance and held his salute for one hour, twenty-two minutes, and forty-seven seconds in remembrance of the day he had been injured in combat.

The date had been January 22, and it had taken what seemed like the longest forty-seven seconds of his life for his battalion to suppress enemy fire long enough to perform a safe extraction. Every month when he arrived at the VA building, he took his position and then started counting to himself, *One-one thousand, two-one thousand, three-one thousand*, not stopping until he got to *four thousand nine hundred sixty-seven-one thousand*, all the while reflecting on his time in the war as well as the countless number of enemy combatants he had killed. The way he saw it, those were the good old days.

When he'd first started with the salutes, some of the locals just figured the old veteran was patriotic, perhaps a bit over the top, but patriotic nonetheless. But as the months passed without any sign of letting up, the whispers began to grow louder around Reese Valley, many questioning whether or not Vic was having a nervous breakdown. Some even thought he was losing his mind.

But not Atticus. He could relate to what the veteran was going through. Not to mention the fact that Vic had been the one who taught him how to make pipe bombs.

The two first had met at Starrocks on Reese Valley Speedway shortly after Vic had been discharged from the military. From the beginning, they'd hit it off as if they were kindred spirits. They would spend hours upon hours chatting about everything under the sun, from popcorn to politics, but the topic that always seemed to bring them the most joy was when they'd discuss the ease with which a freshly sharpened knife could penetrate the human body.

During one of their more animated debates about the type of person it would take to kill someone, each had admitted to having taken another person's life. Vic had gone so far as to say that he was obsessed with death and, for a reason he couldn't begin to explain, was enamored with the look on a dead person's face. What had followed were sixty seconds of silence where neither had spoken, but knew their lives had just become forever intertwined.

CHAPTER 14

Sunday, December 28
Fremont Sunday Street Market on Evanston Ave North
10:58 a.m.

Atticus was up early flipping through the pages of the December edition of *Psychology Today*. What had his attention was an article discussing psychologist Stanley Milgram's obedience theory.

According to Milgram, people will generally obey orders out of a desire to seem cooperative, although sometimes they do because they're fearful. Always looking to push the ethical limits of psychology, Atticus attempted to recreate Dr. Milgram's theory each time he abducted a woman, and at the point where they disobeyed his orders, he murdered them.

By late morning, he was done with his weekend reading, and after getting dressed, he hopped in his SUV and drove over to the street market where he knew to find Vic in his usual spot under the sea of white canopies. He stopped short of Vic's booth when he saw him wrapping up a knife for a man Atticus could tell immediately was a tourist, based on the number of bags filled with souvenirs the man was carrying, not to mention, the thirty-five-millimeter camera with telephoto lens dangling around his neck. A dead giveaway.

Once Vic finalized the sale, Atticus walked up to the Oligopoly game board that was in its usual place atop the whisky barrel at the rear of the booth.

"So, how goes the battle, Sergeant?"

"Same old, same old, my friend. What's shaking?"

"Not a thing," Atticus responded, picking up the dice and rolling them across the white-linen-covered table.

As they did just about every weekend, the two men played Oligopoly for about thirty minutes, breaking only when a customer approached.

"Are your canopy mates still calling the cops on you?"

"Not this weekend, but the day is still young," Vic responded.

Officers had been dispatched to the street market twice during the past three months after vendors on either side of Vic called RVPD on separate occasions to report that he was acting strangely. During one such incident, Vic had been alleged to have walked into an adjacent booth holding a knife and telling the man that the military had taught him how to kill and that he could cut his throat in two seconds if he wanted to. When officers had arrived and spoken to Vic about the allegation, he'd said he was just joking with the man. Still, they'd issued a cease-and-desist order and promised to charge him with making a terrorist threat if he ever threatened anyone again, joking or otherwise.

Vic abruptly backed away from the Oligopoly game board, reached under the table, and retrieved a black leather case. He opened the lid.

"Feast your eyes on this beauty."

The handle of the knife was a work of art, draped in twenty-four-karat gold inlays.

"I picked it up from a little secondhand shop earlier this week."

"Nice handle, but what's the big whoop?"

"You kidding me? This here is a genuine Gentak Makara," Vic responded, cradling the knife in the palm of his left hand and gently rubbing his index finger across the handle. "I've always wanted one of these. I mean, just look at it. This, my friend, is a uniquely crafted piece of art that represents the perfect balance between elegance, function, artistry, and exotic materials."

"Yeah, okay, if you say so. If you don't mind me asking, what something like that set you back?"

"I paid two thousand for it."

"What the hell for?"

"Because it's worth at least six times that much. I convinced this pimple-faced kid behind the counter that it was just a knockoff but, because I was a collector, I'd take it off his hands just to show it off to my friends who wouldn't know the real thing if it cut 'em on the ass."

"And he believed that crap?"

"I have the knife, don't I?"

"And on that note, I'm taking off."

"Appreciate the visit," Vic responded.

"Tomorrow morning."

"What about it?" Vic asked, looking a bit puzzled.

Atticus didn't say anything. Instead, he stood there until the change in Vic's facial expression let him know that his friend had finally caught his drift.

"Behind the gulch," he finally said, looking back over his shoulder before disappearing into the crowd.

CHAPTER 15

Monday, December 29
3322 Leslie Lane
6:30 a.m.

With temperatures in the area dropping overnight, it was hovering around the fifteen-degree mark when Vic and Clover stepped out to begin their usual slow walk along W. Reese Valley Boulevard. It was still dark outside, and with the sun not expected to rise for about another fifteen minutes, maintaining footing on the black ice was a bit of a challenge that time of the morning. They reached the mouth of Reese Gulch at six thirty, and by the time they completed their stroll through the trees and stepped into the alley behind the conservation area, the first glimpse of the sun was starting to break through.

Vic could feel the pace of his heart beat accelerating as he raised the mug to his lips and sipped on his lukewarm coffee that had started to cool from exposure to the brisk morning air. Suddenly, Clover started pulling hard on her leash. There was an object on the side of the road competing for her attention, and even though Atticus had hinted that a body would be found out there, Vic never quite got used to the pure exhilaration of coming upon a corpse and wanted to savor the moment.

Restraining Clover as best he could, he inched closer. And there she was. A dead woman wrapped within the bloodied plastic. He stood there for several seconds staring at the naked body and allowing the mental image to be firmly committed to memory. When he was done, he backed away and placed a call to the RVPD.

"Nine-one-one emergency. Do you need police, fire, or an ambulance?"

"Um, this is Victor McPhee calling, and I need to report an emergency."

"What type of emergency, sir?"

"Um, there's a dead woman behind Reese Gulch."

"You said a dead woman is behind Reese Gulch?"

"Yeah. She's wrapped up in plastic."

"How do you know she's dead, sir?"

"I think I know what a dead person looks like. She's dead!"

"I understand, sir. Police officers are in route to that location and should be there shortly. Please stay there so you can show them where the body is located."

"I'll be here, but they better hurry. I have to get back to my house and raise my flag at seven fifteen," Vic responded before hanging up.

By six fifty, the area behind Reese Gulch was flooded with police cruisers and media trucks, and while the first officers on scene were busy cordoning off both ends of the street in order to preserve the crime scene, Steele couldn't help but notice just how agitated Victor McPhee seemed to be while giving his statement.

For a while now, Steele had had Vic on his radar after noticing that each time a woman was murdered, Vic was among the onlookers at the crime scene, but this time, he was the one who'd actually called RVPD to report the discovery of the body.

The medical examiner, Dr. Douglas Fryatt, arrived on scene at six fifty-five. After a quick review of the body within the plastic, he began making diagrams of the crime scene and taking photographs. After a lengthy discussion with a forensic analyst, it was decided that because of the excessive amount of blood that had pooled in the bottom of the plastic, it would be best to transport the body to the morgue for a more thorough examination, but first, he cut a slit in the plastic to expose the victim's face that confirmed what Steele had believed all along, the deceased was in fact Jennifer Rollins. She was number seven.

Steele and the medical examiner were still talking when the detective felt his cell phone vibrating in his pocket. He stepped away and answered.

"Steele."

"Good morning."

"Hey there, Randy."

"You said you wanted to be notified immediately anytime an envelope containing money arrived in our mailroom. Well, it just happened. This one contained seventy-five dollars with the word *slut* written across the front of each bill in bright red lipstick."

"Ten-four."

CHAPTER 16

Tuesday, December 30
10 Marine View Drive
Reese Valley, Washington
10:00 a.m.

The doorbell sounded, alerting Professor Atticus Dobson that a visitor was standing outside the security gate in front of his home. Not expecting anyone, he took his time walking over to the monitor in the hallway to look at the screen. Detective Steele was standing there, which was only a surprise in the sense that he'd expected to find police standing at his gate much sooner. There was that suspicious scratch on his leg he had yet to determine its origin, and if things played out as he had pictured them in his mind, the reason for the detective's visit was to either slap cuffs around his wrists or, at the least, request a DNA sample.

"Good morning, Detective. To what do I owe the honor of having you show up unannounced at my home?"

"Good morning, Professor. How are you?" Steele responded, speaking into the metal box next to the gate.

Atticus's home sat well back on the lot and was guarded not only by the block wall surrounding the property and the metal gate in front, but also by several tall trees and thick brush that prevented anyone from seeing the house from the street.

"Now, I know you didn't drive out here just to ask me that, and with class being over, I'm assuming your visit isn't academically related. So what can I do for you, Detective?"

Steele was about to answer when Atticus interrupted.

"Tell you what. I was just about to have another cup of coffee. Would you like to join me?"

"That would be great," Steele responded.

"Stand back a foot or so while I open the gate. Once you're inside, stay on the brick pathway. It'll lead you around to the back of the house."

The chain along the bottom rail began to move, and once the security gate opened, Steele walked into the yard, relieved that he didn't have to try to come up with some lame excuse to get into Atticus's house without a search warrant.

"Welcome. That seat right there has your name written all over it, Detective," he said, pointing to a chair at the kitchen table while, at the same time, pulling a cup from the cabinet to pour the detective's coffee. Atticus needed more time to get a read on exactly why Steele was there.

"I must say, this is some piece of property. I didn't realize this much land was back here."

"That's exactly the point of the security gate, Detective. I enjoy my privacy when I'm home."

"You know, my wife always loved this type of home, but they always seemed a bit cramped to me," Steele said, looking around the kitchen and as far as he could into the adjoining rooms.

"Is that right?" Atticus responded, not bothering to turn around, but even with his back to the detective, he knew he was scanning the house. After all, that's what cops do. In any event, with the bookshelf once again cloaking the basement door, none of that mattered.

Atticus handed Steele the cup of hot coffee before taking his usual seat at the head of the table.

"So, back to what I started asking earlier, why exactly did you drive out here to see me, Detective?"

"Well, I thought I'd pick your brain for a minute if you had some time."

"About?"

"I'm going to be straight with you, Professor. We could really use your help in our murder investigation."

What Steele didn't say was that the surveillance team had reported a possible connection between Victor McPhee and the professor. Unbeknownst to Vic, RVPD had resumed conducting surveillance on him even before he left the crime scene yesterday morning, even though, twice in the past, surveillance activity failed to link the veteran to the murders and had eventually been ended. Undercover officers observed Vic and Atticus recently sitting on the pier behind Varley's chatting it up, so if for no reason other than closing the loop, Steele had no choice but to pay the professor a house call.

"After receiving a tip, another body was discovered yesterday. Quite frankly, I'm thinking it's time we have you come down to the office and help us in developing a criminal profile of the type of person we should be searching for."

Atticus didn't respond immediately. Instead, he lifted his coffee cup to his lips and began swallowing several sips before returning his cup to the table.

"I have to be honest with you, Detective. I am a bit perplexed as to why you guys took so long to approach me when I'm right here. I mean, it's common knowledge that I've been pulled all over the country to offer this type of assistance."

"I don't know, Professor. I guess the powers that be allowed their egos to get in the way. But I'm here now. So what do you say?"

"Of course, I'll help, Detective. I'm always willing to help the RVPD. Just let me know when you need me to come down. You'll have to give me a day's notice so I can clear my calendar though."

"Absolutely," Steele responded, finishing off the last of his coffee as he pushed back from the table and stood up. "One more thing, Professor."

"What's that?"

"Would you mind showing me around your home? I've never been in one of these, and if one happens to come on the market, who knows? I may bite the bullet and try to get one for my wife."

"Not a problem, Detective," Atticus responded, figuring the request was coming sooner or later. "It would be my pleasure to show you around."

For the next fifteen minutes or so, Atticus gave Steele the royal tour of his home, walking in and out of the various rooms and pausing as long as the detective wanted in order to fully appreciate and comment on the decor, artwork, and rare artifacts from around the world that the professor had collected during his travels over the years. When they had walked every inch of the dwelling, Steele thanked Atticus for his hospitality and left, never broaching the subject of DNA.

On his drive back to the office, Steele was satisfied that he had seen what he needed without having to apply for a search warrant and had done so without damaging the relationship the RVPD shared with their expert witness. He had seen every inch of the fifteen-hundred-square-foot home, and nothing of significance was in plain sight. The problem, however, was that county records the detective pulled on the residence prior to his visit did not reflect that the former owner, Eugene Hilborn, tried unsuccessfully for two years to get a building permit to construct a passive wine cellar, or that for the next four years, Eugene came home from work and removed gravel from beneath his home and disposed of it by spreading debris across his property. Nor that Eugene spent another year and a half reinforcing the walls of the underground wine cellar with support beams and cement walls, and once it was completed, only three people ever knew the basement existed, Atticus being the only one still living.

The one thing the detective did find interesting during his time at City of Reese Valley Building and Permits were documents he came across showing Professor Dobson's home was part of a blind trust under the name the Smart Company and that the property was transferred to the trust about ten years earlier.

Scene 1

Nordlum Alderwood Mall
12:37 p.m.

Atticus was browsing through the row of sport coats when he suddenly felt the presence of someone coming up from behind. He looked around out of precaution, and after spotting the sales associate approaching, he continued pulling coats from the metal bar for closer inspection.

"I can tell you have really good taste in clothing, sir, but if you don't mind, I'd like to show you some sport coats I just know you'll fall in love with."

"That right?" Atticus responded, while returning the garment.

"My name is Rave, by the way."

"Rave."

"It's really Raven, but I go by Rave."

"Gotcha."

Rave stepped back a few paces.

"Let's see...six four, muscular, with broad shoulders, which means about a thirty-five-inch chest. One hundred eighty pounds and if I'm not being too forward, handsome as hell. How did I do?"

"Oh, you're smooth, Rave. I'll give you that. Okay, let's see."

"Right over here, sir," she said, smiling as she began walking toward another rack. Rave removed a Milano Classic Fit Sport Coat and handed it to Atticus. "What do you think?"

He slipped on the coat and fastened the top button. "Nice, but I need the sleeves shortened an eighth of an inch. How soon can you have it cut?"

Rave smiled. "You'll have it in time for that New Year's Eve party you're obviously getting ready for."

Atticus didn't respond. Instead, he pulled a credit card from his wallet and dropped it on the counter. As he began removing the coat, his attention was squarely on the woman dressed in the white leather pant suit across the store, sitting at the cosmetic counter. Initially, it was the large red purse hanging over her shoulder that had caught his attention, but then he noticed the woman working the counter was applying a heavy coat of bright red lipstick to her lips.

"Excuse me, sir. Here's your card," Rave said, trying her best to get Atticus's attention.

"Sorry. I have a lot on my mind," he eventually responded. "When did you say my coat will be ready?" He took hold of the credit card and returned it to his wallet.

"It'll be ready for you tomorrow afternoon, sir."

"Perfect. Thanks for your help, Rave. And you were right. I do love it."

Atticus walked over to the cosmetic counter where he immediately settled in behind the woman. She was busy looking at the items in the glass case. So busy that for several seconds, she didn't notice he had walked up and was standing no more than three feet away.

After deciding on a fragrance, she pulled her credit card from the red purse and slid it across the counter toward the sales associate and, in that moment, felt the presence of someone standing uncomfortably close. Her initial instincts were to put the person on notice, but when she turned around, all of that changed. Atticus was looking at his cell phone and appeared to be busy scrolling through what she assumed were text messages. Although his head was tilted downward, she saw enough of his face to know he was attractive.

She smiled and quickly turned back toward the sales associate behind the counter.

"What was that you asked me for?" she asked, causing the sales associate to smile.

"Your drivers license, please."

"That's right," she responded, pulling the license from her purse and placing it on the counter. Atticus was watching. Without drawing attention to himself, he carefully aimed his cell phone and snapped a photo. According to the drivers license, her name was Lauren Kelsey.

Lauren paid for her perfume, and as she turned to walk away, she nearly bumped into Atticus, who was now standing even closer.

"Hello," she said, smiling as she walked passed.

"Hello, back at you," he responded, before turning his full attention to the woman standing behind the fragrance counter. According to the silver-plated tag on her lapel, her name was Sam.

"Hello, Sam. I'm looking for a nice perfume. What would you suggest?" he asked.

"Well, sir, you can never go wrong with Chanel," she responded, lifting a sample bottle of Coco Mademoiselle from the counter and spraying some on her wrist. After fanning her wrist for a few seconds and releasing the warm mixture of citrus and white flowers, she raised her arm toward Atticus, who immediately took hold of her hand and gently pulled it toward his nose, never looking away from her eyes.

"Exquisite," he said, still holding onto her soft hand.

"It's one of our newest fragrances, and I just love it. I think it's classy, romantic, and sexy all at once."

"Just like you," he responded, releasing Sam's hand and pulling his credit card from his pocket. "I'll take it."

Loving the attention, Sam smiled as she reached into the glass counter to retrieve the perfume . "I wish you would," she said, her voice much louder than she intended.

"I'm sorry. Did you say something?" Atticus asked, knowing exactly what he'd heard.

Embarrassed, Sam blushed. "Oh, just talking to myself. I have a tendency of doing that on occasion. Your grand total is $230.05."

"Beautiful."

"Here you are, sir," she said, handing the small bag to Atticus along with the receipt and credit card. "Whoever the lucky lady is, she's going to love this fragrance."

"I'm sure she will. You've been most helpful, Sam. Thank you."

"You're very welcome, sir."

"And by the way, my name is Atticus."

"In that case, you're very welcome, Atticus. I hope you enjoy the remainder of your evening."

"Oh, I will."

Atticus turned and walked toward the door and was about fifteen feet from the exit when a woman's voice caught his attention.

"Hello again," she said, walking from between the clothes rack and into the open. It was Lauren Kelsey.

"Hello, back at you, again," Atticus responded.

"I'm Lauren," she said, smiling as she extended her hand.

"Very nice to meet you, Lauren. I'm Atticus," he responded, taking her hand in his.

"You know, I would love to shoot you."

"Already?"

"Okay, okay, okay, that didn't come out right. I'm a professional photographer, and I just know my camera lens would fall in love with you. In fact, it would be magical. And now, I'm rambling. What I'm trying to say is that you are a beautiful man and I would love to snap some photos of you for a project I'm working on."

"And what sort of project would that be?"

"I've been commissioned by the Reese Valley Chamber of Commerce to put together our city's inaugural men-around-town calendar, and I'm always looking for interesting people to shoot. Sorry, I mean, photograph."

"You think I'm interesting?"

"I do. But before we get to the photograph portion, the two of us would have to have a sitdown so I can make sure you're actually a good fit. On the bright side, you've already passed the first test."

"Let me take a wild guess. Physical appearance."

"Guilty as charged," Lauren responded.

"Wow. And you don't think that's shallow?"

"Well, let's see. How much time would you honestly spend thumbing through a calendar filled with photographs that didn't appeal to you visually, be it cars, houses, or as in this case, people?"

"Ouch."

"I rest my case."

"So you really are a photographer."

"I am"

"Tell me, Lauren. What is the best photograph you've ever taken?"

"Wow. It's kinda hard to select just one."

"Come on. If you had to choose, which would it be?"

Lauren thought about it for a moment before responding.

"A sunset in Mexico."

"Mexico?"

"Yes. Cabo San Lucas. I love going there. I'm in Mexico five, sometimes six times a year, depending on what I have going. But no fewer than five times."

"I guess you do like it over there."

"I do. But not as much as my brother."

"What do you mean?"

"My older brother Ryan, the smart one in our family. He used to travel to Cabo just like me then one day, he met a woman and decided to relocate his practice to Mexico. I thought it was just some crazy idea that had popped in his head and would eventually pass, but less than a year of first meeting her, he closed down operations in the States and moved to Mexico. That was about ten years ago."

"All I can say is your brother must really love Cabo."

"That and he really loves Anita, my sister-in-law. She's a sweetie."

"That's quite a story. What type of doctor is Ryan?"

"He performs cosmetic surgery."

"Facelifts."

"Yeah. That and a whole lot more."

"Like what?"

"Well, he performs rhinoplasty, where someone's nose is reconfigured to bring it into better proportion with their face. He also does chin enhancement surgery in order to improve the contours of his client's chin, neck, and jawline."

"Wow!"

"Oh, and my brother also performs breast enhancement surgery if you ever, you know..."

Lauren started laughing. "Just kidding," she said.

"Must be some woman your brother ran into if he was willing to relocate his business to Mexico. My guess is he's probably making a fraction of the money he made in the States."

"You'd be surprised. Ryan lived and worked in Studio City, and several of his clients were Hollywood types who are going to fight for as long as humanly possible not to look their actual age. Plenty of them travel to Cabo just to have my brother give them a little touch-up."

"Who would've thought?"

"I know, right!" Lauren responded, handing Atticus her business card. "Give it some thought, and if you decide you'd like to be in the calendar, call me."

"Interesting."

He was staring at Lauren's business card and noticing the stark difference between the professional headshot she used to promote her photography business and how she looked at the moment.

"What?" she asked.

"You just look so different from the photo on your business card."

"Yeah, about that. I mentioned to the woman at the cosmetic counter that I was thinking about changing my look up a bit, and the next thing I know, I'm sitting on the bar stool, and she's splashing my face with this hideous red lipstick. As soon as I saw it, I knew it wasn't for me. But she was very persuasive. She said it complimented my purse and asked that I try it just for today and see how people respond."

"You're saying you don't wear red lipstick?"

"Oh, heavens no! Tell you what, come with me," Lauren said, walking toward the other side of the store. Sixty seconds later, she and Atticus arrived at the cosmetic counter.

"Excuse me."

"You're back," the woman responded, walking toward Lauren with a warm smile.

"I'm sorry, but this lipstick isn't working for me. Would you be so kind as to remove it?"

"Certainly," the woman responded. "Lipstick is a funny thing. You either love it or you hate it. Sorry this one didn't work. Please have a seat, and I'll take care of it for you."

Once the lipstick had been removed, Lauren thanked the woman and stood up. She stepped away from the counter and turned toward Atticus.

"I want to ask you something and I would appreciate it if you were perfectly honest."

"What's that?"

"When you first saw me, what was the first thing you noticed?"

He knew exactly what had first drawn him to Lauren, but he took a few seconds before answering.

"I would have to say it was your lipstick."

"And now?" Lauren asked, flashing a bright smile.

"Your perfect teeth," he responded without hesitation.

Lauren chuckled. "Thank you, Mom and Dad, for forcing me to wear all that metal headgear as a child," she said, still smiling from ear to ear.

"You do have a beautiful smile," Atticus responded, genuinely meaning every word he said, while at the same time, a bit disappointed that Lauren no longer fit the parameters of his little game.

"Be well, Atticus, and please don't take too long in making up your mind. I have all I need except for the last two months."

"Very nice meeting you, Lauren. I'll give it some thought," he responded, already starting to scan across the aisles for another woman.

Scene 2

Reese Valley City Hall
3:15 p.m.

Social media was having a field day with rumors running rampant about police possibly knowing who the killer was but not disclosing that information to the public. At the same time, calls were flooding RVPD phone lines with reports of a large group of people gathering on Cyrus Way and blocking the entrance to Reese Valley City Hall. The group was becoming unruly, several among them demanding that Mayor Carla Richardson adjourn the city council meeting and come out to address their concerns.

Detective Steele arrived on scene within ten minutes of the first calls hitting the switchboard, and after a brief meeting with the mayor, he decided the best way to calm the crowd was to hold an impromptu press conference. At about a quarter past three, the doors to city hall swung open and out walked Steele with Mayor Richardson following closely behind.

"Good afternoon. If I could have everyone's attention, I'd like to update you on our murder investigation."

"About time, Detective," a voice shouted from somewhere deep within the crowd.

"Yeah! If you know who the killer is, why haven't you made an arrest? And if you have, why haven't you informed the public?" someone else shouted.

"Look. I understand your fears as well as your frustrations. That's why I've come out to answer your questions."

Someone else started to say something, but their voice was squelched when the detective resumed speaking into the microphone.

"I'm going to start out by saying that I too have heard all the rumors about our case. But let me assure you they are just that: rumors. As of now, no arrests have been made, nor have any suspects been identified."

Jolynn Rider was standing directly in front of the podium.

"Detective Steele, I'm going to ask you the same two questions I asked on December 15. One, are the murders related, and two, is there a serial killer lose in our community?"

"Based on our investigative work to date, it does appear the murders were committed by the same person."

"And Jennifer Rollins?"

"Her body was just discovered yesterday, and we're still awaiting forensic examination reports. That said, based on a preliminary examination of her remains, I wouldn't be at all surprised if it turns out that she too was murdered by the same individual."

"That would make seven murders. Certainly sounds like a serial killer to me," Jolynn said, still extending her microrecorder toward the detective.

Steele knew making such an admission would likely cause fear among the residents, but he needed a break in the case and therefore had no choice but to release more information than he typically would. Somebody out there knew the identity of the killer. He just needed to flesh it out. He took a moment to gather his thoughts before speaking.

"I'll be frank with you, folks. As much as this might sound like a cliché, it's extremely important that each of you remain vigilant, and if you see or hear anything, no matter how insignificant it might seem, call my office. If I don't answer, leave a message. We have to catch this guy."

"So you're saying the killer is a man?"

Steele immediately realized his slip. Up to this point, he hadn't disclosed whether the suspect was male or female, but with the cat out the bag, he decided to go for it.

"Yes. I do believe our suspect is a male."

There was a sense of uncomfortableness among the crowd as residents began holding sidebar conversations, many questioning if the time had come to start arming themselves. Suddenly, a high-pitched voice of a woman broke through the commotion.

"You have to catch that maniac, Detective! I heard he's been cutting out the eyeballs of those poor women."

"Is that true, Detective?" someone else shouted.

"Yeah, is it?" another voice chimed in.

"Look. I hope you understand that while I'll provide you with as much information as possible, in order to protect the integrity of the investigation, I really can't delve too far into specifics."

"So, he is cutting out women's eyeballs," a reporter in front stated, resulting in noticeably more shuffling among the crowd.

Steele was mildly knocked off his game by the comment as he scanned the crowd, briefly locking eyes with local residents who for years had put their trust in him to keep them safe.

"I'm going to catch this guy. You have my word," he said, abruptly handing the microphone to Mayor Richardson and walking briskly toward his vehicle, while Atticus, disguised in a wig, sunglasses, and fake moustache, observed everything from his vantage point near the center of the crowd.

Scene 3

RVPD Headquarters
4:05 p.m.

He was not surprised when his cell phone started vibrating the moment he got back to the office. More than that, he fully expected for the person speaking through the voice distorter to be on the other end. He picked up on the third ring.

"Steele."

"I see my little handiwork got you all choked up out there today, Detective. Honestly, I didn't have you pegged as being squeamish. Anyway, have you changed your mind about playing my little game?"

"It was my father."

Atticus was caught off guard when the detective answered. He didn't say anything for a long while, figuring the detective was just trying to extend the call long enough to trace it, a police tactic he never worried about, being that he'd always used burners when placing calls to Steele. Several months earlier, he'd purchased twenty unlocked cell phones for six hundred dollars from a guy at Edgewater Park in Everett and was able to secure the SIM cards he needed from T-Mobile on Reese Valley Speedway. He gathered himself before speaking.

"Just think, the thought of me removing eyeballs from the women was your breaking point. So, tell me, Detective: Did your daddy touch your little private parts?"

"No, nothing like that. He liked my brother more than me and never made any attempt to hide it. Who mistreated you? Was it your father?"

"Nice try, Detective, but this is about you and your issues. Not mine."

"And why is that?"

"My game, my rules."

"Not going to happen."

"Then I guess I'll just have to ratchet things up a bit. Oh, and be sure to let your lovely wife, Madison, know that I really liked that black pant suit she wore yesterday. It was very sexy. The way it just seemed to accentuate that tight ass of—"

"You sick son of a bitch! If you ever come near my fam—"

Click! Atticus disconnected the call then removed the SIM card and used a club hammer to smash the electronic chip into a thousand little pieces. When he was satisfied, he torched what remained of the plastic shell and then flushed the scraps down the toilet.

CHAPTER 17

Friday, January 2
87790 53rd Street W
Reese Valley, Washington
7:45 a.m.

Still feeling himself after yesterday's mental-jostling session with Detective Steele, Atticus peered through the thicket high atop the hill at the end of the cul-de-sac. He had the perfect view of the detective's home. He'd completed his countersurveillance weeks earlier, having followed Steele home one evening after Steele had concluded a press conference about the murders, and after monitoring his travel pattern for the past five days, he had it down.

Like clockwork, at seven forty-five, Steele backed the silver Crown Vic out of the garage and headed to work. He wouldn't be returning home until sometime after five o'clock. Atticus also knew about the detective's wife, Dr. Madison Steele, an optometrist with a robust schedule who was both well-known and adored within the community.

Based on her daily routine, she and their son, Grant, would walk out the front door about thirty minutes from now. She'll make her daily pit stop at the Starrocks around the corner on Reese Valley Speedway, where she'd order her usual morning pick-me-up. Then she and Grant would hop back in the car and head west on Washington, not stopping again until they drive onto the lot of Reese Valley Elementary School. And then it was off to work.

Atticus made it there first. He took his usual seat near the front counter and sipped his coffee as he people watched. Madi and little Grant walked in around eight twenty.

"Triple, venti, quarter-sweet, nonfat caramel macchiato, extra hot with whip, please."

The words rolled effortlessly off her tongue as she placed her order with the barista, and as she spoke, Atticus was busy mumbling the same words under his breath, getting a kick out of knowing exactly what she was going to say. Five minutes later, her order was ready.

Madi picked up her coffee from the counter, grabbed Grant by the hand, and smiled at Atticus as she made her way toward the door to leave. Over the past week, she had become accustomed to seeing him seated near the counter. After all, her detective husband constantly stressed the importance of being aware of her surroundings. And so she was, taking note of not only his presence but also his exceptionally good looks, not to mention the alluring scent of his cologne.

CHAPTER 18

Friday, January 9
RVPD Headquarters
10:45 a.m.

It was midmorning, and all hands had gathered in the briefing room to hear what Professor Dobson had to say. Several were familiar with the assistance he'd provided over the years to police departments. Still, the vast majority of those attending the briefing preferred to do their own investigation without much input from the outside. But having thrown everything at their disposal toward the investigation and not being any closer to identifying a suspect than when they'd first started, even a blind man could see the time had come for RVPD to go a different direction.

"Okay, let's get started," Steele opened. "Most of you already know the professor and the extraordinary work he's done over the years in assisting the law enforcement community. For those unfamiliar with his work, Professor Atticus Dobson holds a PhD in psychology and has taught at RVSU for the past fifteen years. I've had the pleasure of taking a few of his classes and can vouch for his extensive knowledge. Today, he is head of the psychology department and is an expert in cognitive theory, which is useful in explaining human behavior by understanding thought processes.

The professor is an expert witness and has testified in court more than a hundred times in trials involving psychopathic behavior. His expertise has been sought after by police departments worldwide to assist with developing suspect profiles for serial killers."

The detective stopped talking when the door opened and Chief Tillis walked into the briefing room. The two of them exchanged nods, and the chief took a seat in the back. While this was taking place, Atticus was doing everything within his power not to laugh. Here he was, the murderer everyone was looking for, standing before a room filled with police officers and only moments away from giving them pointers on developing a suspect profile.

Steele resumed speaking. "The professor is one of the best at what he does, and I've asked him to spend some time with us this morning to share his knowledge and perhaps point us in the direction we need to be looking in order to once and for all identify our murder suspect. So, without further ado, Professor Atticus Dobson."

Steele turned toward the professor and waved him to the front of the room.

"Thank you, Detective," Atticus said, shaking Steele's hand and spending a few seconds surveying the room. He began clearing his throat as he adjusted his bow tie.

"Well, good morning, officers. It is indeed my honor to be with you this morning, but before we get started, I need to correct the detective's slight mischaracterization regarding my credentials. Let me say that I am nowhere near one of the best. Actually, I'm *the* best in the world at what I do."

Thinking it was a joke, the comment was met with immediate laughter, which abruptly ended when officers noticed Professor Dobson wasn't smiling.

"Now that that's out of the way, let's say we get started."

There was no response from the room, but several officers began looking at one another as if they were in total disbelief at what had just happened.

"What a pompous ass!" a police officer could be heard saying under his breath.

"I also have excellent hearing," Atticus responded while removing a remote control from his briefcase and setting it down on the table. "In any event, for several years now, I've had a suspect profile in mind, but in order for me to assist you, the first order of business is to spend a little time discussing the type of person you've been focusing all of your attention."

Steele took the lead in responding. "As I indicated during my last press conference, we believe our suspect is a male."

"I'll go for that. What else are you assuming about your suspect, Detective?"

"I know he's becoming agitated."

"And you know that how?"

Not expecting the question, the look on Steele's face left no doubt he didn't appreciate the professor trying to put him on the spot in front of the room full of officers. Not to mention, the chief.

"Come on, Detective. Think. I'm sure we covered this in at least one of our classes."

There was no way Steele was going to mention anything about his conversations with the killer. He quickly composed himself before providing a benign answer.

"I'm basing my assumption purely on the fact that the murders appear to be intensifying."

But the professor wasn't quite done with at least attempting to embarrass the detective in front of his colleagues.

"And here I was, ready to be wowed, thinking that you had actually learned something in class, Detective. Tsk tsk."

Steele was fuming but refused to let on that the professor had gotten to him. He could feel police officers around the room staring at him, waiting to see how he was going to respond. But he kept his cool. At least on the outside.

Ready to address the room of police officers while at the same time feeling a certain sense of accomplishment, Atticus smiled at Steele as he lifted the remote from the table. He flipped to the first slide showing a photograph of a chubby-faced man with a neatly trimmed moustache, dressed in a dark pinstriped suit and bow tie. The name *Alfred Adler* appeared beneath the photograph.

"Adler was an Austrian psychiatrist who theorized the main motives of human thought and behavior are an individual's striving for superiority and power, partly in order to compensate for his feelings of inferiority."

Atticus began looking around the room and couldn't help but notice the sea of blank stares.

"I can tell you're not getting it," he said. "Let me try again. The way you identify your suspect is to start with the premise that the driving force behind a person's actions are the desire for personal gain, which Adler referred to as *superiority*, and desire for community benefit, which Adler referred to as *success*. People who strive for superiority have little concern for others and are only focused on personal benefit. Consequently, they are psychologically unhealthy. On the other hand, people who strive for success do so for all of humanity without losing their identity. These individuals are considered to be psychologically healthy."

"I'm sorry, Professor," an officer on the left side of the room interjected. "None of this makes sense to me. I was under the impression you were going to help us develop a more accurate suspect profile."

"I just did," Atticus responded. "Rather than simply focusing your attention on the prototypical twenty-something-year-old, white, male introvert, your time would be better served looking for someone who possesses massive feelings of inadequacy and is striving to compensate for those feelings by exaggerated strivings of superiority over other people. In this case, women. Ladies and gentlemen, your suspect is someone who displays arrogance, or may even come off, as your colleague in the back of the room so eloquently referred to earlier, as a pompous ass."

Atticus looked directly into the eyes of the police officer who had made the comment and held his gaze for several seconds before continuing.

"As much as I'd like to leave you all with a bit of optimism, I would be remiss if I didn't tell you that closing in on your suspect merely serves to reinforce his own notions of inferiority, which means, he's going to push back against those uncomfortable feelings through the only means that seems to bring him relief— killing more women."

CHAPTER 19

Saturday, January 10
Villagers Pizzeria
1:22 p.m.

With her schedule clear for the weekend, Michelle Timmons decided to take the ferry across the water and have lunch with the good folks at Villagers Pizzeria, a trendy spot where she was considered near royalty. So popular at the establishment, the distinguished-looking woman was among a handful of locals with their photograph prominently displayed on the wall just above the bar. Michelle often told her friends that she ate at one and only one table at the restaurant and that the reason she liked this particular table was because it provided her with the perfect view of her photo while she dined. Unfortunately, with the socialite deciding to show up without calling ahead, when she arrived, the restaurant was packed and someone was seated at her favorite table.

Making no attempt to hide her annoyance, Michelle summoned the waiter.

"How long is the wait?" she asked.

The waiter shrugged his shoulders. "My best guess is we're looking at the north side of forty-five minutes."

164

"That's unacceptable! You need to speed things up," she scoffed.

"I'll do what I can, Mrs. Timmons."

"You'll do better than that!" she retorted, storming off.

Atticus was in the middle of enjoying a fourteen-inch Sicilian with homemade sausage, artichokes, bacon, prosciutto, and mushrooms when Michelle suddenly walked up and stood next to him.

"I don't know who you think you are, but you're seated at my table."

"I beg your pardon?" he responded, completely taken aback.

Michelle repeated herself, enunciating each word and speaking in such a loud voice that others in the restaurant stopped what they were doing and turned their attention toward the commotion.

"I said... I—don't—know—who—you—think—you—are, but—you're—seated—at—my—table."

"I don't know what your problem is, lady, but you really need to walk away."

Raising her voice another octave, Michelle shouted, "Scumbag!" as she turned and walked back toward the waiting area near the entrance.

Sensing all eyes were still on him, Atticus began scanning the restaurant. When he looked toward the bar, he noticed a photo of the rude woman among a group of black-and-white headshots on the wall just above the counter. The wheels in his head were already turning as he picked up his cell phone and snapped a photo of the wall display. When he was done, he grabbed another slice of pizza and took a bite, savoring the delicious crispy crust of what he considered an Italian masterpiece.

The waiter approached his table. "Sir, I'm really sorry about that. It was totally uncalled for. And just to let you know, your meal is on us today."

"That's mighty kind of you."

"My pleasure. Would you like anything else? It's on the house."

"No, that won't be necessary. I would however, like a takeout box for the rest of my pizza."

"Absolutely. I'll get that boxed up for you right away."

Moments later, the waiter returned. "Here you are, sir. You'll find plenty of napkins, utensils, and a couple of extra packages of parmesan and crushed pepper in there for you. Again, I apologize for that unfortunate scene and hope you do come back to see us."

Atticus pulled a twenty-dollar bill from his pocket and handed it to the waiter. "Here, this is for you."

The waiter smiled. "Thank you, sir."

"You're welcome. May I ask you a question?"

"What's that?"

"Who are those people up there?" he asked, pointing to the wall above the bar.

"Oh, I guess you can say that's the who's-who wall. When I started working here, someone told me that all of them are really connected with this area." The waiter paused for a moment. "I take it you noticed that lady who was giving you grief is up there."

"I did. What's her story?"

"I just know her name is Michelle Timmons and that she always comes over here on the ferry. I heard she lives in some massive home over in Reese Valley."

"Thanks again for your service. I look forward to seeing you the next time I stop by for lunch."

"Unfortunately, I won't be here. I'm moving back to Cali. Today is my last day, but I appreciate your kind words, sir."

Atticus smiled as he got up and gathered his belongings. "Well, I wish you all the best, young man," he said, starting to make his way toward the waiting area.

He briefly caught eyes with Michelle, and while he tried to ignore her, he couldn't help but notice how icily she was staring at him. He walked passed and actually had a foot out the door when Michelle repeated her earlier insult. "Scumbag!"

Atticus left the restaurant without responding, but as he did, he kept repeating her name to himself over and over and over again.

Scene 1

4:35 p.m.

The final vehicle was loaded and the fog horn sounded, a familiar signal for the engines to come to life. Soon, white water churned from behind the ferry as the large vessel pulled away from the dock marking the beginning of its four thirty-five commute back across the Puget Sound. As soon as he walked out of Villagers Pizzeria, Atticus hustled to his SUV and pulled onto First Street where he parked and waited for Michelle to come out. And when she did, he tailed her as she got in her car and drove the short distance to the holding area at Clinton Terminal, ensuring his vehicle was positioned not only in the same lane, but directly behind hers.

He had a bead on Michelle through his windshield, watching her fiddle with whatever was occupying her attention as she sat in her Tesla Model S. Figuring she would do as most commuters and come to the upper deck, he got out and walked up the metal stairs to the lounge to wait, but when she didn't come up, he moseyed on over to the side of the ferry and took in the beautiful hillside views. One thing was for certain. Michelle wasn't going anywhere, and by the time the ferry made it to Reese Valley, like everyone else, she would be seated behind her steering wheel waiting to drive off the exit ramp.

After safely docking, the gate lowered and cars began parading off the ferry. Michelle headed south on Reese Valley Speedway toward Front Street with Atticus well behind but close enough to keep tabs on her every move. About ten minutes later, she slowed to a stop in front of what had to be the largest waterfront home on Shore Drive. He pulled over to the side of the road and watched as the security gate opened, and after Michelle eased passed the row of Italian Cypress trees framing the manicured grounds, he proceeded slowly passed the residence, making note of her address.

CHAPTER 20

Sunday, January 11
700 Block of Front Street
Reese Valley, Washington
3:00 p.m.

Steele was leaning against the railing on the pier enjoying his vanilla soft-serve and watching the ferry pull alongside the dock behind Varley's when he happened to turn in time to catch a glimpse of the baited ring net disappearing deep into the water. He smiled as he marveled at what a good little crabber Grant had become. This was father-son day, and the two had arrived at the pier nearly four hours ago.

With each pull to the surface, no fewer than three crabs were trapped within the basket. The majority well within the legal limit to keep. Still, Grant insisted that they all be released back into the wild, preferring to trap the crabs merely for the challenge as opposed to actually eating them.

It was starting to get late, and after tossing the last of the trapped critters over the railing, they picked up their gear and headed for the parking lot. After loading up, Steele pulled his cell phone from his pocket and noticed the medical examiner had left him a text message that read, *Call me as soon as you get this message.* Wanting to get the information as soon as possible, Steele dialed Dr. Fryatt's number before leaving the parking lot.

"Hello? Dr. Fryatt speaking."

"Hey, Doc. You got something for me?"

"Thanks for getting back with me, Detective. Normally, I wouldn't have called you on the weekend, but I figured you'd want to know about trace amounts of skin found under Jennifer Rollins's fingernails during her autopsy."

"Sure do. You get a hit?"

"Came back to an Adam McGregor. His DNA was on file from a prior arrest in Los Angeles."

"Los Angeles?"

"Yes, sir."

"Ten-four. Shoot the report over to me when you can."

"Done."

"Thanks, Doc," Steele responded before hanging up.

CHAPTER 21

Wednesday, January 14
RVPD Headquarters
8:00 a.m.

Detective Steele finally had what he considered a viable lead in the murder investigation, and it couldn't have come soon enough. The killer had taken the lives of seven Reese Valley residents. All of them women. And with RVPD seemingly unable to identify the person responsible for the gruesome murders, locals, by and large, were scared to death, many expressing being afraid to sleep at night out of fear that when they awakened, they would find the killer standing over them.

Within thirty minutes of receiving McGregor's name from the medical examiner, Steele was faxed a copy of the suspect's mug shot. A less-than-flattering image of a middle-aged, disheveled man with vacant eyes who obviously lived a hard life. Nowhere close to what Steele expected him to look like. Nonetheless, the detective was a believer in science and as such, would allow forensics to help guide his investigation.

After working steadily for two hours straight, Steele took a much-needed break from searching through the database to glance at the photo of McGregor taped to the upper-right corner of his desk. He sat back in his chair and wondered what possibly could've happened in this man's life to caused him to be such an evil being who killed so callously. And why only kill women?

Around eight, Steele figured it was late enough in the day to reach out to LAPD to get whatever information they could provide on McGregor. He picked up the phone and dialed the number. Unfortunately, he was told by the desk officer that the detective with the most knowledge of the McGregor arrest was Detective T. Z. Allen, who was currently on vacation, but would be returning to the office later in the week. After leaving his callback number, Steele returned to his database queries and discovered McGregor had several charges on the books, including assault and battery, petty theft, and terrorist threats. He also learned that at the time of his most recent arrest in Los Angeles, the man was homeless, he exhibited violent behavior, more importantly, he had ties to Reese Valley.

Scene 1

Reese Valley State University
5:00 p.m.

Professor Atticus Dobson walked into the classroom carrying a briefcase and a stack of paper under his left arm.

"Please forgive my tardiness. The meeting with my esteemed colleagues ran a tad longer than anticipated," he said, walking over to the student seated at the end of the last row and handing the stack to him.

"We'll start off with circulating the syllabus. Please take one and pass them along."

Once at the front of the room, he looked out over the class and noticed Detective Steele on the front row. The same spot where he usually sits.

"Welcome to criminal psychology! I recognize several of you from prior classes. Welcome back! And for those of you taking one of my classes for the first time, a hearty welcome to you as well. You can read the syllabus on your own. I believe it speaks for itself, but if anyone needs further clarification, see me after class. Good? Good. Rather than lecturing this evening, I'd like to spend some time getting a feel for your understanding of criminality. Let me start out by asking you to define criminal behavior. Anyone?"

Cody Reed, a student seated on the left side of the room, blurted out, "It's when some people act like thugs."

"When 'some people' act like thugs. Not really sure what that means. Can you be a bit more specific?" Atticus asked, starting to walk closer to where Cody was seated.

Cody scanned the room and happened to catch eyes with Damon Lewis, the university's star forward and one of only two people of color in the class.

"I'd rather not say," he responded.

"Why not? RVSU is an institution of higher learning, which means we are also here to learn from one another. What exactly did you mean by, some people?"

"I probably shouldn't have said that, Professor."

"No argument here," Atticus responded, walking back to the table at the front of the room.

"Now seems to be the perfect time to lay another ground rule on you. Civility will always be practiced within the walls of my classroom. Understood?"

Again, Atticus looked around the room, periodically stopping to stare into the face of a student here and there as he grinned and adjusted his bow tie.

"One more thing. The very nature of the subject matter we'll be discussing during this course can't help but lead to opposing views. And that's fine. Feel free to debate your differences. In fact, I encourage that sort of engagement. What isn't fine, however, is for anyone to show disrespect toward another student who may hold an opposing view. With that, I'll ask you again, what is criminal behavior?"

Detective Steele raised his hand.

"Detective?"

"Breaking the law," Steele responded.

"Yes. Criminal behavior is an intentional act in violation of the criminal code. Our time together during this course is not necessarily to determine whether or not someone broke the law, but rather to better understand the whys behind people committing crime."

From his seat at the back of the room, Tyler Scott asked, "Does the reason behind someone committing a crime really matter, Professor? I mean, crime is crime and if someone breaks the law they should have to pay for it."

Cody started snickering. "I agree. If you can't do the time, don't do the crime."

"What about mitigating circumstances?" Hannah asked.

"Here we go," Tyler blurted out.

"What's that supposed to mean?"

"I hope this doesn't sound sexist, but I bet I know what side of the ticket you voted for in the last election."

"No, Tyler. Your response was quite foolish, but I didn't think it was sexist," Hannah retorted.

"As you can see, a simple question can generate unlimited responses based on the position one holds, but before we move on, does anyone else have anything to add?" Atticus interjected.

"All righty then. Who among you are in support of capital punishment?"

About fifty percent of the students raised their hands.

"I couldn't help but notice you didn't raise your hand, Detective," Atticus said, turning his attention toward Steele. "Taking into consideration some of your comments at press conferences, I'm a bit confused. Did something change?"

"No, Professor. My beliefs pertaining to capital punishment have not wavered."

Atticus grinned, but rather than press the issue with the detective, he walked over to Cindy Vance, who was also seated on the front row.

"Ms. Vance, I noticed you didn't raise your hand either. Do you oppose capital punishment?"

"Putting another human being to death is wrong, plain and simple."

"Even through lethal injection?"

"Lethal injection? How barbaric!" Cindy exclaimed. "I'm sure you know what goes into ending someone's life through lethal injection, Professor."

"As a matter of fact, I do. But for the sake of your classmates who may not be as fully aware, please enlighten us."

"Well, they typically use three drugs. The first is an anesthetic like sodium thiopental to render the person unconscious. The second drug is pancuronium bromide, which is used to cause muscle paralysis and respiratory arrest, and the third drug is potassium chloride, used to stop the person's heart from beating."

"So where exactly is the cruel and unusual punishment? Now, I'll be the first to admit that I'm nowhere close to being a biblical scholar, but I also know there's a passage in the Bible, I believe it's in Exodus 21. Anyway, it speaks to an eye for an eye in relation to doling out punishment."

"Yeah, I get that."

"Then what's the problem, Ms. Vance? Can we agree that some individuals commit crimes that are so egregious that they deserve to be put to death?"

"Botched executions, Professor. That's the problem. About a month ago, there was this prisoner who wasn't pronounced dead until a whole thirty minutes after the drugs first started flowing through his veins."

With her voice starting to crack, Cindy paused for a moment to gather herself.

"About two minutes after the drugs were administered, the syringe came out of the prisoner's vein and deadly chemicals begin spraying across the room."

Gasps could be heard from every corner of the classroom, but not from Atticus. He knew precisely the incident she was referring to and wasn't moved in the least. Cindy continued.

"But it gets worse. It was reported that the prison guards had to close the curtain so they could reinsert the needle into the prisoner's arm, and although the curtain remained closed for nearly sixteen minutes, he could be heard moaning and groaning the entire time he was back there strapped to the gurney."

Looking around the room, Cindy saw that she had the attention of every student in the room. Suddenly feeling empowered, she stood up from her seat.

"And if you think that example was bad, you're really going to hate this one. There was another execution where the inmate heaved, gasped, and coughed while he struggled to breath for nearly twenty minutes after the lethal drugs were administered. During that time, witnesses saw him clenching his fists and attempting to raise his head off the gurney. Death was not pronounced until about forty-five minutes after the execution started, and the prisoner was likely in pain all of that time."

Again, Cindy looked around the classroom, but this time, she made sure to look each of her classmates in the eyes before slowly taking her seat.

"If that's not barbaric, I don't know what is. So, no, Professor, truth be told, I'm not a fan of capital punishment."

Atticus smiled as he returned to the front of the room and began clapping his hands together.

"Well played, Ms. Vance. And that, class, is how you do that. Own your positions and be willing to defend them."

Atticus looked around the room as he adjusted his bow tie.

"I think this is the perfect stopping point for this evening. Your assignment for our next session is listed in the syllabus so unless there are any lingering questions, I'll see everyone next week."

CHAPTER 22

Thursday, January 15
13901 Shore Drive
Reese Valley, Washington
7:15 p.m.

Although the hollowed-out structure was still smoldering, the ground where the home once stood had cooled to the point where the search for answers could finally begin. Steele desperately wanted to get going on the investigation, limited daylight and all. But it was getting late and once nightfall was upon them, the search would have to be called for the evening.

The widow of a neurosurgeon who had died unexpectedly a few years back, Michelle lived alone. Since that time, she'd become the talk of the town because of the way she ran around spending money rumored to have come from a multimillion-dollar insurance policy she'd presented for cashing before her late husband's body was in the ground. Dr. Jeremy Timmons had died of a heart attack at the ripe old age of sixty-six, and within months of his passing, Michelle seemingly develop a sudden appetite for young men who would often be seen sporting one of her cars up and down the streets of Reese Valley.

The home was a total loss, and all that remained on the lot were two badly scorched brick fireplaces and the burned-out hulls of five luxury vehicles. To assist with determining who may have been inside at the time of the fire, before driving out to the scene, Steele pulled DMV records for all vehicles registered to the address. Based on that information, he knew that Michelle owned a Range Rover Sport, Tesla Model S, Mercedes Benz SL 600, Rolls Royce Phantom, and a Lamborghini Aventador S, purchased two weeks ago. With all of the vehicles being accounted for, the odds increased exponentially that at least one body would be found among the rubble—Michelle's.

After donning his disposable protective coveralls and face mask, Steele and the cadre of investigators commenced their search. They sifted through endless piles of warm ashes cluttered with pieces of burned wood and an assortment of destroyed household effects. It appeared that just about everything Michelle owned had been destroyed in the fire, with the exception of a fireproof gun safe that was photographed in place before being pulled from the ashes and secured in the trunk of a police vehicle.

Within ten minutes of commencing the search, Steele discovered a charred body he immediately assumed was the homeowner but would have to wait for confirmation from the medical examiner to be sure. Less than sixty-seconds later, another investigator on scene called out that she had found a second body beneath the debris. The discovery of the bodies changed everything, and the investigation very quickly turned into a crime scene. It was time for the press conference.

Flanked by Chief Tillis, Steele weaved his way through the crowd of onlookers who had started piling onto Shore Drive shortly after the explosion first occurred. With the incident command post located midway down the block, another two minutes would pass before he reached the podium. It was a little past eight thirty and starting to get dark when Steele finally stepped onto the platform and raised his hand to shield his eyes from the flurry of camera flashes that peppered his face. He adjusted the microphone.

"Good evening. I'm Detective Braxton Steele, Reese Valley Police Department. Being that we are in the preliminary stages of our investigation and there's not much I can offer you at this time, I wanted to at least come over and take a few of your questions."

"Detective, the coroner removed what appeared to be two bodies. Can you confirm that Michelle Timmons was one of the deceased? Also, do you have any idea who the other person was who died in the fire might be?" a reporter asked.

"The bodies pulled from the rubble were so badly burned it's going to take some time for the medical examiner to make positive identifications. Once we receive the ME's report, I'll be in a better position to answer that question," Steele responded.

"Was the fire intentionally started?" another reporter asked.

"We're coordinating our investigation with RVFD, who is taking the lead on determining the cause of the fire."

"Detective, can you confirm reports that there was a loud explosion prior to the fire?"

"Again, our investigation is just getting started. That's all I have for now, but as information is developed, I'll hold additional press conferences to keep you updated. Thank you."

Abrupt movement caught the detective's attention, and when he trained his eyes toward the back of the crowd, he noticed a large man slinging his arms around as if he were trying to clear a path to leave. Several people stood between the man and the podium, making it difficult to see his face clearly. But even from such a distance, observing the man's gait was all it took for the detective to figure out who he was.

CHAPTER 23

Wednesday, January 21
RVPD Headquarters
8:00 a.m.

Ever since receiving McGregor's name from the medical examiner the other day, Steele had used every resource at his disposal at unearthing any and everything he could on the man. He'd learned that, in addition to being saddled with a ton of credit problems, McGregor's rap sheet was about as long as the Nile, albeit mainly petty offenses. Database queries also disclosed he had worked at the US Military Sealift Command in Everett, Washington, as a civil service mariner for several years but made no mention about why he'd left that position.

The military base was about fifteen minutes away from the detective's home, and while he could've easily stopped by there on his way to the office to see what he might be able to glean from McGregor's personnel files, he knew privacy rights would limit his ability to get his hands on anything of potential value, making the trip to the base likely not worth the effort. Instead, he scrolled through his cell phone until he located the phone number for Rence Murphy, one of his old military buddies who he recalled was stationed at the Sealift Command at one time. He dialed the number, and Murph answered on the third ring.

"Tell me something good."

"Hello stranger," Steele replied.

"Braxton?"

"Yep."

"Well, I'll be! What's it been, five, six years?"

"Come on, man. Two years max. Even still, that's far too long. How's retirement treating you?"

"What is that? I'm working harder these days than I did in the service. Anyway, what's on your mind?"

"You ever heard the name Adam McGregor? He used to work at the Military Sealift Command as a civilian, and I was wondering if the two of you might have been there at the same time."

"You kidding me? Everybody on base knew McGregor."

"So you know him."

"I know of him. That guy was always trying to pick a fight with somebody, and it didn't matter whether they were military or civilian. Or their rank, for that matter. Why do you ask?"

"His name came up in my investigation."

"That can't be good."

"No, it's not. Anyway, I can't seem to find any information regarding the reason he stopped working at the base and was hoping you could fill in the blank."

"They fired his ass."

"For what?"

"Assault. He cut his supervisor on the shoulder with a pocketknife. Wasn't serious, but it was bad enough. Word was he was drunk when he did it. I also heard the man suffered from schizophrenia."

"Got it. You wouldn't happen to know where he may have gone after he lost his job, would you? Right now, I have nothing in terms of his whereabouts. Anything will help. Name of a family member or friend he may have stayed with. Anything."

"I know he had a girlfriend, and the two lived together in an apartment somewhere in Reese Valley. She was always coming up to the base to pick him up after work."

"Name?"

"Her first name was Trish. Not sure about the last name, though. I think it was, Thompson. Just can't say for sure."

"That helps. I'll do some digging and see what I can come up with. Hopefully, she's still local."

"Good luck with that one. I heard that within a month of McGregor losing his job at the base, he went home drunk one evening and beat the hell out of her. Apparently, the neighbor next door called the police when they heard all the screaming coming through the walls."

"Interesting. I didn't see anything about that when I ran his criminal history."

"That's because his girl refused to press charges, nor would she tell police officers the name of the person who beat her up. From what I heard, her only interest was getting as far away from McGregor as the gas in her car would allow."

"That explains that."

"Like they say, love is a funny thing. Anyway, I was reaching for the doorknob when you called so I'm going to have to get out of here."

"Many thanks, my friend."

"You got it. And another thing…"

"What's that, Murph?"

"Don't take so long to call the next time. We should spend some time catching up. Life is way too short."

"You got it. Be well, my friend," Steele responded before hanging up.

Scene 1

RVPD Headquarters
9:00 a.m.

The note on his desk indicated Detective T. Z. Allen left a message requesting a callback. Eager to find out what the LAPD knew about McGregor, Steele immediately picked up the phone and dialed the number.

"Detective Allen."

"Good morning, Detective. Detective Steele, RVPD calling."

"Hey there, Detective. I just got back in the office this morning and saw where you had called me."

"How was your vacation?"

"Too short. Me and the wife spent seven days on the island of Tahiti. We had a quaint little bungalow right there on the beach, looking at nothing but blue water as far as the eye could see. And the tropical cocktails—unreal! You ever been there?"

"Can't say I have."

"Well, I highly recommend it if you ever get a chance. Anyway, what can I do for you?"

"I was calling about an investigation I was told you worked on a while back involving a suspect by the name of Adam McGregor. His name has come up in my investigation, and I wanted to see what you could tell me about him. I saw on his criminal history report where you guys had him in custody a few of times."

"Yeah, he certainly knows the inside of our lockup. What are you working on?"

"I've tied him to my murder investigation through DNA."

"Interesting. His DNA came up in a murder investigation out here as well."

"Can you tell me about the case?"

"In a nutshell, early one morning, an anonymous call came into LAPD reporting a woman being assaulted in the alley behind a nightclub near the 6300 block of Hollywood Boulevard. When officers arrived, they discovered the body of a deceased African American woman in her midtwenties wedged between the trash dumpster and the building. She was later identified as Gwen Stevenson, a freshman student at the University of Southern California. The cause of death was strangulation. The medical examiner's report showed that DNA evidence, including human tissue, was found under her fingernails, which was traced back to McGregor."

"You think he's good for it?"

"That's just it. You've seen his record. No doubt this guy is a royal pain in the ass, but aside from a single charge of terrorist threats where he physically assaulted a Canadian tourist who tried to photograph the homeless man, everything else on the report are nonviolent offenses, such as petty theft, and nuisance charges for pissing in public, something he'll tell you in a minute he enjoys doing. I guess I'm just surprised that he's coming up in these types of crimes. McGregor is a drunk and appears to have psychological problems. He actually does more harm to himself than to others, but as we both know, you can't put anything past anyone. In any event, we're looking for him too."

"You didn't happen to receive currency with the word *slut* written across the front in red lipstick following the death of that USC student, did you?"

"Negative. Nothing like that. Is that what's happening in your case?"

"Yes. Several women have been killed in Reese Valley over the years, and each time, an envelope filled with money as I described arrives at our headquarters following the murder."

"Now, that's a twist."

"What about the condition of the woman's body when your folks found her?"

"She was fully clothed and had not been sexually assaulted. Outside of the hand impressions found on her neck, there was no evidence of trauma on any other part of her body."

"Got it. How about letting me know should you locate McGregor. I'd really like to talk to him."

"Sure thing. And I trust you'll let me know if you happen to catch him first."

"Absolutely. I really appreciate you getting back with me, Detective Allen."

"You bet, and please, call me T. Z."

"You got it. Thanks again, T. Z. We'll be in touch."

Thirty minutes later, Steele was in his office going over case notes when Randy knocked on the door and walked in clutching a lab report.

"Excuse me, Detective."

"Hey there, Randy."

"We have confirmation that Michelle Timmons was in fact one of the victims of the Shore Drive fire. The second victim was a young man named Chase Silverman."

"Timmons, I get. But who is Chase Silverman?"

"Beats me. And get this, the kid was only sixteen."

"Sixteen?"

"I know, right?"

"There has to be a story there. Anyway, RV Fire come back with an official cause yet?"

"Not yet."

"Ten-four. Thanks for the info. I'll ensure we make proper notification."

"Anytime," Randy responded, turning and leaving the office.

Scene 2

Reese Valley State University
5:00 p.m.

Atticus walked in and placed his briefcase on the table. Almost immediately, he was met with thunderous applause. Throughout the day, the talk around campus had been about how, for the third successive year, the professor was the recipient of the Distinguished Teaching Award, an honor bestowed upon instructors who epitomize the highest levels of performance and excellence. As he always did, Atticus stood in front of his students and adjusted his bow tie.

"Stop it," he said, gesturing toward the class with both hands to settle down. "Just kidding. More applause, please."

The class again erupted in ovation but, this time, much louder than before.

"Thank you, thank you, thank you. That was really nice of you, but now, I think it's high time we get going. This evening, we'll be discussing the psychological effects of domestic violence on children, a subject near and dear to my heart."

Shuffling paper immediately became the dominant sound in the room as students began opening their binders and peeling back the pages of their notepads. Taking copious notes was a wise thing, if, for no other reason, to jot down the answers to quizzes the professor occasionally popped on his students right before ending class for the evening, something he did often as a way of determining who was paying attention. The unannounced pop quizzes also served as motivation for students to show up for class regularly.

"Studies have shown that children exposed to domestic violence exhibit many more behavioral and emotional problems when compared to other—" Atticus abruptly stopped speaking and took a deep breath. After several seconds, he started up again.

"When compared to other children. Such abuse has an adverse impact on cognitive functioning, where many of these same children experience difficulty as adults when it comes to dealing with violence and conflict resolution."

He stepped from behind the table and walked over to stand close to where Detective Steele was seated.

"More than fifteen million children in the United States live in homes where domestic violence is the norm. These children are at a much greater risk of perpetuating the cycle as adults and becoming abusers themselves. Moreover, children growing up in these types of households are prime candidates for certain mental health conditions, such as depression and anxiety."

"That's so sad," Cindy exclaimed.

"Yes, Ms. Vance. It's very sad. I think I'll take some time here to get you all involved in the discussion. Let's apply this to crime being committed within society. What are your thoughts about a suspect who commits a crime where it's later learned that he or she was a victim of child abuse? Detective Steele, I'm assuming that, at some point during your illustrious career, you've run into such a scenario. Am I correct?"

"I have," Steele responded.

"As I suspected. Would you be so kind as to share with the class one of those experiences?"

"It's just like you said, Professor. Some of the suspects we've arrested over the years were later discovered to have been abused themselves as children."

"In your opinion, Detective, does the fact that someone was abused as a child serve as a mitigating factor when it comes to sentencing?"

"That depends."

"On?"

"On several factors. But that's really a matter for the court."

"Let's switch gears. Were any of you abused as children?"

"Should you really be asking those types of questions? That seems a bit personal, Professor Dobson," Sarah Fleetwood responded.

"Being abused as a child is nothing to be ashamed of, Ms. Fleetwood. And let me be clear. A child is not responsible for the actions of an adult, nor did they ask to be abused. I was abused as a child, and yes, it still affects me," Atticus responded, taking a few deliberate steps toward Sarah.

"You appear to be doing just fine to me, Professor. I mean, you earned your PhD and seem to be a well-functioning individual," Jake Sorenson offered.

"I thank you for saying that, Mr. Sorenson. Unfortunately, the impact of childhood abuse leaves invisible scars that can last a lifetime."

Atticus walked over and again stood in front of Detective Steele.

"What do you think, Detective?"

"What do I think about what?"

"Do you know of anyone who may have suffered abuse as a child and are now experiencing difficulty as an adult?"

The detective paused before responding.

"Can't say I do, Professor."

"Well, let's consider your fellow police officers? Earlier I discussed the carryover effect of childhood abuse. When we assess engagements between police officers and the public that occasionally spiral out of control, do you believe that at least some of that dynamic can be attributed to abuse the officer may have experienced as a child?"

"The police officer? What about actions on the part of civilians that sometime contribute to the escalation?"

"Please forgive me, Detective. I didn't mean to insinuate that police officers were the sole cause of some of these encounters going south. So, back to my question, do you believe the possibility exists for childhood abuse to have a negative impact on the way individuals conduct themselves later in life?"

"I have no idea, Professor, nor do I believe the manner in which you are framing your questions is appropriate for a classroom setting."

"Again, please forgive me, Detective. My intent was certainly not to put you on the spot."

Atticus smiled as he turned and walked back to the table at the front of the room. He pulled on his sleeve to expose his watch.

"I think we'll stop here. Remember: your essays are due next week, and I'm looking forward to reading your scholarly work. With that, enjoy the remainder of your evening."

Within sixty-something seconds, all students had cleared out of the classroom. All except for Steele. Atticus looked up and noticed the detective approaching the table.

"I would like to again apologize if I put you on the spot, Detective. That was not my intention."

"No worries, Professor. But I thought I'd pick your brain about that bomb that went off on Shore Drive."

Steele placed his items on the table next to the professor's briefcase.

"Means and motive, Detective. Means and motive," Atticus said, pushing his glasses higher up on his face.

"That's really not helping me, Professor."

"This is a small town, Detective. How many people around here have explosive-ordinance experience?"

"Again, that doesn't get me any closer to narrowing the list. We have a military base down the street. On top of that, more than a couple of our residents are veterans."

"Come on, Detective. Surely, you know of at least a few people around here that have a short fuse. Now, if they just so happen to be former military with explosive-ordinance experience in their background, I'd say that's a good place to start."

Steele didn't respond. Instead he stood there wondering why he'd just wasted fifty-five seconds of his life talking with the professor who did little more than state the obvious. He was already thinking about bringing Victor McPhee in for another round of questioning ever since he noticed the veteran leaving the press conference on Shore Drive. Vic was a strange duck with an uncanny ability of arriving at crime scenes well before police officers, and because of it, he was a perpetual person of interest. Add to that, he was a bomb expert.

Steele gathered his items.

"Thank you, Professor."

"Always here to help the RVPD," Atticus responded, his eyes fixed coldly on the detective's back as he walked toward the door to leave the classroom.

CHAPTER 24

Thursday, January 22
RVPD Headquarters
9:26 a.m.

Detective Steele stood on the other side of the one-way glass located on the west wall of interview room two for several minutes. He watched as the veteran sat apathetically in the chair with his hands lying flat and motionless atop the table. Police brought Victor McPhee in for questioning earlier in the day, and from the moment they'd picked him up, he'd made no attempt at mincing his words, making it absolutely clear that he was not happy to be there. Around nine thirty, Steele walked in.

"Good morning, Mr. McPhee. I appreciate you coming down to answer a few questions."

"Right. Like I had a choice. Anyway, I don't have anything to say to you."

"You don't even know what I wanted to ask."

"Don't matter. The answer will still be the same. I don't have anything to say."

"Look, Mr. McPhee. I'm going to just put it out there. You are under no obligation to speak with me, but until I get some answers, you can kiss your privacy goodbye, and I'm not talking about covert operations. Everybody is going to know we're looking at you."

Steele got up from the table and walked over to the one-way glass. Almost immediately, the door to the interview room opened, and two police officers walked in.

"You're free to go. These fine officers will drive you back to your home."

"You can't do that. I'll sue you for harassment!"

"Then I guess we'll be getting video footage of you walking up the courthouse steps when you go to file your lawsuit. Like I said, you're free to go. Have a nice day, Mr. McPhee."

"What do you want?"

"I want to ask you a few questions."

"About what?"

"About the bomb explosion on Shore Drive."

McPhee stood up and took a few steps toward the door before returning to the table and sitting back down. Steele nodded toward the two police officers. It was a signal for them to leave.

"I didn't have anything to do with that bombing, and you're sure as hell not going to pin that on me."

"Let's start with discussing your time in the military, Mr. McPhee. You were an ordinance expert, correct?"

"Me and about a million other people. So what?"

"And you've participated in training seminars on explosives, correct?"

"Look, Detective. I've also talked to people about responsible gun ownership. Does that mean it's my fault when people get shot? I'll say it again; I didn't do it!"

"What were you doing last Thursday?"

"How in the hell am I supposed to know that? I can barely remember what I did yesterday."

"Well, let's see. I held a press conference on that day where I talked about the explosion on Shore Drive. I was wondering if you happened to see it?"

"Yeah, I saw it."

"You wouldn't happen to recall what television channel aired the press conference, would you?"

"Can't say I do, Detective."

"So you don't know what channel you were looking at when you saw the press conference?"

"I never said I was looking at the television. I was there, Detective. I was on Shore Drive when you gave your press conference."

Steele was sure he'd seen McPhee in the crowd on that day but thought he'd test his veracity.

"Did you know the victim?"

"Not personally, but hell, who around here didn't know what she was about?"

"I'm not following. What was she about?"

"You know. She liked them young boys and was always throwing around her money. That sorta thing."

"So you didn't know her?"

"That's what I said, Detective."

"And the two of you never had any run-ins?"

"No, Detective. We never had any run-ins."

"You do know we're going to catch whoever did this."

"If you say so, Detective."

"Tell me something. What do you think should happen to the person responsible for the explosion?"

"Hell, I don't know. Lock their ass up and throw away the key."

"So, you'd sentence them to life in prison?"

"Yeah, why not? You can kill the bastard for all I care."

Steele stood up and walked over to the one-way glass, and again, the door swung open, and the same two police officers reentered the interview room.

"Thanks for your time, Mr. McPhee. You're free to go. These officers will drop you off."

"Oh, and I guess they'll be following me around town like two lost puppies, right?"

"Nobody's going to follow you."

McPhee hopped up and started walking toward the door. Just before he stepped into the hallway, he looked back over his shoulder. It was impossible to not notice the scowl on his face.

"You really need to stop, Detective. This shit is getting old."

"Thank you again, Mr. McPhee," Steele responded.

The detective posed the same question to McPhee that he routinely used whenever he wanted to gauge a suspect's potential involvement in a crime. And it always worked. Right off the bat, guilty suspects typically made excuses as to why someone might commit a crime and how they would be better off in therapy or simply given a second chance. On the other hand, individuals having absolutely nothing to do with the crime were quick to throw the book at the perp. Based on his responses, Steele was fairly certain McPhee was not the person responsible for the bomb explosion on Shore Drive.

Scene 1

3322 Leslie Lane
11:05 a.m.

McPhee was fit to be tied as he watched the police officers back out of the driveway. Detective Steele said he would not be under surveillance, but he didn't believe that for a minute.

"Enjoy the rest of your day, Mr. McPhee," the officer in the passenger seat called out.

"Yeah, yeah, yeah, and the doughnut shop is right around the corner."

Both officers started laughing loudly, but neither bothered to respond. No sooner than the car was off the block, McPhee walked inside, pulled his cell phone from his pocket, and started dialing.

Atticus answered on the second ring. But he didn't say a word.

"Hey, it's Vic."

"Hey back at you. How goes the battle, Sarge?"

"Why didn't you say anything when you picked up?"

"Why should I? You called me."

"Yeah, whatever. Anyway, I need to talk to you."

"Okay."

"Aren't you going to ask me what I want to talk about?"

"I figured you'd tell me sooner or later."

"Why are you being such an asshole?"

Atticus started laughing. "I'm just jerking your chain, Sarge. When and where?"

"Starrocks on the speedway. Meet me there around three o'clock."

Scene 2

Starrocks
8601 Reese Valley Speedway
3:02 p.m.

Atticus was already seated at a table near the front door when Vic walked in.

"You're one hundred twenty seconds late, Sarge."

"Not really. I said, around three," Vic responded, taking a seat at the table and grabbing the cup of coffee Atticus had ordered for him.

"That you did, Sarge. That you did. Anyway, what's on your mind?"

Vic shifted in his seat and started looking around the coffee shop, pausing to briefly study the faces he hadn't seen in there before.

"What are you doing?" Atticus asked.

"They picked me up this morning and hauled me down to the station."

"For what?"

"Detective Steele tried to get me to say that I had something to do with that bomb explosion that happened on Shore Drive."

"What did you tell him?"

"Nothing. He started asking me stuff like did I know that Timmons woman and if I had a problem with her."

"Really?"

"That's right. Then he started talking about my bomb training and my time in the military when I was handling explosives."

"Did he, now?"

"That's right. I immediately saw through him, though. Then I reminded the detective about that little military base over yonder and how ridiculous it was to think that I was the only person around here who knows about bombs."

"Well, if I'm being honest, I can see why they would want to talk to you."

"What in the hell is that supposed to mean?"

"Think about it, Sarge. You're an expert when it comes to bombs."

"So what! Anyone with the ability to read can easily pull up instructions for making a bomb from the internet. It's not all that difficult. And let us not forget: I even taught you how to make one."

"Touché."

"You're damn right, touché. So don't be coming at me with that crap."

Atticus started laughing and pounding his hand on the table.

"I wish you could see your face, Sarge. You look like you're about to explode, no pun intended. But on a serious note, you're going to have to watch your every step. Don't say anything else to them, and above all, don't trust anything they try to tell you."

"But I didn't do it."

"And you think that matters? Look, Sarge. People are starting to get rattled around here, and the police are feeling the heat. They need to get on top of this case before it really gets out of control."

"Yeah, I get that. But I still didn't do it."

"You're not listening to me, Sarge. Somebody's going down. If they ever pick you up again, just keep your mouth shut. The more you say, the more you're giving them to use against you."

"But won't that make me look guilty?"

"We're way past that. Why do you think they dragged you in there in the first place? Obviously, you already look guilty. You get what I'm saying?"

"Yeah. I get it."

Atticus stood up and finished off the last of his coffee.

"Good. See you around, Sarge."

Scene 3

87790 53rd Street W
Reese Valley, Washington
6:20 p.m.

Steele and Grant were sitting in the living room playing video games and having a good old time when Madi started coming down the stairway. The room was immediately taken over by the smell of her sweet perfume. Partway down, she stopped and pretended to be clearing her throat until she commanded the detective's attention. Steele turned his head toward the stairway and just smiled.

Madi always illuminated whatever space she happened to be in but on this particular evening, her face was aglow, and not just from the one-carat-weight diamonds in her ears. She loved celebrating her birthday. Stunning from head to toe, she was dressed in an off-white satin mini slip dress exposing her beyond gorgeous legs. And with her hair pulled back, coupled with just enough makeup to accentuate her natural beauty, Madi was the epitome of class.

Steele leaped up off the couch and hurried over to the stairs to meet her as she stepped off onto the ground floor.

"Wow!"

"You like?"

"Oh, I like," Steele responded, taking his wife in his arms and planting a tender kiss on her cheek.

"Yuck!" Grant blurted out, giving his parents a good laugh.

"You say that now, son, but just wait until you kiss a girl for the first time."

"No, Dad. I'm never going to kiss a girl. Girls are yucky."

"You think I'm yucky, sweetie?" Madi asked, turning down the corners of her lips.

"Don't be sad, Mommy. Girls are yucky. Not you."

"Thank you, sweetie. Mommy feels better now."

As Steele and Madi again burst out in laughter, there was a sudden knock on the front door. It was Casey Phillips, Grant's babysitter and the only other person the couple trusted to watch over their son. Within five minutes, Steele and Madi were on their way, and at around seven o'clock, they pulled into the parking lot across from Varley's Reese Valley Landing.

Their reservation was for seven fifteen, but with restaurant traffic being light on this evening, they were immediately seated at their favorite spot. The center-most location along the expansive bank of windows overlooking the Puget Sound. The ambiance was perfect and the Steele's couldn't help but smile, sitting across from one another and allowing their fingertips to straddle the candle in the center of the table, seemingly mesmerized by the rhythm of the flame dancing boldly against the backdrop of the dimly lit restaurant.

Steele was the first to speak.

"Have I told you lately just how beautiful you are?"

"You have. But I certainly don't mind hearing it again," Madi responded, a bright smile forming across her face.

"We'll, let me tell—"

"Good evening. My name is Heath, and I'll be taking care of you this evening. Can I start you out with something to drink?"

Madi started laughing, knowing her husband was just about to start laying it on heavy.

"Absolutely," she finally responded. "I'm thinking about ordering a bottle of Pinot Noir. What can you tell me about the Ponzi Tavola?"

"Honestly, I don't drink red wine, but a lot of people seem to like Ponzi Tavola. It's without question one of the most sought-after wines we serve," Heath responded.

Madi looked across the table toward Steele.

"Works for me," he said.

"We'll take a bottle of the Ponzi Tavola," she said, smiling as she looked up at the waiter.

"Excellent choice. Can I bring you any appetizers?"

"Yes. We'll have the Dungeness crab and shrimp dip. We'll also have an order of the crispy fried calamari."

"Again, excellent choices. I'll get those started right away."

"Thank you, Heath," Madi responded.

For the next hour or so, the Steele's enjoyed their night out, exchanging pleasantries and eating from each other's plate as they dined on cedar pan seared Alaskan halibut, planked wild sockeye salmon, and a northwest seafood cobb salad. Around eight forty-five, Heath returned to the table carrying a cupcake with a single candle stuck in the middle, which not only caught Madi by surprise, but also caught the attention of Atticus who happened to be in the restaurant at the same time, and while he wasn't close enough to overhear the conversation taking place between the detective and his wife, even with limited lighting, he clearly saw the waiter mouth the words *happy birthday*.

Steele and Madi filled the next fifteen or so minutes with additional small talk while finishing off the last of the wine. At around nine fifteen, the couple were on their way to the parking lot where unbeknownst to them, they walked right by the table Atticus had vacated only moments before. After a short drive, they were standing in their living room squaring up with Casey when Steele's cell phone suddenly started vibrating.

He pulled it from his pocket, and immediately, his mood changed. One look at the screen and he knew the person using the voice distorter was going to be on the other end. After thanking Casey, Steele began walking upstairs, preferring to wait until he was alone before answering.

"Steele."

"I must say, Detective, Madison looked exceptionally beautiful tonight. Would you be so kind as to wish her happy birthday from me?"

Click! Atticus disconnected the call and immediately walked to the basement to destroy the burner phone.

Madi stood on the porch and watched after Casey until she was safely in her car and pulling away from the curb. After locking the front door, she checked on Grant who was fast asleep, and after kissing her little son on the forehead, she quickly made her way to the master bedroom.

"Was that him?"

"Have a seat. We need to talk, Madi."

"What's wrong? You're scaring me."

"He mentioned you by name," Steele responded, purposely leaving out the part about any connection Varley's might have with the murder investigation.

"What?"

"He didn't threaten you, but I'll feel more comfortable if police officers are close by when I'm not around."

Understandably shaken, Madi sat down on the edge of the bed.

"Is our family in danger?" she asked.

"No. We're going to be fine. I can promise you that."

He responded without hesitation, coming up with the best answer he could think of on the spot. But he was concerned. In fact, this was unfamiliar territory for the detective, being the first time in his law enforcement career that his family had been pulled into one of his investigations. He dialed the number for Chief Tillis. With the murderer bringing up Madi, the time had come to let his boss in on the phone calls. It was also time to ask the chief for permission to assign police officers to shadow Madi and Grant so that he could continue focusing his full attention on the investigation.

CHAPTER 25

Friday, January 23
RVPD Headquarters
7:30 a.m.

His cell phone started vibrating the moment he pulled onto the RVPD parking lot, and as if on cue, the painful, high-pitched ringing in his ears returned. Instantaneously, the muscles in the back of his neck tightened. Already having convinced himself the killer would be on the other end, Steele pulled the phone from his pocket. He stared at the number on the screen, waiting until the fourth ring to answer.

"Hello, Colonel."

"Hey."

After an awkward silence where it became evident the detective was not going to be the first to speak, the colonel asked, "So how's your wife?"

"Madison is doing fine, thanks for asking. To what do I owe the pleasure of your call, Colonel?"

"You're right. I guess I'm rambling. Anyway, do you remember that big kid named Raymond from your T-ball team back in Germany?"

"Coach?"

"Come to think of it, I guess you fellas did call him that."

"Raymond Jones. What I remember most is that he's on death row for murdering a district attorney in cold blood. What about him?"

"Well, some woman named Velma stopped by here yesterday asking if I knew how to get hold of you?"

"She say what she wanted?"

"From what I gather, Raymond is her nephew, and I guess his number is up."

"There's nothing I can do to stop his execution if that's what she's thinking."

"Hold your horses! According to that Velma lady, Raymond wants to tell his story to someone before he leaves this earth. She says he knows you're a detective, don't know how, but he apparently only trusts you with his story. She says he's never spoken to anyone about the night he killed that fella, not even the police."

"I don't know, Colonel. I have a lot of things going on right—"

"Dammit! You're always busy! Anyway, I promised I'd pass along the information. And I did. Your buddy is still being held at the Quarry, and apparently, the date is fast approaching for putting him to death. And before you ask, nobody knows the exact day. Could be a month from now, a week, a day, or even hours, if any of that even matters to you. Tell your wife I said hello."

"Her name is—"

Before Steele could get his words out, the colonel abruptly disconnected the call and rather than focus on his father's usual rudeness, the detective started contemplating whether or not to travel to the Quarry, the one prison he spent his entire career trying to avoid. Like most others in law enforcement, he too had heard the rumors surrounding the warden's prison ministry. Over the years, a total of twenty-three inmates had hanged themselves while in prison, and in each case, they were ministry participants.

According to unverified information obtained from an inmate who spoke on condition of anonymity, rather than a ministry in the traditional sense of the word, the warden's program was more like a cult where he personally taught Bible classes comprised primarily of African American men. The one rule participants were expected to adhere to was that everything discussed was expected to remain within the group and not shared with anyone, including other inmates who were not part of the program. Inmates who accepted Christ as their Lord and Savior were told that man was incapable of passing judgment on another man and that the Bible teaches us that individuals are responsible for self-accountability in proportion to the crime they had been convicted of.

Carefully selected Bible verses were consistently drilled into the heads of inmates taking part in the ministry that, in accordance with the warden's translation, illustrated that God didn't create man for the purpose of being kept behind bars like animals in cages and that, as true believers, every inmate knew exactly what they needed to do in order to free themselves. Although the inmates were never specifically told that they should take their own life, anytime one of them committed suicide, the warden gathered the group to pay homage to their departed Christian brethren who showed tremendous courage in refusing to be held captive by man's flawed rules and, as a reward for their bravery, were granted access to the only place where their freedom could never again be taken away.

CHAPTER 26

Saturday, January 24
Pensacola International Airport
8:45 a.m.

Detective Steele was somewhat apprehensive about leaving Madi and Grant alone, but Chief Tillis assured him that his family would be properly looked after while he was away for the weekend, though he didn't bother sharing his travel plans with his boss. His reason was simple. He knew the chief would question his judgment about wanting to visit with an inmate serving time on death row, and he just didn't feel like getting into it. Madi, on the other hand, knew the history between Steele and Raymond Jones and, because of it, felt it was only right that he honored his former teammate's request and visit with him one last time.

Steele figured he'd kill two birds with one stone by flying into Pensacola, dropping in on the colonel, and then making the six-hour drive down to the Quarry to see Raymond. To this day, it was hard for him to believe Coach was a convicted killer on death row awaiting execution and as he thought about the day he'd learned about the shooting, that sickening feeling in the pit of his stomach came rushing back as if he were learning about the incident for the very first time.

He took the red-eye, and when his plane touched down at eight forty-five, Steele picked up his rental car, threw his carry-on in the back seat and hopped on the I-110 South. It was early, so he figured he'd spend at least a few hours catching up with the colonel, being that the two hadn't seen each other for several years. The thing is, neither seemed overly eager to be in the presence of the other, making their brief sporadic phone calls their sole means of communication. Thirty-five minutes later, he was knocking on the desperately in need of painting front door of his father's home.

Steele heard the sound of footsteps and imagined the colonel marching across the living room floor as if he were on base. Suddenly, the sound from within the home abruptly stopped, and the detective figured the colonel was standing just on the other side of the door staring at him through the peephole with those wicked eyes. He could feel him. After about thirty seconds, the deadbolt lock could be heard turning and then there was a loud creaking sound as the front door swung open.

"So you finally decided to pay your old man a visit."

"Hello, Colonel," Steele responded.

"I really don't appreciate surprise visits, but since you're here, might as well come on in."

Steele walked through the door and was immediately confronted by the pungent smell of cigarette smoke, so strong that not only did he taste the nicotine, but his throat was burning. As was fairly common for someone in his profession, he quickly glanced around the room to familiarize himself with his surroundings. He immediately spotted the flag in the acrylic box sitting on the coffee table flanked by a military photo of his twin brother Brice on one side, the colonel in uniform on the other. But the object in the living room that was impossible not to see was the ten-by-fifteen-foot, floor-to-ceiling American flag that completely covered the width of one entire wall and half of another.

"Push those newspapers to the floor and have a seat over there on the couch. I wasn't expecting company, which is why I haven't gotten around to picking up around here. Don't know why I was even telling you that. This my damn house."

"So how have you been, Colonel?"

"Decided to run out to the Quarry, did you?"

"Yes, sir. Thought it was the right thing to do."

"Well, that's mighty decent of you, Braxton, but why did you stop by here?"

"Again. Thought it was the right thing to do. Besides, we haven't seen each other in quite some time."

"And who do you think is to blame for that?"

"I didn't come here to argue with you, Colonel. I just thought it would be nice for the two of us to see if we can sit and talk. You know, try our hand at working through some things."

"What the hell for?" the colonel shouted, standing and walking toward the kitchen.

"Can I get you something to drink?"

"No, sir."

"Mind if I smoke?"

"No, sir."

"Good because I was going to do it anyway," the colonel said, sitting back down and lighting his cigarette.

"Have you heard from your brother?"

Steele didn't respond immediately. On the one hand, he thought his father was purposely engaging in selective amnesia, but after witnessing what his mother had gone through with her memory loss, he was starting to believe the colonel was entering the early stages of Alzheimer's.

"Brice is dead, Colonel."

The colonel stood up and walked across the room. He took a long drag on his cigarette and gazed at the flag-covered wall.

"I bet you have no idea what this here flag symbolizes. But your brother sure does. Yes, sir, Brice is a soldier. The kind of man who made this country great!"

Steele sat quietly watching the colonel rubbing his fingers back and forth across the flag as if he were in a trance.

After a solid sixty seconds of complete silence, the detective had no choice but to accept the fact that his attempt at striking up a meaningful conversation with the colonel had fallen flat.

"Perhaps it wasn't such a good idea for me to just drop by unannounced. Guess I'll get on the road. Besides, I still have about a six-hour drive in front of me."

But the colonel wasn't moved. He continued staring at the flag while puffing on his cigarette, electing instead to ignore the sound of quick and steady footsteps as Steele walked briskly toward the front door. Once he was seated and buckled up, he looked toward the house and noticed the colonel was standing on the porch with the cigarette still dangling from the side of his mouth.

Not wanting to drive off without saying goodbye, Steele lowered the driver-side window and waved.

"See you around, Colonel. Take good care of yourself."

"Oh, I'm going to do that. You just make sure you call next time and don't just be showing up on my doorstep," the colonel countered, not bothering to remove his hands from his pant pockets.

Steele raised the car window and slowly backed out of the driveway and onto the street. After one final look toward the porch, he put his car in drive and began heading toward Louisiana. Toward the Quarry, the second-largest maximum-security prison in the United States with seventy-five hundred prisoners and two thousand staff personnel, including Warden Orson Thaddeus Cornwell, who in addition to the allegations surrounding his prison ministry, was best known for forcing prisoners to perform menial jobs for him and his cronies.

It was just after four o'clock when Steele pulled off Highway 77 and started driving along the bumpy, mile-long dirt road toward the entrance, and by four forty, he cleared security and was sitting in a small damp interview room. A short time later, the door swung opened, and a prison guard escorted Raymond Jones into the room. All six foot seven inch, two hundred fifty pounds of him.

His enormous hands were cuffed to a thick chain that was wrapped around his waist, providing the guard leverage while escorting him into the room. Raymond's immense size was what had earned him the nickname Coach. That and the fact that although he was only five years old, he was still almost as tall as Coach Clemmons.

"Sit down on that chair and keep your hands in your lap at all times! That clear?" the guard commanded.

"No prob," Raymond responded.

The prison guard turned his attention toward Steele.

"I know you're a cop, but you follow the same rules as everybody else. No touching of any kind under any circumstance. Got that?"

"Got it," Steele responded.

The guard backed up several feet and leaned his back against the wall.

"Hello, Coach."

The guard quickly stepped forward.

"Hold up! Don't you dare refer to him as anything other than Jones, or Inmate Jones. Honestly, I prefer you call this asshole exactly what he is. An asshole. We clear here?"

Steele didn't bother responding and, instead, promptly returned his attention to Raymond.

"My father said you had something to say to me."

"That's right. I wanted to get the truth out about why I did what I did," Raymond responded.

"Why tell me? There's really nothing that I can do for you."

"I'm not asking you to do anything for me, Braxton, I mean, Detective Steele."

Raymond sat quietly for a moment before he resumed speaking.

"From the time we were kids, I could tell you were going to grow up to be a decent person. Look, I don't trust the criminal justice system. But I trust you."

"I'm curious. How did you know I was a detective?"

"I saw you on television giving a press conference."

"You do know that everything we say in this room is being recorded."

"Don't matter."

"And the prison guard will be able to hear our conversation?"

"Like I said, don't matter."

Steele sat back in his chair, and for the next twenty-two minutes, he listened to Coach unload. Raymond began telling the story of how his father, Norman, had been convicted of a crime he didn't commit. Norman, a college recruiter, had been in another state over twenty-three hundred miles away at the time of the incident, making it virtually impossible for him to commit the crime. Although surprised at being picked up by police officers for questioning, not to mention being told that he closely resembled the police sketch artist's facial composite, being a law-abiding citizen and knowing that he was innocent, Norman had figured it wouldn't take very long to clear up things once police officers had an opportunity to verify his alibi. After forty minutes of questioning, Norman was told by officers that he needed to take part in a police lineup and that once that was completed, he would be free to go.

In an unfortunate turn of events, the witness had identified Norman as the individual who committed the crime, and in spite of what should have been an iron-clad alibi, he had been held over, found guilty in a jury trial, and ultimately sentenced to twenty-five years in prison. Because the family had relied solely on Norman's salary for their subsistence, his incarceration set in motion a whole host of problems for the Jones family, including Raymond's mother, Janice, having to work two jobs just to make ends meet. On the anniversary of Norman's first year of incarceration, Raymond had gone to the prison to break the devastating news to his dad that Janice was murdered at work the night before when three teenagers wearing ski masks walked into the local Quickly Mart and shot her in the face at point-blank range before taking money from the cash register.

On his own and without any foreseeable way of making enough money to pay the mortgage or other expenses associated with home ownership, after burying his mother, sixteen-year-old Raymond had put all the items he could scrounge in storage and moved in with his aunt Velma. Several weeks later, on the seventeenth of December, the home the Jones family had occupied for the past thirteen years was repossessed. But the bad news was just getting started.

At nine o'clock that same evening, Velma had received a call from the prison advising that Norman committed suicide. She was told that prison guards found his lifeless body in his jail cell during their rounds and that he had apparently slit his own throat with a shank. She was also told that a note was discovered lying next to his body that had simply read, "Keep your promise, Raymond!"

Days had turned into weeks, weeks to months, and months to years, as rumors swirled about how shortly after the successful prosecution of the highly charged case involving Norman Jones, while still an ADA, Clinton Hayes had received creditable evidence that would've likely exonerated the defendant, but not wanting to place his pending promotion to DA in jeopardy, Hayes had chosen to withhold the information from the defense and, instead, allow Norman to remain in prison without any regard for how his self-centered actions might impact the Jones family. Word had even gotten back to Raymond that the primary reason Hayes was being considered for the top job in his office was due to the high volume of cases he had successfully prosecuted over the years. The problem with that, however, had been that Hayes also had a reputation of not having any qualms when it came to knowingly putting innocent individuals behind bars in order to beef up his numbers.

On the evening of the fifth anniversary of the day his father allegedly committed suicide, Raymond had slouched in the front seat of his silver Ford Taurus parked two doors from the Hayes residence, and at eight fifty-eight, he'd spotted the headlights of a car rapidly approaching from the rear. He could tell the vehicle was beginning to slow and assuming it was Hayes, Raymond started his car and waited. His hunch had been confirmed when brake lights flashed bright red before him.

The vehicle had made a turn into the driveway, and when it had, Raymond pushed down hard on the gas pedal before quickly coming to a stop in front of the home. Hayes was still holding his cell phone to his ear, apparently so involved in his conversation that he never saw Raymond walking toward him with a forty-five caliber in his hand. Still preoccupied, the DA had opened the driver side door, and that's when Raymond reached his arm into the vehicle and fired off three quick rounds, all striking the DA in the head.

After making sure Hayes was dead, Raymond had called Cranston PD and told them what he had done. He also told the dispatcher that he would wait in front of the Hayes' home to be arrested. Twelve minutes later, officers had arrived on scene and took Raymond into custody, where, once at the station, he'd provided officers with both a verbal and a written confession to the murder.

That was the last time Raymond had ever spoken a word about the murder. Before today.

"Why didn't you want anyone to know why you did what you did?"

"Wouldn't have mattered. They knew my father was innocent and they put him behind bars anyway."

"I have to ask you, Coach. Being on death row and looking back now, do you have any regrets?"

"Not a one."

Raymond exhaled as he leaned back in his chair, and in that moment, it would've been impossible for anyone looking at the man to not notice that something had happened. Every muscle in his body appeared to have relaxed. At the same time, his eyes softened to the point of where he looked like a completely different person. Suddenly, that broad smile of his spread across the entirety of his face and the dimly lit interview room seemed to light up.

"Thank you, Detective."

"For what?"

"For listening. Now, long after they put me to death and people are talking about what a horrible person I was, which I'm sure they will, at least, you'll know a bit more about why I did what I did."

Steele leaned forward, and when he did, the prison guard stepped toward the table but then suddenly stopped. Seconds later, he backed up and resumed his position against the wall.

"I know you know better than to try and whisper in here, Detective, but I'm going to make an exception this one time." The guard chuckled. "At this point, I could care less what you and that asshole talk about. We'll be sticking that big-ass needle in his arm soon enough. Go ahead. Knock yourself out."

Steele leaned across the table toward Raymond.

"Any truth to those rumors about the warden's prison ministry being linked to inmate deaths?"

Surprised by the question, Raymond sat quietly with a stunned look on his face for several seconds before responding in a barely audible voice.

"Death row inmates are kept away from the rest of the prison population, but there's no such thing as a secret in the Quarry. Years ago, one of the guards tried to get me to participate in the warden's little prayer meetings, and when I refused, they threw me in the hole for more than ninety days. I lost count just how long I was down there because I stopped making scratches in the wall at ninety. So, yeah, I heard about inmates killing themselves after somehow becoming brainwashed from those meetings. That's why I wasn't having no part of it."

"Got it," Steele responded.

Both men leaned back in their chairs.

"Remember when I said I had no regrets about what I did?"

"Yes."

"Well, I guess you can say it was sort of like intentionally pushing the red button."

"What's that supposed to mean?" Steele asked.

"When you get home, look up a psychologist by the name of B. F. Skinner. Read his research on operant conditioning. You'll understand."

"Enough of this psychobabble!" the guard interrupted, briskly stepping toward Raymond. "Time to return to your cage, asshole!"

The guard grabbed hold of the belly chain and yanked Raymond up off the chair. Within no time, the two were standing at the door with the prison guard straining against the much larger man, trying to push him out of the interview room. But Raymond resisted long enough to say, "A man's gotta do what a man's gotta do."

There was a sudden stillness in the interview room, that is, until the silence was broken by the sound of metal doors being slammed shut from somewhere deep within the prison walls.

Detective Steele pictured Raymond being ushered through the corridor with that broad smile still plastered across his face. And then it all made sense. More than anything else, he didn't want to die without anyone ever knowing his rationale for murdering the district attorney, and now that Coach had told his story, he was ready.

CHAPTER 27

Today ended pretty much like the rest, plenty of leads to chase down but nothing of significance warranting latching onto. Steele was looking forward to this evening's class if, for no other reason, that just so that he could focus on something other than the murder investigation. After calling Madi to ensure police officers were still parked out front, he returned his cell phone to his pocket and prepared for this evening's lecture.

Ten minutes later, Atticus walked in and placed his briefcase on the table. He looked over at the clock, and seeing that there was still a whole five minutes before the official start of class, he abruptly walked out and returned shortly carrying two cups of steaming hot coffee. He sat the cups on the table and then turned to greet his students.

"Evening, everyone," he said, smiling as he adjusted his bow tie. "As you can tell, I'm really going to be downing the caffeine this evening. Long day, long day. But that's all right. We'll get through it. Anyway, this evening we're going to spend some time unpacking contributors to why people become lawbreakers."

Atticus pulled his notes from the briefcase, while students opened their notebooks in preparation of this evening's lecture.

"The precursors to crime are complex due to a whole host of factors," he said. "Poverty, parental neglect, low self-esteem, alcohol, and drug abuse, all play into this phenomenon. And then there are those within our society who are at a greater risk of becoming offenders simply because of the circumstances they were born into. Moreover, some in academia go so far as to suggest that were we to simply devote increased attention to social conditions, such as creating better schools and improved employment opportunities, people would become more content with life, and as a byproduct, we'd see a decrease in overall crime."

Atticus stopped speaking in response to the sudden loud laughter coming from the back of the room.

"Excuse me, gentlemen. Is it something you'd like to share with the rest of us?" he asked.

Obviously embarrassed to have been caught talking, the students immediately ended their private conversation and turned their attention toward the front of the room.

"Okay, where were we?"

"Professor Dobson?" Steele called out.

"Detective Steele. Yes?"

"I couldn't help but notice you didn't mention recompense."

"Never heard that word before," a student on the left side of the room said in a low voice, but still loud enough for others to hear.

"What the detective is referring to is revenge. Am I correct, Detective?"

"Correct," Steele responded.

"Revenge is absolutely one of the reasons someone might resort to committing crime. As I said earlier, there are a multitude of contributors. Did I answer your question, Detective?"

"You did."

"Most excellent."

"I do have one other thing I'd like to ask if you don't mind."

"Of course. What is it, Detective?"

"A death row inmate once told me that he wasn't remorseful in the least about the murder he committed. He went on to say that he rationalized his crime along the lines of purposely pushing the red button. Since we're discussing reasons why individuals commit crime, I thought I'd get your thoughts on what he might have meant by that comment."

Atticus smiled as he toyed with the edges of his bow tie.

"B. F. Skinner. That's who he was referring to."

"I believe that is the name he mentioned."

Atticus grabbed his lecture notes from the table and shoved them back in the briefcase.

"You know, although Dr. Skinner's research is not on my list of discussion items for this course, I feel it perfectly aligns with this evening's lecture. Tell you what. Put your pens and paper away and just listen. You will not be quizzed on any of what I'm about to share, but I feel it will be extremely useful to you in better understanding precursors to crime, not to mention reasons why individuals may commit crime in spite of the consequences."

For the next thirty-something seconds, there was a noticeable increase in the classroom noise level as students began shuffling papers while, at the same time, scooting their chairs across the linoleum floor.

"Professor Skinner was an advocate of behaviorism best known for coming up with the concept of operant conditioning. He was also what I would call a tinkerer. The professor would develop various gadgets where, oftentimes, he'd use lab animals in his experiments. In one such experiment, to test his behavior modification theory, rats would be rewarded with items like food and water anytime they pushed against a blue button. There was also a red button used in the experiment. The sole purpose of this particular button was to apply negative reinforcement. To deter the behavior. When a rat pushed the red button, it would receive a shock treatment."

Atticus came from behind the table and began a deliberate walk around the perimeter of the classroom.

"Now let me ask you: Which of the buttons would you push if you were one of the rats used in Professor Skinner's experiment?"

Laughter erupted in the room as students began vocalizing their thoughts.

"That's an easy one. I'm team blue button all the way," a student shouted.

"You got that right! I bet those little hairballs learned how to distinguish colors really fast," a second student responded.

Atticus continued circling the classroom, nodding his head in approval while allowing students to continue expressing their feelings.

"It would only take me one time of pushing that red button. After that, I'd glue my hand to the blue button. I mean, I'm not stupid," another student exclaimed.

Atticus began clapping his hands together.

"So why is it that people commit crime when every indication is that their actions will be met with dire consequences? Detective Steele provided us with one such reason why someone might do this when he mentioned revenge."

Atticus returned to the table at the front of the room. After a vigorous discussion, he raised his hand high in the air.

"By a show of hands, who in here has plans on killing someone after you leave class this evening?"

Loud laughter again erupted throughout the classroom.

"No, I'm being serious here," Atticus interrupted. "While none of you may be actively plotting to commit murder, the situation where someone totally disbands their normal behavior and decides to take another person's life in spite of the consequences exists for each of us. And that is what it means to purposely push the red button."

There was quiet in the room as all eyes were glued on the look of disgust that had appeared across Professor Dobson's face. It was as if for a brief moment, he had forgotten where he was. Atticus just stood there, glaring at Detective Steele with a look of hostility that was intense as a laser beam cutting through hardened metal.

But Steele was preoccupied with his thoughts. Coach was heavy on his mind. Suddenly sensing that something wasn't quite right in the classroom, he looked up just in time to catch

Atticus staring coldly at him. Seconds later, Atticus raised his wire-rim glasses higher up over the bridge of his nose and adjusted his bow tie. Then he smiled as if nothing out of the ordinary had ever happened.

"Well, let's say we call it an evening. Hopefully, you got something out of our discussion and don't feel we just went off at a tangent."

Atticus looked toward Detective Steele.

"Good stuff, Detective. Your input never ceases to amaze me."

After staring at the table for several seconds, the professor gathered his items and abruptly walked out of the classroom, leaving students sitting in their chairs and wondering what just happened.

CHAPTER 28

Thursday, January 29
Nordlum Alderwood Mall
12:37 p.m.

The professor was in the parking lot out front of Nordlum, thinking about last night's class discussion. He still couldn't believe it. Of all the things to interject into the class discussion, Detective Steele wanted to talk about the research of Professor Skinner. Atticus knew the research well, but unlike lab rats that might undergo a behavioral change and shy away from the red button just to get some measly food pallets and water droplets, the only reward he was remotely interested in was that derived from exacting revenge on anyone who had the audacity to cross him.

He suddenly felt the detective's presence. It felt so real. Atticus reached his arm across the console but then immediately pulled it back. He knew his mind was simply playing tricks on him.

"I can't stand you, Steele, you smug son of a bitch!" he shouted, slamming his clinched fist hard against the dashboard.

Lost in his tirade, it took him several seconds to notice the person standing next to his car window. The young man happened to be passing between cars when he heard yelling coming from the

SUV. Thinking someone might be needing assistance, he stopped and took a peek inside the tinted passenger-side window. But it was short-lived.

The look on Atticus's face must have frightened the young man or, at the least, left no doubt that he needed to mind his own business and move along. Taking heed, the young man darted off without looking back, while Atticus monitored his every move through the rearview mirror, remembering the last time he had been here. It was December 30, the day he just knew he had identified the perfect woman.

Lauren had easily checked off all the boxes right up to the point when she'd told Atticus that wearing red lipstick really wasn't her thing, making her no longer the ideal target. Frustrated at not having identified his next victim, he took solace knowing that the game was still in play and that, in time, he was going to find exactly who he was looking for. After a peek in the mirror to make sure he looked presentable, Atticus stepped out of the SUV and began walking toward the luxury department store.

He yanked open the glass door, stepped in, and walked straight over to the cosmetic department. He felt as if he was being drawn there, and as it turned out, the person Atticus was looking for was standing right before him. In fact, she had been there all along. He walked up to the counter and waved to the woman who'd sold him the bottle of perfume when he had been in there about a month ago. Recognizing him immediately, she smiled, and a short time later, Samantha Stillwell made her way over to where Atticus was standing.

"Hello, Sam."

Sam smiled and playfully covered her name tag with her hand.

"I wonder if you would've remembered my name were it not on display for the whole world to see."

"Come on now. How could I ever forget the name of someone as captivating as you."

"I guess we'll never know, will we?"

"Looks like you'll just have to trust me."

Sam blushed as she allowed her ruby-red lips to form a perfect smile across her face.

"So, what can I do for you today, good-looking?"

"I don't know. Thought I'd just peruse the aisles and see if anything in here grabs my attention."

Sam had no idea that rather than dropping some lame pickup line on her, Atticus was speaking literally. She smiled as she leaned forward and placed her elbows on the glass counter, while at the same time, started playfully batting her eyelashes.

"So, how's that working out for you?"

"Too early to tell. Join me for dinner and drinks after you get off work."

"Just like that?"

"Just like that."

"Let me know if I'm missing something here, but didn't I assist you with your purchase of Coco Mademoiselle for that special lady of yours just a little while back?"

"You did."

"Well?"

"Let's just say it didn't work out."

"Hopefully, it wasn't the perfume."

"Not at all. It was just time for the both of us to move on."

Sam smiled.

"Okay, Atticus. I'm off at eight thirty."

"You remembered my name."

"Come on now. How could I ever forget the name of someone as captivating as you," Sam responded, repeating his words back to him.

"Nice. Meet me at Benedict's at nine."

"You meet me there. Gotta go, good-looking. See you at nine."

Looking up and noticing a woman approaching, Sam rubbed her petite hand gently across Atticus's forearm before turning and walking toward the customer patiently waiting at the far end of the cosmetic counter. With his mind finally focused on something other than what occurred in class last night, he stood there for a while longer, smirking as he watched Sam turn her attention toward the customer. She was perfect.

The thing is, Sam had always been perfect for his game, and had he not locked onto Lauren the way he did, he would've noticed just how perfect she was. Thinking back, Sam was wearing red lipstick on the day she sold him the perfume. But that's water under the bridge. All that mattered now was that fate had brought the two of them together again.

Scene 1

Benedict's Restaurant
7114 2nd Street
Reese Valley, Washington
9:00 p.m.

Atticus was reaching for the door when he heard footsteps approaching from behind. It was Sam.

"Wait for me, good-looking," she said.

"Hello, Sam. Your timing is impeccable," he responded, opening the left side of the double door for her to step in. "I hope you're hungry."

"I am. But what I have a taste for right now couldn't possibly be on the menu."

Atticus let go of the brass handle and allowed the door to close.

"It's not a must that we eat here. Do you have another place in mind?"

Sam smiled as she nuzzled up against his chest and reached her arms around his waist.

"How about we just go back to your place?"

He couldn't believe his good fortune. From the time he'd walked into Nordlum earlier in the day and seen Sam behind the cosmetic counter, his plan had been to somehow coax her back to his residence, and now, she was volunteering to go there on her own. Sam truly was beautiful, and while it was well past sunset, the two floodlights high above the entrance was more than enough to illuminate the bold contours of her bright red lips.

Scene 2

10 Marine View Drive
Reese Valley, Washington
11:30 p.m.

Sam woke up around eleven thirty. Groggy and disoriented. At first, she thought she was having an out-of-body experience. She prayed it was only a dream. But her gut told her something wasn't right.

The last thing she remembered was sipping from the glass of Pinot Noir and how wonderful the wine meshed with her palate. She couldn't remember if she'd ever finished the drink. And now, she was horizontal on a cold cement floor with a weighted shackle affixed to her left ankle, legs and wrists bound, and virtually blind under a canvas hood pulled tightly over her head. All of a sudden, she sensed someone was near, and while she couldn't see a thing, she knew it was Atticus. She could smell his cologne.

"Why are you doing this, Atticus?" she screamed from behind the canvas hood as she squirmed wildly on the cement floor, causing the chain to rattle in concert with her movements.

"Why am I doing this? Are you kidding me? I'm not the one who paints their lips red!" he yelled, staring at the stick of red lipstick he'd removed from Sam's clutch purse.

He walked across the basement and slammed the lipstick down hard on the workbench before returning to where Sam was laying on the floor.

"But that's neither here nor there. The important thing now is that you listen very carefully to what I'm about to say."

"Please! Don't hurt me!"

"I don't want to hurt you, Sam. That's why I'm trying to explain what needs to happen in order for that not to occur. Now please listen carefully."

"Let me go!" Sam screamed, again squirming along the floor as far as the chain would allow.

Atticus placed his foot in the small of her back and pressed down hard. Sam wailed so loudly her voice reverberated off the basement walls.

"Stop! You're hurting me!"

"Then stop moving, Sam. I will not repeat myself again. I told you it was important that you listen. Trust me: what I'm about to say benefits you more than it does me, so listen up. That extra weight you feel on your leg is actually a six-foot chain shackled to your ankle that's going to severely limit your mobility. But you'll still be able to get to everything you'll be needing down here. Also, there are motion-sensing video cameras throughout this room, all pointing at you from every angle you can possibly imagine."

Atticus began tapping his finger against the plastic casing of the camera.

"Please don't do—"

"This is your last warning, Sam," Atticus calmly interjected, cutting her off in midsentence. "Don't interrupt me again. Now, I want you to form a picture of a clock in your mind. The camera I'm standing next to happens to be at twelve o'clock."

Atticus took a few steps to his left, leaned over and grabbed hold of the bucket. He began scraping it slowly back and forth across the cement floor.

"You hear that, Sam? This is a metal bucket. You'll need it when that sudden urge hits you to relieve yourself. It'll be at three o'clock."

He moved around and stood next to Sam's feet, then picked up a handful of burlap sacks, and started pulling them slowly back and forth across her naked body. She winced the moment the itchy fibers made contact with her skin.

"It gets rather cold down here at night, Sam, so you'll need these sacks to keep warm. They'll be at six o'clock."

She heard him move again, and when the footsteps stopped, she could tell he was standing near her stomach.

"Okay. Now I'm standing at nine o'clock, Sam. I'll put your food here."

Atticus crouched to the floor and grabbed hold of her wrists. Using the knife, he sliced through the zip ties.

Sam instantly became hysterical and started screaming, but quickly stopped when Atticus released her wrists, allowing her arms to flop down hard on the cement floor. She could tell the zip ties were gone and her hands were free, but she was too afraid to move.

"You're in total control as to how long you stay alive, Sam," Atticus said in a measured voice as he reached down and cut the zip ties from around her legs. "In a moment, I'm going to remove the sack from over your head. Everything you need is here for you. All you have to do is remember where I placed everything in relation to the face on a clock. Now, this is very important. You must promise that you'll never open your eyes again. You do that, and I promise not to kill you. Can you do that, Sam?"

Sam didn't respond. Instead, she resumed screaming. Only much louder this time around.

"I asked you a question, Sam. Will you give me your word that you'll keep your eyes shut at all times?"

"Yes," she managed to say between sobs.

"I can't hear you, Sam. You need to speak much, much, much louder."

"Yes!" she screamed, still crying uncontrollably.

"That's good, Sam. That's very good. I'm going to trust you at your word. Hopefully, you won't disappoint me."

Atticus got to his feet and immediately grabbed hold of the hood. In a single move, he pulled it up over Sam's head and stood there for several seconds without saying a word. For whatever reason, he couldn't take his eyes off of her. Sam was still strikingly beautiful in spite of the dark mascara streaks running horizontally across her face. Her eyelids twitched as she used every ounce of her strength to keep them shut.

After standing over her for several seconds watching tears stream freely from the corner of her eyes, Atticus bent over and with the back of his hand, gently touched her wet face. Startled, Sam pulled away and nearly opened her eyes instinctively, but somehow managed to keep them shut.

"You really are a beautiful woman, Sam. I just hope you keep your promise," he whispered, before backing away and leaving the basement.

CHAPTER 29

Friday, January 30
10 Marine View Drive
Reese Valley, Washington
3:30 p.m.

The ferry was at the midway point between Whidbey Island and Reese Valley when Atticus looked out over the stern back toward the rugged terrain. It was always such a beautiful sight, especially on a clear day like today. After making sure no other passengers were close enough to see what he was doing, he pulled the burner phone from his pocket, inserted the voice distorter, and began punching in the numbers. The detective picked up on the third ring.

"Steele."

"I've taken another woman."

Click! Before Steele could respond, Atticus hung up. He disconnected the voice distorter and returned it to his pocket. Then he removed the SIM card from the back of the phone and flicked the components overboard, laughing out loud as both were quickly gobbled up by the choppy wake. Completing what he set out to do, Atticus returned to his car to wait out the remainder of the trip across the water. Besides, he was still a little buzzed from an afternoon of wine tasting and just wanted to sit back and relax.

A longtime member of the O & S Founder's Club, it was that time of year for the wine club release and rather than have his bottles shipped to him, Atticus decided to make the trip across the water and pick up his wine in person. Besides, he hadn't been back to the tasting room since the day he had been so rudely interrupted by Jennifer and her little posse, but once inside, he had no problem picking up right where he left off, enjoying a glass of 2013 Boushey Vineyard Syrah. In fact, he enjoyed several glasses. The ferry docked at Reese Valley Landing around two forty-five and by three thirty, Atticus was sitting in his living room uncorking a bottle of 2008 L'Entente Red.

The day was still young, and having finished off the bottle of wine, Atticus decided to review the tape to see how Sam was doing in the basement. A short ten minutes into the recording, she opened her eyes and started pulling on the chain, trying her best to break loose as she looked frantically around the basement. He continued watching the tape for the next fifteen minutes or so before fast-forwarding to the thirty-minute spot. Again, Sam's eyes were wide-open, and she was still pulling hard on the chain. He began zipping through the tape again, this time stopping at the one-hour mark. Her eyes were still open, but she was no longer trying to break loose from the restraint. She had given up.

After sitting at the kitchen table and becoming more irritated by the moment, Atticus got up and walked briskly toward the bookshelf in the hallway. He slid it aside and as soon as he opened the basement door, Sam started screaming. But he ignored her.

In fact, he didn't even want to look at her as he made his way over to the metal cabinet and removed two knives from the drawer.

"I asked you to do one thing, Sam, and you couldn't do it. One. Little. Thing."

Sam was freaking out and screaming much louder now. The veins in her neck seemingly about to burst through the skin.

"Why? Why are you doing this?" she yelled.

"It didn't have to be like this, Sam, but you broke your promise. All you had to do was keep your eyes shut. One. Little. Thing. And you couldn't do it. So now, we're here. Slow or fast, Sam?"

As soon as he started walking back across the basement with a knife in each hand, Sam tried to back away, doing all she could to create distance between Atticus and her. She reached as far as she could, straining to get hold of the camera affixed to the tripod, but it was just out of reach. She grabbed the metal bucket and flung it toward his head forcing him to dodge the flying object.

"Not smart, Sam," he said, letting go of the knife in his right hand and allowing it to clink against the cement.

Atticus picked up the bucket and hurled it back toward Sam, striking her on the knee and causing her to cry out in pain. He continued to close the gap and was now within two feet. The moment she reached for her leg, he transferred the knife to his right hand as he circled around, grabbed her by the head, and pinned her tightly against his chest. Before she could react, he pulled the knife from left to right across the front of her neck, creating a deep bloody gash.

Still needing to identify a location for his next abduction, Atticus walked over to the metal cabinet and grabbed the dice. Making sure they landed in a place where blood had not yet run, he shook them around in his hand and then tossed the ivory cubes hard against her body. When they finally settled, each dice displayed a single pip.

"Snake eyes!" he shouted, retrieving the dice from the floor and making his way back across the basement. He pulled the top hat from the box and began moving it around the Oligopoly game board stopping on the second spot. Once the location was determined, Atticus picked up one of the plastic trays and shoved it in his pocket. Then he picked up the photo of his mother.

"What do you think, Mommy, dearest? Are you proud of me? Oh, not yet? Well, that's okay. I already know where the next one's going to come from."

He walked across the basement and placed Judith's photo on the cement floor near Sam, making sure it was facing exactly as he wanted. Then he picked up the knife and removed Sam's eyes, making sure Judith had a front-row seat.

"You are so, so beautiful, Sam," he said, placing her eyes in the plastic tray.

When he was done, Atticus rolled her in plastic wrapping and placed her body at the rear of the freezer next to the burlap sacks. He stepped out only to return a short time later with a baffled look on his face. He was still gripping the knife tightly as he walked across the metal grate and stood next to the body.

"I can't part with you just yet, Sam," he said, bending over and cutting a slit in the plastic to expose her face.

"There. That's much better."

Atticus stood there for about three minutes just staring at Sam. When he had his fill, he left the meat freezer, walked over to the metal cabinet and removed two hundred sixty dollars. Using Sam's red lipstick, he wrote the word *slut* across the front of each bill.

CHAPTER 30

Monday, February 2nd
RVPD Headquarters
11:15 a.m.

Steele was seated across from Chief Tillis, discussing Adam McGregor being a suspect in the Shore Drive bomb explosion when his cell phone started vibrating. It was T. Z. Allen.

"Steele."

"Hey there, Steele, T. Z. here. You have a minute?"

"You bet. What's going on?"

"Two of my officers were approached this morning by a homeless man offering information on McGregor in exchange for five bucks to buy some food. He said he knew the police were looking for him. Apparently, McGregor left town a few days ago and headed up to Seattle."

"Appreciate the heads-up.

"You got it."

Steele disconnected the call and brought the chief up to speed. Now, it was time to hold a press conference and let the public know about McGregor.

Scene 1

Everett, Washington
1:20 p.m.

Atticus was in line at Narratively Coffee when his attention was drawn to a conversation two guys standing in front of him were having about whatever they were looking at on their cell phones. The conversation was on the verge of becoming disrespectfully loud as the young men continued carrying on as if they were the only ones in the coffee shop. Curious as to what all the commotion was about, he peeped at one of the cell phone screens and realized that what had their attention was a police press conference. Detective Steele was standing at the podium in front of RVPD addressing news reporters.

Having downloaded live TV streaming service years earlier, he pulled his cell phone from his pocket and tuned into the press conference, making sure to keep the volume turned all the way down as to not disturb other customers. He stared intently at the detective's lips, and while only succeeding at making out every third or fourth word on the small screen, logic told him the detective was conveying information about the Reese Valley murders. Figuring he'd catch up on the news when he was able to get in front of a television later in the day, Atticus was about to shut off his phone when a photograph of a man suddenly appeared on a split-screen. The name below the photo read *Adam McGregor*.

"What the hell!" he blurted out, attracting the attention of nearby customers.

He was certain he saw Steele mouth the words, "Person of interest," which Atticus knew was code for *suspect*. He couldn't believe it. The likeness between himself and the man on the poster was unreal. McGregor looked like a vagrant. Still, Atticus saw the man as an unkempt version of himself. Puzzled, he took a screenshot, swiftly capturing the photo.

Now at the front of the line, Atticus called out his order and then stepped aside and started caressing his face, using his thumb and forefinger to trace the outline of his chin. Several years ago, he had the shape of his chin altered by having some of the soft tissue below the skin removed in order to create a cleft chin, or chin dimple, a particular look he always believed signified masculinity. He began picturing the homeless man with a chin dimple.

"This is nuts," he mumbled.

And then there were the eyes. McGregor's eyes were hazel. But so were his under the solid-black contact lenses he wore anytime he was in public. Atticus first started wearing the lenses when he was a teenager, thinking the color black symbolized evil. Exactly what he thought of himself.

Still a bit thrown off by the suspect photo, he picked up his latte and found a seat on the gray couch next to the brick wall. After setting the cup down on the table, he reached his hand under his pant leg and rubbed across the scar that while nearly completely healed, never failed in putting the thought in his head that RVPD might just have his DNA. He was still gripping his leg two minutes later when he abruptly stopped. He realized Detective Steele had just mouthed the words *homeless* and *Seattle.*

Recalling that homeless shelters maintain a list of those who check into their facilities, Atticus immediately turned his attention away from the press conference and began pulling up every homeless shelter in Seattle. Each time he dialed a number, his ruse was always the same: that he desperately needed to locate a family member who may have checked into the facility, and on the eighth call, he was on the phone with someone at the Interfaith Family Shelter who knew of a man by the name of Adam McGregor.

"Oh, thank God!" he said to the man. "I've been looking for my cousin for weeks. Is he close by? I really need to speak with him."

"I'm sorry. I don't think I ever got your name."

"Please forgive me. My name is Sucitta Nosbod," Atticus responded.

"Well, Mr. Nosbod, your cousin stopped by here yesterday and tried to check in. Unfortunately, we were filled to capacity, and I had to turn him away."

"So he's not there?"

"Not at the moment. I told him to check back with me today to see if we have space to put him up. Not sure if he's going to take me up on that, but who knows? He may be out there on the sidewalk as we speak. Some of our homeless actually start getting in line before sunup just for a shot at getting in for the evening. Sorry I couldn't be of more assistance to you, Mr. Nosbod."

"No worries. It was worth a try. I was really just passing through town and thought I'd give it a shot while I was here. Hopefully, he'll reach out to his family one of these days. You've been a big help, though."

"Thank you for saying that. You take care now."

"You too. Thanks again."

Atticus finished his latte and left the coffee shop. Fifty-five minutes later, he pulled over and parked alongside an industrial building about a half block away from the homeless shelter. He slapped on the wig and fake moustache, then glanced in the rearview mirror, making sure everything was in place.

He hurried over to Second Avenue occasionally having to sidestep someone fast asleep on the sidewalk, undoubtedly dog tired from aimlessly roaming the streets trying to remain a step or two ahead of the coldness that was notorious for lulling the human body into a state of stillness for those caught napping in the night. The sign posted next to the steps showed that the Interfaith Family Shelter opened its doors at three o'clock daily and had a capacity of fifty people, meaning, beginning with the fifty-first person in line, countless men, women and children with nothing to do and nowhere to go, would have to hustle to find safe haven for yet another night. And this evening was expected to be cold. Biting cold. All day, the temperature hovered in the midthirties but was expected to be in the low teens by the end of the night.

Taken aback at just how long the line to get into the shelter was, Atticus briefly stared into the pale eyes of individuals with seemingly nothing to look forward to but despair. But right now, his primary concern was whether McGregor would be found among them. He continued making his way down the sidewalk, stepping around empty cans and discarded candy wrappers as he counted off the people in line with each step. When he reached the eighty-third person, he spotted someone who resembled the man in the police photo standing near the end of the line. He was number eighty-eight. Atticus pulled his cell phone from his pocket and looked at the photo, then back at the man. It was definitely McGregor.

He was severely underweight, wearing tattered jeans and a soiled tan bomber jacket. He looked crusty, and it was apparent he hadn't bathed in several days. McGregor was beyond filthy, and other than the black plastic bag he straddled with his feet, it appeared his only possessions were contained within the oil-stained duffel bag dangling over his left shoulder.

After observing him a while longer, Atticus resumed his walk down the line until he was standing side by side with the man. McGregor smelled of alcohol. But more than that, he smelled sick. His thin, graying hair was stuck to his scalp. He also had fresh scabs on his nose and forehead.

"The line starts back there," he said, slurring his words while pointing his shaky finger toward the end of the line.

"I hope you know there's no chance of you getting in there this evening. Too many people out here, buddy," Atticus responded.

"Why the hell do you care? You seem to be doing okay for yourself."

Atticus pulled two crisp one hundred-dollar bills from his shirt pocket and started waving them in front of McGregor's face.

"This money will pay for food and a couple of days at the WoodSpring Suites where you'll enjoy a warm room, clean linen, and a nice hot bath. The good thing is that it can be yours."

"What's the catch?"

"Let's just say I'm a nice guy who wants to help out a guy who appears to be down on his luck."

"Yeah, right."

"All righty then. Guess I'll see if someone else would rather sleep in a hotel room than out in the cold."

Atticus stuck the money in his pocket and started walking away. Out the corner of his eye, he noticed McGregor was watching him.

"Wait a minute!"

Atticus stopped and turned around.

"Well, now. You should've taken my offer when I first made it. Now I want something in return."

McGregor dropped his duffle bag and started scratching his head with both hands.

"What I gotta do?"

"I have some handiwork that needs to be done around the house. You interested?"

"Do I look stupid, mister? Hell, yeah, I'm interested."

"All righty then. My car is parked around the corner. You knock out a couple of things around the house and the money is all yours. I'll even drop you off at the hotel when you're done."

Atticus turned and started slow walking toward his car, leaving McGregor standing there.

"Hey, hold up, mister. I'm right behind you."

It was all orchestrated. While he had no doubt the money flash would be sufficient in getting McGregor to come to his house, a mystery still existed as to why the man surfaced as a suspect in the first place. In any event, Atticus now had McGregor under his control, and he would see to it that Detective Steele never got him in an interview room.

CHAPTER 31

Wednesday, February 4
Reese Valley State University
5:00 p.m.

Needing to make a few last minute revisions to his lecture notes, Atticus skipped going to the faculty lounge and arrived at class about twenty minutes earlier than normal, surprising students who walked into the room and noticed him sitting behind the table. The professor was lost in his thoughts and never once looked up from his computer. Still, like clockwork, the moment the clock struck five, he walked from behind the table and stood before the class.

"Good evening," he said, smiling broadly while adjusting his bow tie. "Our focus for this session is emotional intelligence, or EQ, as it is commonly known. Who can tell me what we mean by a person being emotionally intelligent?"

Cody raised his hand.

"Mr. Reed."

"I believe it's when someone is really in tuned with their emotions."

"Correct. And that's helpful why?"

Cindy raised her hand.

"Yes, Ms. Vance."

"People with high levels of EQ are better communicators."

"Right again. There are five basic features of EQ, namely, self-awareness, self-regulation, empathy, motivation, and social skill. It's been suggested that individuals possessing high levels of these competencies are not only able to regulate their own emotions, but the emotions of others. All things being equal, that typically leads to improved communication between people. Do you see the linkage?"

Atticus glanced around the classroom. He noticed the vast majority of students were nodding their heads in affirmation and scribbling on their notepads.

"Okay. Considering this is a criminal psychology course, we're going to set all of those positive attributes of EQ aside for a moment and unpack this construct from the standpoint of someone using it for destructive purposes. I realize this may sound a bit radical, but believe me: there is in fact a dark side to EQ."

Steele leaned forward in his seat. Although he was familiar with EQ, his understanding was nothing like how the professor apparently planned on discussing it. Atticus dimmed the lights in the classroom and flipped the power button on the projector. The first slide popped up on the screen.

"While it is true that individuals who possess high level of EQ are more effective both on and off the job, evidence has also shown that people who are masters at honing their emotional skills, are also better at manipulating others."

"That doesn't sound so positive to me, Professor," Cindy said.

"Exactly my point, Ms. Vance. When someone has out-and-out control of their emotions, they're able to easily disguise their true feelings. Let's take this a bit further. If someone has the ability to tap into another person's feelings, what's to say they won't hoodwink another person into doing something they may not normally do? What this means is that an individual who possesses a high level of EQ may very well on the one hand turn out to be someone like the detective over there who's life mission appears to be upholding the law, or they could just as easily become a menace to society. Do you have anything to add, Detective Steele?"

"Nothing at all," Steele responded.

"All righty then. Let us now turn our attention to psychopathic behavior. What would you say to my assertion that psychopaths are actually geniuses?"

"Yeah, right," Steele responded.

"I take it you have a differing opinion, Detective Steele."

"Psychopaths are not geniuses, Professor."

"Well, let's see, Detective. Can we agree that it would take someone with an extremely high level of intellect to talk another person into doing something totally against their will?"

"Let's just agree to disagree, Professor."

"Oh, that's taking the easy way out. Just how would you describe psychopaths, Detective?"

"Sickos."

Atticus walked over and stood directly in front of Steele's desk.

"Sickos?"

"Sickos," Steele repeated without hesitation.

Atticus pressed the button on the remote, and the projector screen went dark. On his way back to the front of the room, he flipped on the light switch before taking a quick look at the clock on the wall. There was still more than thirty-five minutes to go before the end of class. He slipped the remote in his jacket pocket and sat on the edge of the table.

"How about the rest of you? Anyone else in here think of psychopaths as sickos?"

Caught off guard by the question and immediately feeling the tension in the room, students purposely looked away, not wanting to catch eyes with the professor. But not Steele. The detective and the professor had locked in on one another and were engaged in a serious game of mean mugging.

"Everybody out!" Atticus shouted, still looking diabolically at the detective.

There was about five seconds of complete silence before he spoke again.

"I apologize for that. I have no idea where that came from. Anyway, what I really meant to say was, that's enough for this evening. I'll see everyone next week."

Once again shocked by the professor's sudden mood swing, students got up and began swiftly making their way toward the exit while just as he did last week, Detective Steele ensured everyone was safely out before he left.

Once the room was clear, Atticus gathered his belongings and walked over to Detective Steele's empty seat. He stood in front of the desk for a long time staring as if the detective was still seated there. Suddenly, he turned to the wall, violently flipped off the light switch, and stormed out the room.

CHAPTER 32

Thursday, February 5
87790 53rd Street W
Reese Valley, Washington
5:00 a.m.

Unable to sleep, Detective Steele tossed and turned throughout the night. The day had finally arrived. Having grown tired of staring at the ceiling, he hopped up, walked downstairs, and picked up the TV remote. Absent of any last-minute appeals or stays of execution, he knew what the featured story was going to be once he turned on the television.

He pressed the power button and started flipping through the channels. As expected, Raymond Jones had been put to death overnight by lethal injection for the murder of District Attorney Chuck Hayes.

Steele leaned back on the couch and reflected on the day he'd sat across from Coach at the Quarry, having walked away from that conversation knowing that not only did he fully accept his fate, but he was also ready to leave this earth.

And then the detective smiled, as he imagined Coach walking down the brightly lit hallway toward the execution chamber with that shit-eating grin still plastered across his face. No fear. No regrets.

Steele rolled off the couch and immediately got down on his knees as he began praying for his childhood friend.

"May Christ Who was crucified for you bring you freedom and peace. Amen."

Scene 1

48854 Deerfield Place
Reese Valley, Washington
4:00 p.m.

Madi and Grant made it home around four o'clock, and as she was inserting the key, she noticed the package sitting on the front porch next to the chair. Surprised to see it laying there, she picked it up and quickly stepped inside, making her way to the kitchen to answer the phone that started ringing the moment she opened the front door. Nearly out of breath, she got to the phone on the fourth ring.

"Hello?"

Her sister, Rachael, was on the other end crying hysterically.

"What's wrong, Rach?" Madi asked, cradling the phone between her ear and shoulder, while still holding her purse in her left hand and the package under her right arm.

Rachael didn't respond. Instead, the crying grew louder.

"I'm on my way," Madi assured her, immediately hanging up the phone and setting the package on the counter. She grabbed Grant by the arm and hurried out the door, forgetting to lock up. Fifteen minutes later, she and Grant made it over to Deerfield Place and were knocking on Rachael's door.

"Come in," Rachael said, still crying loudly.

Madi opened the door and walked inside.

"Give me a sec," she said, hurrying upstairs to get Grant situated. In a flash, Madi was seated on the couch next to her sister.

"What's wrong?" she asked.

"It's Mr. Pickles," Rachael responded. "He never came home last night, and I think he may be gone for good this time."

Since losing both their parents ten years ago, Rachael had never been the same. Almost immediately, she'd become withdrawn and, for the most part, had lived in isolation since that time. Mr. Pickles seemed to be her saving grace. She loved that cat more than anything and having him near provided that vital sense of balance to her life.

"He'll be back, Rach," Madi whispered in her ear as she held Rachael tightly, and the two gently rocked back and forth on the couch.

Two hours had passed since Madi first arrived, and it was starting to get late. Madi knew she would have to be leaving soon. As if on cue, Mr. Pickles walked through the pet opening at the bottom of the kitchen door and made his way to the living room.

"See, Rach, I told you he'd be back."

Madi lifted the Siamese cat from the floor and sat him on her sister's lap before calling for Grant to come down stairs.

"I think I'll leave you two lovebirds alone to make up."

Rachael was all smiles as she sat on the couch hugging her cat.

"Where did you run off to, Mr. Pickles? You gave me a good scare."

Madi opened the door and right before stepping out, she smiled and blew her sister a kiss.

Rachael smiled. "Love you, Madi."

"Love you more, Rach," she responded, before closing the door.

Scene 2

87790 53rd Street W
Reese Valley, Washington
6:30 p.m.

Madi and Grant didn't make it back home until around six thirty and from the moment they walked through the door, there was only one thing on Grant's mind. The package. He had that knowing grin and just couldn't stop eying it. Each time he walked past the counter, he'd reach up and touch it with his little hand. When he'd first spotted the package on the porch, the first thing he'd noticed were the colorful stamps. All eight of them. He saw that as a sure sign the package was meant for him being that he'd be turning eight tomorrow.

Madi too noticed the excessive amount of postage stamps. But there were other signs that also triggered her suspicion. For starters, the package didn't have a return address anywhere on it. But more than that, it was only addressed to *Steele*, which she found especially odd being that the detective never received business mail at their home.

She picked up the package for a closer inspection. Something just didn't feel right, and her initial instinct was to just drive it down to the local post office. But it was already closed for the day. Besides, she was running late and really needed to get dinner started. She decided to place the package back on the counter and let her detective husband decide what to do with it once he got home from work. She could always return it to the post office tomorrow if need be. Unfortunately, with all she had gone through with trying to comfort her sister coupled with Steele not walking into the house until well after ten that evening, Madi forgot to mention anything about the mysterious package.

It was just past midnight, and everyone in the house was sleeping peacefully. Except for Grant. He was lying in bed, anticipating what present could possibly be waiting for him in the package downstairs. After about thirty minutes of not being able to fall back asleep and the anticipation becoming virtually unbearable, Grant sneaked out of bed and tiptoed quietly downstairs for a little peek inside the package. His parents taught him that the moment the hands on the clock passed midnight, it was the beginning of a whole new day, so technically, it was officially his birthday.

Like any kid his age, all he wanted was a quick look. For months, Grant pleaded with his dad for a new baseball glove and to him, the six-by-twelve-inch package seemed about the right size. He would be careful not to mess up the wrapping so that he could reseal the package after he verified that what he wanted more than anything else in the world was in there. He was dying to know.

Grant raised up on his toes, pulled the package off the counter and sat it on the chair seat. He could feel his little heart jumping with excitement as he turned the package on its side and began gently easing back the flap.

CHAPTER 33

Friday, February 6
87790 53rd Street W
Reese Valley, Washington
12:34 a.m.

Boom! Once the seal was broken and without forewarning, the package exploded, releasing shrapnel in every direction imaginable and immediately killing the curious youngster a mere thirty-four minutes into his eighth birthday. Steele was awakened by the sudden blast. That sound was all too familiar from his days in the military. He prayed it was only a dream. But it wasn't. The detective knew for a fact he was wide awake. Another thing he knew for a fact was that a bomb had just exploded within the confines of his home.

Madi was trying to tell him something, but the screeching sound of the home alarm was ringing so loudly in his ears that he couldn't make out her words. It didn't take long before the bedroom became engulfed by the smell of gunpowder that reeked of sulfur. Remembering that Grant was down the hall, Steele leaped out of bed, grabbed his service weapon, and bolted toward the door.

His hearing returned about the same time he arrived at Grant's bedroom, and that's when the sheer panic in Madi's voice finally registered.

"Where's Grant?" she screamed.

Steele turned and darted down the stairs. Seconds later, Madi heard the unmistakable sound of anguish echoing through the home from the lower level. Flesh and blood coated the kitchen cabinets while Grant's lifeless body, nearly cut in half, slumped over what remained of the chair. Grant had taken a direct hit because of his close proximity to the package when it exploded.

First responders arrived within fifteen minutes of the blast, and three hours later, the residence was still crawling with investigators. Fragments were strewn everywhere as analysts methodically combed through the home, peering into every crack and crevice and carefully placing debris and dust particles into brown paper bags. By seven o'clock, analysts had collected a trove of bomb-making components, including shrapnel, wire, pieces of blasting cap, and labelling from the nine-volt battery that was used in rendering power to the device.

Jill Atwood stood in the doorway just outside the living room, trying her best to fend off tears. But she was losing the battle. Although this was not her first rodeo, more than any crime scene in the past, she found herself having to corral her emotions as she noted the aftereffects of the bomb ripping through Grant's little body. As it turned out, it was she, and not Madi who would be the last to see Grant before his body was removed from the home. Steele shielded Madi from looking into the kitchen when the two made their way downstairs, and although it pained him to not allow her to hold Grant one last time, the integrity of the crime scene needed to be maintained. More importantly, having already gone into the kitchen and witnessing the devastation, the last thing Steele wanted was for Madi to have those gruesome images of their son's remains trapped in her mind forever. Something that he would just have to find a way of dealing with.

The Atwoods and the Steeles were friends off the clock, with each spending time at the other's home for social events. Their sons even attended the same school, and while Jill stood there tormented over having to break the news to her child that his little buddy would never again be seated next to him in class, her heart was breaking for what the Steele's must have been going through. After what seemed like forever and a day, she hesitantly walked over and placed her arms around their shoulders.

"I'm so sorry, Madi."

Madi slowly turned to look over her shoulder. Her face was drained, and because she hadn't stopped crying since the explosion, her eyes resembled little puffer fish. Although she was far too distraught to speak, she managed to nod her head.

Jill leaned in close to the detective's ear.

"We're going to catch whoever did this. I promise you."

Steele didn't respond. Instead, his barely blinking eyes were fixed on the living room wall. Those watching assumed he was in shock. But he wasn't. He was enraged. The thing is, none of his colleagues had an inkling that at that very moment, Detective Steele was on the verge of completely losing it.

He sat on the couch in total stillness, trying his best to remember the suite of coping skills Dr. Beale had taught him when he'd been a child to use in staving off the monster within. But nothing seemed to be working. The tension throughout his body was just too great. Making matters worse, the pressure in his head was so intense his eye sockets felt as if they were convulsing.

The piercing sound in his ears was back and as penetrating as ever. Steele knew that unless something gave, and quickly, he was going to scream at the top of his lungs right there in front of everyone. Suddenly, he remembered. The only way of getting through the current episode was to mentally detach from everything. To block out the world around him.

Jill had a strange look on her face as she watched the detective squeezing his eyelids shut with all his might. She saw his lips quivering ever so slightly, and although it took her a moment to catch on, she eventually realized that what the detective was doing was counting to himself. About three minutes after he started the routine, Steele opened his eyes. He didn't speak a word, but appeared to be breathing normally again, a clear sign that he was at least regaining his composure.

Over the next several hours, the yellow tape used in creating a barrier around the Steele residence was pulled down as the last of the crime-scene investigators removed their equipment from the residence, marking the conclusion of on-site analysis, but the restart of a journey along a path of pain and heartache for the detective and Madi. They waited more than an hour after the last investigator cleared out before leaving.

Nevertheless, when they backed out of their driveway to head for the ferry landing, news crews and several of the locals were still gathered out front, each hoping to catch a glimpse of the couple. The Steele's had suffered yet another loss of a child. And now they were not only devastated for the second time but left splintered, while wondering if the mourning would ever end.

CHAPTER 34

Wednesday, February 11
400 First Street
Langley, Washington 98260
7:00 a.m.

Five days had passed since the bomb exploded in their home, wrecking their lives and leaving the Steeles feeling completely empty, with their faith the only thing solid enough to latch onto. They hadn't slept since the day Grant died, and with preparations finalized, there was no need in prolonging the inevitable. It was time to leave Whidbey Island.

They checked out of their room at the Inn at Langley around seven, and after a short sixteen-minute drive down the Langley loop and Washington-525 South, they pulled onto the back of the MV Suquamish. Neither spoke a word during the entire commute back across the Puget Sound, instead, the detective and Madi quietly stared out the windshield of their car which was now sandwiched between the other one-hundred-plus vehicles on the parking deck. At a little past eight, the Olympic-class ferry blasted through the early morning fog and pulled alongside Reese Valley Ferry Terminal.

A short time later, they arrived home, and without knowing what to expect, Steele opened the front door and apprehensively stepped inside. He was grateful to see that his colleagues had taken the initiative to restore their home as best they could to its original condition. After stepping aside for Madi to enter, Steele walked over to his leather chair next to the picture window and flopped down hard, allowing himself to be swallowed up by the arms of the oversize piece of furniture that seemed to collapse on contact, folding itself around the detective.

He reached over and picked up the hourglass from the table, flipped it over, and extended his arm, carefully positioning it between his face and the window as he gazed toward the outside, allowing his eyes to find their focus through the quintillion particles of white sand free falling into the bottom glass cylinder. Steele and Madi had given the hourglass to his mother, Kandace, as a gift several years earlier, and after she'd succumbed to Alzheimer's following a lengthy battle with the disease, they'd brought it to their home as a way of maintaining connection with the woman they both loved so dearly. It didn't take long before tears began to stream down his face, and the longer he sat in the leather chair, the more difficult it became to breath. He felt as if a giant anaconda had wrapped itself around his body, and the more he thought about Grant's pending memorial service, the more the giant reptile seemed to squeeze. Incrementally tightening its grip.

At the same time, Madi was dealing with her own set of struggles. After forcing herself into the kitchen, she walked over to the table brought there to replace the one destroyed in the explosion. She reached out and touched the edge of the table with her hand, and almost immediately, her mind began to roam wildly, shifting from one negative thought to the next. She stepped behind the table and gently rubbed the wall, sliding her hand lightly across the freshly applied paint while sensing the texture through her fingertips.

Suddenly, she became nauseated, and her legs felt weak. Like wet noodles. Unable to continue standing on her own, Madi leaned back against the wall and allowed her body to collapse onto the kitchen floor where she lowered her head and began crying silently into the palms of her hands as she prayed.

"Jesus, You said, 'Blessed are those who mourn, for they will be comforted.' I need You now, Lord. Amen."

Scene 1

Grace Presbyterian Church
2:00 p.m.

The polished black limousine made a right turn onto Harbour Pointe Boulevard before slowing to a stop in front of the church about a car length behind the hearse. A short time later, the detective, Madi, and Rachael stepped out and into the mass of people. Once the crowd parted, they began making that dreaded march up the church steps. This was where the family worshiped. Selected in part because of the symbolism between the church name and the name they had given the daughter they lost years earlier, but also because the Steele's felt connected with the congregation from the time they first stepped through the doors.

The sanctuary was filled to capacity with every seat taken and standing room only at the rear. Flowers seemed to occupy every inch of the church floor, so much so, the miniature-sized casket literally disappeared amongst the mass of vibrant color. Many in attendance were crabbers who routinely met the detective on the pier behind Varley's Reese Valley Landing for their crab-and-chat session, the locals referred to as crabbing with a cop, or CWAC. They, like everyone else, had come to pay their respects.

About an hour into the memorial service, and with Pastor Jeremiah Davies only a few words into the benediction, there was a loud popping sound outside, causing the pastor to abruptly stop speaking and several of the jittery people seated in the sanctuary to shuffle in their seats as they turned their attention toward the back of the church. A few even stood up and started heading toward the exit until the pastor's commanding voice rang out over the loud speaker.

"In God, I trust and am not afraid. What can man do to me?"

Reese Valley residents were on edge. They had been so ever since the bomb explosion, and it didn't take much for nerves to become rattled. Looking out and seeing that his words seemed to have calmed the congregation, the pastor continued for another fifteen minutes or so before bringing the service to a close by citing from 1 Peter 5: 7–10.

"Cast all your anxiety on Him because He cares for you. Be alert and of sober mind. Your enemy the devil prowls around like a roaring lion looking for someone to devour. Resist him, standing firm in the faith, because you know that the family of believers throughout the world is undergoing the same kind of sufferings. And the God of all grace, who called you to His eternal glory in Christ, after you have suffered a little while, will Himself restore you and make you strong, firm and steadfast. To Him be the power for ever and ever. Amen."

After the parting view, everyone vacated the sanctuary to allow the Steele family some private time with Grant. Rachael kissed her nephew on the forehead and, after praying over the casket, began walking toward the exit door. The detective and Madi stood somberly at the casket absorbing those last moments with their child. Madi gently stroked his little face before bending down and kissing Grant on the cheek.

"My beautiful little boy," she said between sobs while removing the silver locket from around her neck. Leaning in, she tucked it in Grant's jacket pocket and then kissed him one last time.

"You and Ania are finally together," she whispered in his ear before turning and hastily walking toward the exit.

Steele wanted to follow behind his wife, but he could tell the funeral director was getting anxious, obviously wanting to move things along. With his life seemingly flashing before him, the detective stared at his son, thinking about how something as simple as catching a crab had brought Grant so much joy. Steele loved the fact that he and Grant had been close. That the two of them had shared a special bond that he could only dream of ever having with the colonel. Still, there was so much more the two wanted to do together, none of which would happen now. He reached into the casket and adjusted the little tie around Grant's neck. After standing there for a while longer, Steele leaned over and kissed Grant on the forehead.

"I am so sorry I couldn't protect you, son. Please forgive me."

Steele gave the tiny casket a few quick taps with his fingers before looking up and nodding toward the funeral director. As he began walking up the aisle toward the exit, a loud slapping sound caused him to stop in midstride and the hair on his arms to stand up. He trembled as a cold chill washed over him, and without turning around, he knew that the loud sound was the lid on Grant's casket being closed shut for the very last time. After remaining motionless for several seconds, Steele resumed his walk toward the exit doors, making his way down the steps, and finally into the back seat of the limo for the fifteen-minute funeral procession over to Cypress Lawn Memorial Park.

For whatever reason, he looked out the window and happened to catch a glimpse of a face in the crowd. He could've sworn he saw Professor Dobson, but there was no way to be certain. There had to be at least three hundred people milling about on the sidewalk in front of the church, and the only visible portion of the person's face he could make out were the eyes. Still, that was enough to discern that something was amiss. Unlike the vibe coming from the crowd of well-wishers there to support the Steele family, whoever this person was, their eyes were shrouded in utter disdain, and as the polished black limousine pulled away from the curb, they were staring straight into the cabin from somewhere deep within the crowd.

Scene 2

Reese Valley State University
5:00 p.m.

The classroom chatter was appreciably louder than usual, and as expected, Grant's memorial service was the topic of discussion. It would've been nearly impossible to find anyone residing in or around Reese Valley who wasn't aware of the bomb explosion that had killed the little boy. The local news and social media made sure of that.

In typical fashion, Professor Dobson walked in just before five o'clock. He laid his briefcase on the table, and students immediately quieted down as they began reaching for their pens and notepads in preparation for the evening's lecture. After fumbling around with his briefcase, Atticus walked from behind the table and started adjusting his bow tie.

"Good evening, everyone. Let me start out by apologizing for my little slip of the tongue last week. My mind was somewhere else when I told everyone to get out of the classroom. Again, I didn't mean it, and just thought I needed to clear the air. Think about it. You don't get voted best instructor on campus for nothing, do you? Anyway, that's that."

Hannah raised her hand.

"One moment, please, Ms. Cohen. The second thing I wanted to talk about involves Detective Steele. As you can see, your classmate isn't with us this evening. While everyone in here is likely aware of the unfortunate incident that occurred at his home where his son was killed, what you may not be aware of is that the memorial service took place earlier today."

"Yeah. I drove down Harbour Pointe this morning on my way to work and saw all the people pulling into the parking lot at Grace Presbyterian Church. I figured it probably had something to do with that," Tyler said.

"That's exactly what that was, Mr. Scott. I heard someone say the kid's memorial service was scheduled for today and was going to be held at that church. Now, back to you, Ms. Cohen. I believe you had a question."

"Professor Dobson. I just know Detective Steele and his family are hurting during this difficult time, and I was wondering if we could take a moment and pray for them."

The question caught Atticus by surprise, and before he knew it, he started feeling tension in the muscles along the back of his neck. Although he was irritated as hell, he figured he'd just brush off the request with a line such as prayer in a classroom setting might be offensive to those who do not carry such spiritual beliefs.

"About that," he said. " I'm thinking some in here might be— on second thought, that sounds like an excellent idea, Ms. Cohen. Would you be so kind as to lead us in prayer?"

"Thank you, Professor."

Hannah pulled her Bible from her backpack and flipped it open.

"Revelation 21:4. He will wipe every tear from their eyes. There will be no more death or mourning or crying or pain, for the old order of things has passed away."

She closed her Bible and returned it to her backpack.

"If everyone would please bow their head, I will now lead us in prayer."

Hannah prayed at length for Detective Steele and his family while everyone in the room sat quietly with their heads bowed and their eyes closed. All except for Atticus. The professor spent prayer time looking from student to student while chuckling to himself.

About ninety seconds later, Hannah brought her prayer to a close.

"Amen."

After a chorus of responding amens, students began raising their heads and directing their attention toward the front of the room where Atticus was standing.

"Amen," he belatedly blurted out once he realized all eyes were on him. "That was very thoughtful of you, Ms. Cohen. In fact, all of you are to be commended for your kindness. I'm sure your prayers are uplifting the detective at this very moment wherever he might be."

It didn't take Atticus long to notice all the sad faces around the room. Several students were even sniffling and wiping away tears.

"You know…I don't feel much like lecturing this evening. Must be the weather. Anyone one else feeling like that?"

Every single student raised their hand. Some going so far as to extend both arms high in the air.

"All righty then. I guess I'll see you next week."

As soon as the last student walked out, Atticus picked up his briefcase and made his way over to the side of the room where Detective Steele usually sat. He stood there for a long time just staring at the empty seat. When he was done, he flipped off the lights and walked out.

CHAPTER 35

Thursday, February 12
87790 53rd Street W
Reese Valley, Washington
7:45 a.m.

Detective Steele walked outside and onto his frost-covered driveway and breathed deeply, taking in the frigid Reese Valley morning through his lungs. With each warm breath he exhaled, tiny artistic clouds danced gracefully before his face. He knew he hadn't given himself sufficient time to grieve and, in fact, wished he could just unplug from it all and curl up in a corner. But sitting around the house wasn't going to bring him any closer to catching his son's killer. And that, he also knew.

Hurting and emotionally drained, he drove in complete silence down Harbour Pointe Boulevard with his eyes focused straight through the windshield. Twenty minutes later, Steele pulled into his parking stall at RVPD and walked through the lobby doors. Although nobody expected to see him at work only a day after burying his son, there was just this *thing* about Detective Steele that separated him from the rest. It was indescribable, but everyone knew it was there.

Steele managed a half smile as he nodded in response to the overwhelming show of support from colleagues who, one by one, walked up to offer their condolences.

"Thank you, everyone. Madi and I can't begin to express just how much we truly appreciate the love and support you've shown us during this difficult time. And in case you're wondering, the answer is yes. I'm okay to return to work, and that's all I'm going to say about that. Thank you, again."

Steele turned and walked briskly across the lobby, straight into his boss's office. The desk officer had already notified Chief Tillis that the detective was in the building, and while the chief would've preferred that Steele take some time off, he really wasn't all that surprised to see him. Dedication aside, he knew he would have to keep an eye on the detective, if for no other reason than to ensure his return to the office so quickly following the brutal murder of his son wouldn't compound the issue by resulting in unintended consequences for the department.

"Have a seat, Steele."

"No, thank you, Chief. I just wanted to let you know I'm on duty."

Chief Tillis got to his feet, but didn't respond right away.

"I honestly don't think you should be here. Right now, your focus should be on your family."

"I appreciate your concern, but where exactly will staying home get me? Last time I checked, the person who killed my son isn't running around there."

Again, the chief took his time in responding as he tried to get a read on his ace detective. And Steele's eyes said it all. He knew the man standing before him would not take no for an answer. Not only was he on duty, he was on a mission.

"Fair enough. You let me know if you change your mind and need some time off."

The two men stood facing one another. Looking into each other's eyes for about thirty seconds, with neither speaking another word. But none were needed. Suddenly, Steele turned and left the office, making a beeline toward the bank of elevators on the far side of the lobby.

Scene 1

8:25 a.m.

The moment Detective Steele walked off the elevator, thoughts of yesterday came rushing back where every step he took down the hallway brought him that much closer to the scent of lilies. The same smell that permeated throughout Grace Presbyterian Church during Grant's memorial service. By the time he reached his office, the scent was overpowering, and he knew exactly where it was coming from.

He opened the door, and just as he expected, his office was filled with flowers. They were everywhere. Just like the mound of sympathy cards piled high on his desk and shielding every inch of the surface with the exception of the portion occupied by Grant's photo. The detective slid into his chair and started pushing the pile of cards aside, all the while vowing not only to read each and every one of them but also to personally acknowledge those who had taken the time to offer their sympathy.

Steele continued to sit at his desk in total darkness with only Professor Atticus Dobson on his mind. He was the real reason the detective returned to the office less than twenty-four hours after burying his son. While the professor had a reputation of being one of Reese Valley's most respected citizens, one of the first rules in crime solving is to focus attention on individuals with an ax to grind, and Atticus certainly seemed to fit that bill.

Although there was nothing concrete to go on, it was just a feeling Steele had. Most of it having to do with the way the professor always seemed to stare at him in class. Like he hated him with a passion, and while he had no idea why the professor might feel that way, when it came right down to it, Steele really didn't care. The only thing that mattered was whether or not Atticus had it in him to send a pipe bomb to his home.

Steele recalled Atticus taking part in some highly classified study several years ago where the military consulted with psychologists from around the country. But in order to be a part of the think tank, the psychologists were required to submit to a background check so that they could be issued appropriate clearances, which meant their fingerprints were on file. Steele called in a marker, and even before hanging up the phone, Professor Atticus Dobson's fingerprint card was being pulled. He was assured the information would be on his desk within a day or so.

Steele got up out of the chair, walked over to the wall, and flipped on the lights. Then he opened the drawer and removed the file he kept at the very back. It was labeled; Professor Atticus Dobson. There was just something about him that rubbed Steele the wrong way. So much so, the detective started keeping notes on Atticus.

The notes were short and to the point, and outside of the occasional mentioning of Vic and him being spotted together, the majority of the notations involved the professor's strange behavior in class. The most recent was dated February 4, two days before Grant was murdered.

Steele fired up the RVPD database and started cross-checking the name Dobson, searching for anyone outside of the professor with that last name. There had to be more to the professor. More than just how he portrayed himself. After what seemed like an endless hunt, Steele started locating Dobsons living in nearly every state, including in Washington State.

The first Dobson he found was Judith. She was Atticus's mother, and according to public records, she had died in a motor vehicle accident several years ago. Steele pulled up records on Chauncey Dobson, Atticus's father. According to what was listed in the files, he too was deceased.

The third and final individual he located with that last name who seemed to have ties to the local area was Chauncey's sister, Shannon. Steele couldn't find any record reporting her death, so there was a good chance she was still living. He just had to find her.

He pulled Shannon's credit report and instantly uncovered all sorts of useful information. The report listed her birth date, social security number, and her home address. There was also a telephone number for Shannon listed. Steele picked up the phone and dialed her number.

"Speak to me," she said, answering the phone on the third ring.

"Hello. This is Detective Braxton Steele with the Reese Valley Police Department. I'm trying to locate Mrs. Shannon Dobson."

"May I ask what this is about?"

"Are you Mrs. Dobson?"

"Well, that depends. Like I said, what's this about?"

Steele knew Shannon Dobson was the person on the other end of the call, but since she wasn't under any obligation to speak with him, he played along in order to get whatever information she was willing to divulge.

"I'm just trying to locate Mrs. Dobson to ask her a few questions. That's all."

"I'm Shannon Dobson," she finally said after a brief silence.

"Hello, Mrs. Dobson. I'm working an investigation where the last name Dobson came up. Let me say from the beginning that I do not consider you in any way to be a suspect in my investigation."

"Well, that's mighty nice of you, Detective, seeing that I haven't done anything wrong. So what is it you want to ask me?"

"Do you have any relatives living in Reese Valley?"

"I did at one time. Me and my brother, Chauncey, moved out here from the east coast way back when. We're originally from New Hampshire. Anyway, my brother passed away two years ago. Lung cancer. So it's just me now."

"I'm sorry to hear that."

"Don't be. It was his own fault. Damn fool just wouldn't give up the cancer sticks even though he knew they were killing him. Anything else you want to ask me?"

"You know anybody by the name of Atticus?"

Shannon let out a long, deliberate sigh before responding.

"I haven't heard from, thought about, nor have I seen Atticus in years."

"Are the two of you related?"

"Oh, hell no! Although that uppity-ass bastard grew up thinking we were. Thing is, he probably still thinks we're related. I guess he's just too important to call anybody. Maybe one day, I'll tell him my brother really wasn't his daddy. That'll knock his ass down a few pegs."

"What did you just say?"

"You heard me. Atticus was a test-tube baby. Chauncey had a low sperm count, and he and Judith really wanted a kid, so they went the route of in vitro fertilization. I think the place where they went was called Lindenwood Fertility. Anything else, Detective?"

"No. You've been most helpful. Thank you, Mrs. Dobson."

Steele hung up the phone and immediately turned to his computer and typed in the words *Lindenwood Fertility*.

CHAPTER 36

Sunday, February 15
Fremont Sunday Street Market on Evanston Ave North
10:00 a.m.

Atticus made it to the street market around ten o'clock, and after strolling the grounds for a bit, he walked up to Vic's booth. Almost immediately, he could tell the veteran was stressing about something. His face was contorted, and both of his fists were clenched tightly atop the table.

"You okay, Sarge?" he asked.

"Why wouldn't I be?"

"I don't know. You just seem a little tense."

"What if I were? There's nothing you can do about it."

"And you know that for a fact?"

"I know enough."

Atticus laughed and started slapping his hand down hard on the table.

"I don't see what's so damn funny!"

"You are. But that's not why I'm here. Just keep your eyes open in the morning, Sarge."

"Wait! What? Are you saying what I think you're saying?"

Atticus didn't respond.

"Don't you be messing with me, Atticus."

"Like I said, Sarge. Keep your eyes open in the morning."

For the last several weeks, the thought of dead women had literally hijacked the veteran's dreams. It was both his obsession and the reason he relied so heavily on Atticus to continue tipping him off whenever one would be out there. And he always wanted to be the one who found them. Well before police arrived and draped the body with a tarp.

Being the person who discovered the body had its advantages. Namely, it allowed the veteran an opportunity to spend a little one-on-one time with the dead women. A chance to stare into their faces and commit the images to memory. Something he couldn't get enough of. And as he watched Atticus walk away, Vic was already thinking about tomorrow morning, wondering what color hair this one was going to have.

Scene 1

10 Marine View Drive
Reese Valley, Washington
8:30 p.m.

After gathering Sam's clothing, Atticus did as he had done so many times in the past with the garments of other women who had died in his basement; he took them out back to the fire pit and tossed them into the flame. After adding a bit more gasoline, he took a seat on the large rock under the olive tree and waited patiently until the fire extinguished on its own, leaving nothing but a pile of thick gray ash. He knew anytime he burned his victim's clothing and other items, carbon dioxide and other greenhouse gasses were being released into the atmosphere, and while he often chided others about not taking global warming seriously, at the moment, not getting caught with evidence from a crime was of much greater concern to the professor than trying to save the planet.

Once it was dark outside, he pulled Sam's body from the freezer and stuffed it in the back of his SUV. Twenty minutes later, he was just outside Reese Gulch. He was starting to slow down to make his turn when he spotted an unmarked unit near the mouth of the alley. He could spot an undercover police vehicle from a mile away.

Figuring RVPD was probably hiding in the shadows, he drove by the alley without stopping. As soon as he turned the corner his suspicions were confirmed. He spotted a second unmarked unit pulled to the side of the road. It was actually well-hidden and had the light from the officer's cell phone screen not flashed and caught his attention, Atticus likely would've driven by without seeing it. In any event, it was time for plan B.

CHAPTER 37

Monday, February 16
3:00 a.m.

Vic tossed and turned throughout the night, his mind working overtime thinking about what might await him when he took his morning walk in just a few hours from now. He'd barely slept. Nor had he wanted to. Right now, the only thing he wanted was to see the body of a dead woman.

He turned his head and looked at the clock on the nightstand. It was only three o'clock. For the next hour, the old veteran did all he could to fall asleep, but that proved to be an exercise in futility. He was just too amped up.

About fifty minutes later, he crawled out of bed and got dressed, catching Clover off guard and totally throwing her off her daily routine. After washing his face and brushing his teeth, he walked into the kitchen and made a fresh pot of coffee, but it was way too early to leave the house. He tried tidying up a bit while humming Motown songs out loud. He knew them all. From the Temptations to the Supremes and everything in between. But that soon became boring. He took another look at his watch. Sunrise was still an hour and a half away.

Downing that second cup of coffee seemed to only make matters worse, and in addition to the anxiety he was feeling, a case of severe jitters had now joined the party. Deciding he had about enough of fumbling around with the empty coffee cup, Vic stood up and walked over to the cabinet.

He grabbed a screwdriver from the drawer and stuck it in his pocket, then walked into the living room, and pulled the sofa about three feet away from the wall. After folding back the dusty throw rug, Vic pulled the screwdriver from his pocket and pried up the loose floorboard, something he hadn't done in more than a year. He removed the metal box. Then he returned to the kitchen and placed it on the table.

The lid was rusted tight, but after a few hard tugs, he was able to pop it off. The metal box contained the articles of each and every woman murdered in Reese Valley. Vic reached into the box and removed a handful of old newspaper clippings and laid them on the table, arranging them in no particular order.

"Time for more coffee," he told Clover while walking over to the counter to pour his third cup for the morning. He returned to the table and once again glanced at his watch. One more hour to go.

"Eeny, meeny, miny, moe," he rattled off, lightly tapping the articles with his index finger and stopping on the one dated December 29. He lifted it from the table. Just holding the wrinkled news article in his hand refreshed his recollection of the incident.

"Ah, yes. I remember this one, Clover. This here is Jennifer Rollins."

Vic took another sip of coffee and smiled, thinking back to the sheer exhilaration he felt when he first stumbled upon the woman's body wrapped in bloody plastic. The hands on his watch continued advancing, and after a while, the sun peeked through the clouds. It was time to go. He hooked the leash to Clover's collar, and shortly thereafter, the two were out the door. They walked at a much faster stride than usual, Vic's mind understandably focused more on finding the body than on exercising. He and Clover sped through Reese Gulch as rapidly as his feet would allow. Within minutes, they were in the alley.

Vic walked along the back street, looking in all directions. But there wasn't a body in any of the familiar locations. He walked back to the beginning and made a second pass. Nothing. He made a third pass, and then a fourth. Still nothing. He tried convincing himself that he must be overlooking something, so he returned to the beginning and made a fifth pass. When he came up empty again, the veteran was beside himself.

Thinking perhaps Atticus hid the corpse under the thick brush, he let go of the leash and started picking up tree branches and tossing them aside. He was starting to panic, and the longer he sifted through the brush without finding a body, the more the panic sat in. The morning air was crisp, but Vic was sweating like a pig.

For more than an hour, he stomped through the brush, stepping around boulders and over the stream that ran through the gulch. His heart was pumping at a blistering pace as he sprinted from fallen tree to fallen tree, hoping to find a body under at least one of them. And when he continued coming up empty, he had to accept the fact that nothing was out there. Frazzled, he sat on a fallen tree trunk to collect his thoughts, but the only thing he could think of was that Atticus had deceived him.

Vic got to his feet and summoned for Clover to come near. He grabbed hold of her leash and started walking up the alley toward home. Twenty-minutes later, he was in his front yard raising the flag to the top of the pole. When he was done, he got down on a knee and started rubbing Clover's ears.

"Yeah, I bet he thought that shit was funny. But that's all right, girl. He's gonna find out soon enough what happens when you screw with Sergeant First Class Victor McPhee."

Scene 1

10 Marine View Drive
Reese Valley, Washington
8:00 a. m.

Ludwig van Beethoven's Piano Sonata No. 14 in C-sharp minor, "Moonlight," played softly over the kitchen speakers while Atticus sat at the table sipping piping-hot coffee and nibbling on a maple-pecan Danish. He couldn't get his mind off of last night. With his plans foiled for getting rid of her body, he decided to just keep Sam in the basement. Actually, the decision was made for him. After spotting the undercover police cars hanging out at the gulch, attempting to leave her out there was entirely out of the question.

By nine o'clock, he was busy saw-cutting through the cement floor and removing dirt from the basement. Three hours later and with the prep-work completed, Atticus hustled over to the Home Depot on Highway 99 to pick up the items he'd be needing for his project. The time had come to shut off access to the space beneath his home.

When he returned, he pulled Sam's body from the meat freezer, dragged her across the cement floor, and rolled her over into the six-by-four-by-three-foot-deep hole. Then he walked back over to the freezer and snatched the power cord from the wall socket before stepping inside and removing the small plastic containers from the shelf.

One by one, he peeled back the lids and took a final look at the frozen eyeballs before tossing each of the containers into the hole. He marveled at knowing exactly which of the women the eyes had come from. After disposing of the final plastic container, he backfilled the hole with approximately seventy-four cubic feet of wet cement.

His last order of business before securing the basement was to update the manuscript to account for the deaths of Jennifer Rollins and Samantha Stillwell, and once he was done, he placed the manuscript in a manila envelope and stuck it in his pocket. He looked around the basement one final time then walked up the stairs and flipped off the lights to begin the process of drywalling over the door opening and applying a little touch up paint here and there.

Another thirty minutes to permanently affix the bookshelf to the wall over the spot where the door used to be and—voilà!—for all intents and purposes the basement disappeared, leaving driving over to the post office to drop the manuscript in the mail the only remaining item on the to-do list.

CHAPTER 38

Tuesday, February 17
55403 101st Street SW
Reese Valley, Washington
10:15 a.m.

It took some time, but Steele was able to come up with a potential address for Dr. Gipson. Forty-five minutes later, the detective walked up the cobblestone pathway to the home and pulled on the brass door knocker. He flashed his badge when a middle-aged woman answered the door.

"Good morning. I'm Detective Braxton Steele with the Reese Valley Police Department. I'm looking for a Dr. Rutherford Gipson."

"Dr. Gipson is my father. He lives out back in the guest house. My dad had a stroke about six years ago. After that, my husband and I brought him here to live with us."

"I see. I wanted to ask him a few questions that have to do with the fertility clinic he used to run. Do you think he would be able to answer my questions?"

"You kidding me? He's as sharp as a tack! He really doesn't talk much about the fertility clinic, especially since he was forced to shut it down, but I don't think he'd have any problem with answering your questions."

"Thank you."

"I'm sorry. How rude of me. I'm Laura Becker."

"Thank you, Mrs. Becker. I'd appreciate that."

Laura opened the door and waved the detective in.

"This way, Detective," she said, walking toward the back door near the kitchen stove. "You drink coffee? I'll bring you a cup if you like."

"No, thank you. I've had my fill for today. Any more and I won't be able to sleep tonight."

Laura laughed. "Yeah, it can have that effect on some people. But not me. I'll drink coffee right up to bedtime and still sleep like a baby."

Laura led Steele across the grassy area in the backyard, and after walking off several steps, she knocked on the door of the small granny unit.

"Why are you knocking on the door like that, Laura?" a voice from within the unit yelled out.

"Excuse me, Dad. I have a Detective Steele standing here with me. He would like to ask you some questions about the fertility clinic."

The door flung opened, and a frail-looking man with hair as white as snow was standing there. He was dressed in dark-blue overalls and a white T-shirt.

"I shut it down, so what do guys want now?"

Steele held out his credentials for Dr. Gipson to see.

"Hello, Dr. Gipson. I'm Detective Steele, and I'm not here about anything having to do with you shutting down your clinic. I do, however, have a few questions about former clients of yours, and I was hoping you could help."

Dr. Gipson stood in the doorway for several seconds, staring at the detective as if he could see right through him.

"What's the name?" he finally asked.

"Dobson. Judith and Chauncey."

Dr. Gipson pushed the door open.

"Come in. I'll try to help you if I can," he said, stepping aside for Steele to enter. "Laura, sweetie, would you be a dear and get me and the detective some coffee?"

"I already offered the detective a cup, Dad. He didn't want any."

"He'll have a cup. I'm sure the detective wouldn't want an old man to drink alone. Right, Detective?"

"That's right," Steele responded.

Laura chuckled. "What I tell you, Detective? I'll put on a fresh pot."

"Not much room in here, but we can sit and talk on that couch over there."

"Thank you, Dr. Gipson."

"Now, what exactly is it you would like to know about the Dobsons?"

"I wanted to ask you about their son who was conceived in your clinic."

"You mean sons."

Steele didn't respond immediately. The detective prided himself on maintaining a poker face during interviews, but his facial expression changed suddenly, and Dr. Gipson spotted it right away. He could tell the detective was thinking. Dr. Gipson stood up, walked over to a table in the corner of the tiny home and plucked a magazine from the bottom half of the stack. He sat down and flipped it open, removed a yellow file folder, and handed it to Steele.

"Here. When I shut down my clinic and was done with talking with the authorities, I destroyed all of the patient files. Except this one. It is the file I kept on the Dobsons. I was able to remove it before the FDA started ransacking my office. Nobody knows it even exists."

"I have to ask. Why this file?"

"You have no idea what I was up against at that time, Detective. They were already shutting me down for allegedly violating FDA regulations regarding donor eligibility. The last thing I needed was to further complicate matters."

Steele opened the file and started flipping through the pages.

"What's the deal with this rap sheet for Matthew Fowler?"

There was a sudden knock on the door. Laura walked in carrying a wooden serving tray with two cups of coffee along with sugar, cream, and a couple of plastic spoons.

"Here you are, gentlemen. Nice and hot," she said, placing the tray on the table in front of the couch.

"Thank you, honey," Dr. Gipson responded.

"Yes. Thank you, Laura."

"Both of you are more than welcome. You know where to find me should either of you need anything else."

Laura smiled then turned and headed back toward the main house. Once she closed the door, Dr. Gipson resumed speaking.

"Matthew Fowler was listed in our files only as sperm donor K-104. He was, and likely still is, an extremely handsome man. According to his profile, he had an IQ of 160, a bachelor's degree in neuroscience, a masters in artificial intelligence, and was working on his PhD in neuroscience engineering at the time. He supposedly had a passion for crystallography, algorithms, and fitness. In short, Matthew Fowler was perfect in every way imaginable, which is why his sperm was so highly sought after. With me so far, Detective?"

"I think so."

"Like other clients who came to see me, the Dobsons had exhausted all other options, which is why they wanted to try to conceive through in vitro fertilization. And we were successful. You can say we were perhaps a bit too successful. Judith became pregnant with twins. Two boys. But all they wanted was one child. They were adamant about that."

Dr. Gipson stopped talking. He stood up and walked over to the window and stared out onto the grassy area.

"I thought that with time they would change their minds. But they didn't. In any event, they gave one up for adoption. How they decided which one to keep is beyond me. I never heard anything about the boy they parted with, but the one they kept, well, they named him Atticus. The only reason I know that is because Mr. Dobson came into my office one day madder than hell."

"About what?"

Dr. Gipson returned to the couch and sat silently with his hands in his lap. After about thirty seconds, he resumed speaking.

"This intern we had working for us at the time sent a letter to the Dobsons that contained classified information about our program, including the actual name of donor K-104. Mr. Dobson read the letter and decided to conduct his own background check on the donor. I still don't know how he did it, but somehow he found out that Mathew Fowler, AKA donor K-104, was a very disturbed man. As it turned out, Fowler was nothing like the person he purported to be. His profile was complete garbage, and we failed to catch it! We had no idea the man suffered from schizophrenia. He also had a narcissistic personality disorder as well as a criminal history."

"That's unbelievable."

"You think? He was on parole when he first started showing up at our clinic. Apparently, he spent time in prison for burglary. Like I said, Mr. Dobson learned all of this but wanted to keep it under wraps. He told me I had done enough damage, and if his wife ever learned the truth about the donor, he'd personally see to it that I regretted it."

"And now you're handing the file over to me."

"Look, Detective. I'm getting up in age, and someone needs to know about this. After I shut down the clinic, I spent the next several months following up on Matthew Fowler, and what I learned scared the living hell out of me. It seems Fowler started experiencing psychotic episodes around the age of twenty, well before the time he started donating his sperm. I also learned that Fowler is currently serving two life-sentences on a double-murder conviction."

"Tell me, Dr. Gipson. Is it possible that the twins conceived by the Dobsons share the same DNA?"

"It more certainly is. Anyway, I really hope you find something you can use in that file, Detective."

Dr. Gipson stood up and walked over to the door.

"No need in going back through the house. That side gate over there will lead you back to your car. I'll tell Laura bye for you."

"Thank you, Dr. Gipson. I appreciate your time."

Steele stepped out and was midway across the lawn when Dr. Gipson called after him.

"One more thing, Detective. There's a page in the file indicating sperm from donor K-104 was used in fathering forty-two children. That, sir, is not a typo."

And before Steele could respond, Dr. Gipson closed the door.

CHAPTER 39

Thursday, February 19
8601 Reese Valley Speedway
8:40 a.m.

After Atticus followed Madi from Starrocks, he pulled to the curb across the street from her office and watched as she unlocked the door and walked inside. She was alone, and he wanted to get in there before her clients started arriving for their appointments. He slipped a black V-neck sweater over his shirt and then covered his hair with the wig. After waving to a jogger who passed by the driver-side window, he slapped on the fake moustache and checked himself out in the rearview mirror to ensure it was on correctly.

Atticus pulled into the lot and parked in the spot adjacent to one labeled, Dr. Madison Steele, OD. He walked in, but Madi was so deep in thought she didn't immediately notice that someone was standing there. Taking note of his presence, she reached over and grabbed a handkerchief to dab her eyes as she walked from behind the desk.

"Hello, I'm Dr. Madison Steele."

"I'm sorry. Did I catch you at a bad time?"

"No, not at all. How may I help you?"

"I've been seeing spots in my eyes."

"Let's have a look," Madi said, gesturing with her hand for Atticus to take a seat in the examination chair about ten feet away in the adjoining room.

"No, I'd rather just talk about what's going on if you don't mind. I'm not ready to have anyone poking around in my eyes just yet, but I'll gladly pay you for your time."

"I must say this is a first. But if that's what you want, I'll try my best to help. What questions can I answer for you?"

"First off, is this something I need to be worried about?"

"Based on your description of what you're experiencing, it sounds to me like you have floaters, which are not that big of a deal. That said, without actually examining your eyes, the best answer I can give you is it depends. And this is why I say that. At one end of the spectrum, floaters may be simply the result of aging, and while they are a nuisance, they're totally harmless."

"Fair enough," Atticus responded. "Now let's hear the bad stuff."

"In rare occasions, floaters can be symptomatic of a number of eye problems, including retinal tears, retinal detachment, and bleeding within the eye."

"Wow!"

"I know that sounds alarming, but again, without an eye exam, there's really no way I can assess what's going on in there."

"I really just wanted to let you know how sorry I am for what happened to your son".

"Excuse me?" Madi exclaimed.

Taken aback, her facial expression left no doubt the comment threw her for a loop.

"Why would you say something like that?"

"I saw it in the newspaper."

Madi tried her best to remain calm, but on the inside, she was totally unnerved.

"I never got your name."

"Nosbod. Sucitta Nosbod."

There was about thirty seconds of silence where neither Atticus nor Madi spoke a word.

"You know, Doc, I used to see a shrink."

"Why did you stop?"

"Because it wasn't working."

"I'm sorry to hear that," she said, hoping her response wouldn't be the one thing that set the man off.

"I've done some really bad things in my life, Doc."

His words were chilling. Madi looked over her shoulder toward her chair, but knew there was no way for her to reach the panic button. She contemplated running for the exit but wasn't sure if she could make it or what he might do if she tried but failed.

"Do you believe in God?" he asked.

Madi's fear level was way off the chart and she wanted to scream, but she continued to fight through it.

"Yes, Mr. Nosbod. I do believe in God. I also believe that He forgives us of our sins."

"I don't think God will never forgive me for the things I've done."

Atticus stuck his hand in his pocket while Madi, unsure of his intentions, quickly backed away.

Seconds later, he pulled out a wad of dollar bills. "Settle down Doc. How much do I owe you?"

"Nothing. It's on the house."

"I truly am sorry for what happened to your son," he said, walking across the office and out the door.

When she was certain he was gone, Madi picked up her cell phone and called her husband. Seeing who was calling, Steele picked up on the first ring.

"Is everything okay?"

"I'm fine, but this man came in here today acting strange. I mean, it was weird."

"Is he there now?"

"No. He just left."

"What happened?"

"Well, for starters, he didn't come here for an eye examination."

"What did he want?"

"To talk."

"To talk? About what?"

"At first, he said he was seeing spots in his eyes. But then he pivoted and started saying stuff like he was sorry about what happened to our son."

"What?"

"I know. He said something about seeing it in the newspaper."

"Did you get his name?"

"He said his name was Sucitta Nosbod."

"Nosbod?" Steele repeated, typing the man's name on the keyboard.

"Yes. Sucitta Nosbod. What's that tapping sound?"

"It's nothing. Did he threaten you in any way?"

"No."

"Do you think you can identify him if I bring some photos home for you to look at?"

"Perhaps."

"Okay. I'll see what I can find on him."

Madi suddenly became quiet.

"There's something else, isn't it?"

"He just looked fake to me. There's that sound again. What is that?"

"It's nothing, Madi. You said he looked fake. Fake how?"

"I'm not sure. He looked made up. Like he was wearing a wig. I thought his moustache was fake too. Oh, and he was wearing these really dark contact lenses."

"Okay. I want you to start keeping your door locked so anyone coming to your office will have to ring the doorbell to gain access. I don't want people just walking in on you. Not even clients with appointments."

"That's a great idea. In fact, I'm going to lock my door right now. I'll be fine, sweetheart. See you at home a bit later."

"See you later."

Shortly after he began searching for the strange name in the database Steele realized Sucitta Nosbod was an anagram, and that the man who walked into Madi's office was actually Professor Atticus Dobson. It suddenly made sense, and if the detective's instincts were right, the oath he'd sworn to when he'd first joined the department wouldn't matter. At least, not right now anyway. He just needed one additional piece of information.

Steele picked up the phone and dialed the lab. Randy answered on the second ring.

"Hello, Detective."

"Hey, Randy. I need for you to take another stab at that evidence from both bomb sites. Maybe your guys missed something."

"I highly doubt it, but stranger things have happened. What is this about?"

"Just check it out for me. We can talk later."

"On it. I'll let you know what I find."

He hung up and immediately felt the pressure. The giant anaconda was back and had once again enveloped his body, compressing the detective with all its might. Steele knew what he knew but wanted confirmation. Now just a waiting game, he settled into the tension of the moment, while his mind proceeded to rove.

He thought about what Dr. Gipson said about the possibility of twins sharing the same DNA. He thought about the possibility of the professor and Adam McGregor being related. He thought about the pain and anguish Madi had gone through in losing a child for the second time. He thought about the plans he'd had for Grant and him that would never happen, all because of the cowardly act of someone deciding to send a pipe bomb to their home. He thought about the possibility of the professor being that person. But the one thing Detective Steele didn't have to give any thought to was what he was going to do to whoever was responsible for all the hurt Madi and he were going through.

Two hours later, Randy walked in and closed the door. He had an uneasy look on his face.

"I have no idea how they missed it, but I can say without a doubt, the same DNA can be traced to both devices," Randy said, handing Steele the report.

Steele began skimming through the document.

"The power source. How in the hell could something like this happen, Randy?"

"Beats me. I am at a loss, and we can certainly hash that out later. You mind cluing me in on what this is about?"

"I believe Professor Atticus Dobson is the person behind the pipe bombs."

"Hold on a minute! That same Professor Dobson you brought in here to brief us a while back?"

"Yes."

"I'll be honest. I was thinking this new information tied McGregor to both devices. What about him?"

"I believe McGregor and Dobson are related."

"What?"

"Long story. I'll explain later. Anyway, I know this is a longshot, but I just got this print card in the mail. It's from when Professor Dobson was working with the military on some secret project. I know there's that single print hanging out there that you guys haven't been able to put to bed. Check out these prints and see if anything pops."

"Say no more. This won't take very long."

About thirty minutes later, Randy was back carrying a second report. He stepped in and closed the door.

"It's him! I don't know how this can even be possible when the DNA from both bomb sites are the same, and Adam McGregor is the person we matched it to. You said these two guys are related?"

"I believe they're twins who share the same DNA."

Randy just stood there. His eyes began darting back and forth, and the look on his face said the wheels in his head were turning.

"I'll be damn," he said. "That's it! Although it's rare for twins to share the same DNA, it can happen."

"That's exactly how it was recently explained to me."

"So you're thinking McGregor really has nothing to do with this?"

"I don't believe he does. McGregor is a bum, Randy. Honestly, he never really fit."

Steele got quiet as his facial expression suddenly turned dark.

"Who knows about these reports?"

"Me. And now you," Randy responded.

"Keep it that way. I don't want them becoming part of the file."

Randy walked across the office and started looking out the window. Although he and the detective maintained a professional relationship at work, the Steeles and the Polks were about as close as friends could be. In fact, they were like family. Randy and his wife, Alyssa, had been Grant's godparents. Because of a medical condition, the Polks were unable to produce children of their own, and Grant had come the closest to filling that void for them. Since his murder, outside of the Steele family, nobody mourned more than the Polks.

Over his twenty-three years as a forensic analyst, there was never a case where Randy wanted to identify a suspect more than this one. The two men stared at one another for about sixty seconds before Randy left the office, and although neither spoke, plenty had been communicated with each keeping their respective thoughts to themselves. After a brief stop by his desk to call Pastor Davies, the forensic analyst hastily left work and drove straight over to Grace Presbyterian Church.

Randy desperately needed to see the pastor. Since Grant's death, he would periodically make an appointment with the pastor anytime he felt the need for spiritual guidance. He knew he was at a crossroads, struggling to live in accordance with his faith while at the same time, engaging in self-talk that had him questioning what he might do if it were he and not police officers who were first to encounter the person responsible for murdering his godson. And now that he finally had a name, he was terrified.

Scene 1

10 Marine View Drive
7:15 p.m.

Steele swung by the house to switch cars and was just about to back out of the driveway when he pulled out his cell phone and dialed Dr. Beale's phone number. As soon as she answered, he quickly hung up. He knew she could talk him out of what he was about to do, which is exactly why he didn't want to hear her voice. Not tonight. He also knew the last class Atticus taught on Thursdays ended at seven, and although he had no idea what time he would make it home, the detective was in no rush. He would wait there for as long as it took.

At seven fifteen, Steele pulled his car off the road and parked in front of the double-wide vacant lot about three-hundred feet west of the professor's home, and because there were no street lights on the entire block, the detective was able to easily make his way back to the professor's home without being seen. He remembered the tall hedges from when he'd paid a visit to the professor on December 30, and while the greenery surrounding the property was perfect for camouflaging the unsightly block wall, the hedge also provided cover for anyone wanting to hide not only from passersby but also from those within the home.

A keen observer, Steele also knew there was a chain running along the bottom rail of the security gate. Before taking his position between the rain-drenched hedge and block wall, he pulled a twelve-inch piece of wire from his pant pocket and threaded it through two of the links. He knew that, by doing so, the gate wouldn't open all the way, and the professor would have to exit his vehicle in order to override the security mechanism.

The temperature was forty degrees outside, and the rain was beginning to swirl in the howling wind. At a little past eight, Atticus pulled up to the gate. Although the interior of the vehicle was illuminated only by the dashboard light, Atticus still could be seen pushing on the remote control. As expected, the gate failed to open.

Steele, wearing gloves and dressed in all black, watched from his crouched position as Atticus began pounding hard on the remote, frustrated that the security gate continued opening only about a foot or two before reversing track and returning to a closed position. Suddenly, he flung the driver-side door open and, in a huff, opened his umbrella.

He stepped out into the pouring rain and began reaching toward the security control panel, and when he did, Steele pounced on him from behind like a hungry lion lunging at prey. He wrapped a metal chain around the professor's neck and pulled him to the ground behind the hedge and out of view of anyone who might happen to drive down the street. Once there, Steele continued pulling hard on the chain until he rendered Atticus unconscious.

Steele stepped from behind his cover, leaned into the SUV, and turned off the lights. Then he killed the engine. Within a minute or so, Atticus was completely immobilized by hand and leg cuffs. Steele also covered his eyes and mouth with duct tape.

The detective was still on his knees, leaning over Atticus and staring at him for about ten seconds. Suddenly, he raised his arm and unleashed a vicious openhanded strike to the professor's temple, not enough to kill him, but certainly enough to ensure he wouldn't wake up during the time he left to go pull his car up to the security gate. He removed the cell phone from Atticus's pocket, and after powering-down the device, tossed it on the ground next to the hedge.

It was around eight forty when Steele first started hearing the faint bumping sound coming from the trunk. The rain muffled the sound a bit, but he could still hear good enough to know Atticus was starting to wake up. Suddenly, his cell phone starting rattling in the passenger seat. He picked it up and looked at the screen. As expected, Randy was returning his call.

Steele cranked up the volume on his car radio before he answered.

"Thanks for getting back with me."

"You got it. Would've called earlier but I had to make a run," Randy responded.

"I need access to the warehouse tonight."

Neither Steele nor Randy said a word for the next several seconds.

"My uncle recently changed the digital lock. The new code is eighty-six, forty-five, eleven, three. How much time you need?"

"About an hour."

There was more silence. About ten seconds this time.

"That building gets pretty cold at night. You want the heater on?"

"Yes."

"I'll flip on the switch from my phone. It should be nice and toasty for you when you get there. Just be sure to lock up when you leave."

Steele disconnected the call, and ten minutes later, he drove onto the lot and pulled alongside the large metal door. Atticus was wide awake by now. He could be heard grunting and struggling to free himself from the restraints.

It was raining cats and dogs when Steele stepped out of his vehicle and popped the trunk. He stood there for a moment staring down at Atticus, who was clueless as to what was happening to him. Not that he hadn't caused more than his fair share of pain and heartache to others to deserve whatever fate might lie before him. Still, that did little to taper his consternation.

Who was doing this? How many were there? He just didn't know. The last thing he remembered thinking about before passing out was that he was being carjacked, but when he woke up in the trunk of a moving vehicle, Atticus knew immediately that whoever was responsible for his current circumstances wanted much more from him than just his Mercedes SUV.

Steele didn't say a word. Actually, there was nothing to say. After a while, he reached into the trunk and, with one hand, snatched Atticus out by the leg cuffs, causing his body to slap down hard against the ground. After shutting the trunk, he began dragging the professor across the rain-soaked gravel toward the building. Once inside, Steele slid a chair out from a nearby table, yanked Atticus up off the floor, and shoved him down hard on the seat before using more handcuffs to secure his wrists to the metal arm rests.

Steele began removing the duct tape. First, he ripped the tape off the professor's mouth. Then his eyes.

Atticus's eyes widened in surprise when he saw Steele standing there.

"What the fuck, Detective! I thought some badasses had abducted me, but seeing you here, I can't tell you how relieved I am. Shit! I was starting to get worried. Anyway, knowing you the way I do and how you always strive to live up to that oath of serving and protecting, I'm feeling pretty damn good about now. So tell me. What exactly are we doing here?"

Steele didn't respond. Instead, he pulled another chair from the table and sat down about thirty-six inches away from Atticus. The throbbing in his ears was about as painful as he could ever remember. In fact, it had been there for several hours. Ever since Randy showed him the supplemental lab report.

There was no reason for Grant to die the way he had, and nothing anyone could ever say or do would change that. And now that he was seated only feet away from the individual he believed was responsible for his son's murder, the detective only had one thing in mind. The longer he sat there staring at Atticus, the more those horrific images neatly stored within his brain seemed to surface.

He smelled the smoke. He saw the blood. Worse, he saw Grant's lifeless body.

The images were so vivid in his mind that it was as if the pipe bomb had just exploded. Still, he didn't say a word. As far as Steele was concerned, the time for talking had long passed.

Atticus figured he could just bullshit his way out of his dilemma by resorting to his usual manipulative tactics, and while in the back of his mind he wondered if the detective had figured out that it was he who sent the pipe bomb to his home, he sure as hell wasn't about to ask. That would be a sure admission of guilt. After weighing his options, Atticus broke the silence by laughing out loud and trying to make light of the situation.

"Let me guess, Detective. You didn't like that grade I gave you last semester, so you brought me to this dreary warehouse to rough me up a bit."

There was a slight smirk on his face while he assessed whether or not he was making any headway with the detective. But Steele's demeanor was unchanged. He just continued siting there, deep in his own thoughts.

Failing to get the response he hoped for, Atticus went in again.

"No, that's not it at all. I bet your daddy hurt your feelings again, and for whatever reason, you've decided to take your frustration out on me. Is that it, Detective Steele? If so, let's just get this over with. I got shit to do."

Suddenly, Steele inched his chair a little closer to Atticus, and within seconds, screams filled the warehouse as he lifted Atticus's left hand off the arm rest and bent his thumb backward, pressing it flat against his wrist. Then he started pressing each of the remaining fingers backward from the index to the pinky, a full one hundred eighty degrees away from its normal position until the bone cracked and protruded through the skin, while Atticus, now in full panic mode, shrieked and pulled with all his might against the cuffs.

Unmoved by the obvious pain Atticus was in, Steele grabbed hold of the other hand and began pressing those fingers backward one at a time. He was just about to break the pinky finger when he noticed Atticus had fainted. He waited a few seconds, then pushed hard on the little finger just like the rest, before walking over to the washroom and returning with a bucket filled with water. He hurled the water at Atticus hitting him in the face, and the professor immediately regained consciousness.

Steele turned the chair around backward and sat down. While still maintaining his silence, he leaned over the backrest and again stared hard at Atticus. The thought of Grant crossed his mind. And again, he fought back against the urge to hop out of the chair and just choke the life out of Atticus.

Five minutes passed, and the detective was still sitting there silently. His eyes focused on nothing but Atticus. In a trice, he stood up, pushed his chair aside, and stepped forward. Without foreshadowing, he quickly raised his foot and came down hard on Atticus's left knee, breaking the bone and causing the leg to bow out the back. Be it from pain or the immense stress he was under, Atticus fainted again. Steele stood there for a few seconds, as if he were waiting for Atticus to wake up. Then he raised his foot again and brought it down even harder. This time on the right knee.

Atticus was out cold for a couple of minutes, and when he opened his eyes, the first image he saw was Detective Steele, still staring at him, but now from a distance of only about twenty-four inches away. Steele got up, snatched Atticus out of the chair, and pushed him to the ground. Then he began dragging him toward the long block wall that provided separation between the two distinct sections of the building. They arrived at the opening about thirty seconds later, and there was an immediate noticeable change in room temperature. It was a bit warmer.

Steele yanked him around the corner of the block wall where the room temperature was warmer still. In fact, it was starting to get hot. Atticus started looking frantically around the warehouse, turning his head from side to side. And then his eyes settled on the row of large, gleaming, cremation chambers.

He gasped loudly. Then he started swallowing saliva as quickly as he could, trying his best to lubricate his parched throat. Fear seized his every thought upon realizing that, rather than being brought to a warehouse like he first believed, Detective Steele had brought him to a crematorium.

Atticus noticed the thick metal door on one of the units was open. He saw the fire dancing around the interior of the chamber. All at once, the color suddenly drained from his face. He knew from his research that the temperature within the furnace could easily reach upward of eighteen-hundred-degrees Fahrenheit during the period the body was being reduced to gases and bone fragments, and for a split-second, he hated himself for being as knowledgeable as he was about the cremation process.

Steele took his foot and shoved Atticus a bit closer to the portable cremation storage rack where he had a bird's-eye view of the detective removing a cremation container from the shelf and placing it on top. Atticus knew by the look in Steele's eyes that there would be no turning back. What he didn't know, however, was how long he would be made to suffer before finally being put out of his misery and based on what he had already endured, coupled with what he imagined was in store for him, dying quickly seemed like a pretty good deal.

After standing over Atticus for another twenty seconds or so, Steele reached his hand around his back and pulled out a handgun. He fired two quick rounds, both striking Atticus in the head and killing him instantly. After picking up the two bullet casings, Steele removed the cuffs from Atticus's wrists and legs and then stuffed his body inside the cremation container.

He rolled the storage rack up to the chamber and shoved the corrugated container deep into the flame. Standing there watching in complete stillness while the fire swallowed up the container, Steele reflected on that day at the Quarry and what Coach had said just before the prison guard forced him out of the interview room, and for the first time, he understood what his childhood friend had meant.

The ringing in his ears stopped about the same time the pain dissipated. Suddenly, a sense of serenity washed over him.

"A man's gotta do what a man's gotta do," he uttered, barely audible but very, very matter-of-factly, before slamming the chamber door shut and walking away. Moments later, Steele was on the road and headed back to Reese Valley. He pulled his cell phone from his pocket and punched in the numbers. This time, Randy was waiting for his call.

"Heater work okay for you?" Randy asked.

"Yes," Steele responded.

"Any metal?"

"Two pieces."

The call took less than five seconds, but Randy heard all he needed. He would swing by his uncle's crematorium in a few hours and sift through the remains with a magnet to pull out bullet fragments and any other metal that may have been left behind. Once the process was finalized, Professor Atticus Dobson's cremated ashes would be stored in an unmarked urn to be later disposed of in a single mass grave along with other unclaimed remains.

CHAPTER 40

Friday, February 20
Reese Valley Herald
10:00 a.m.

Fresh back from her working vacation, Jolynn walked down the hall and pulled a document from the fax machine. She was just about to leave the mailroom when she happened to notice the thick manila envelope. She pulled it from the bin, immediately taking note of just how heavy it was. The envelope was about one and a quarter-inch thick. She ripped open one end and tilted it on its side. After a few shakes, the manuscript slid out and into the palm of her hand.

Jolynn returned to her desk, sat down and started turning through the thick stack of paper. The manuscript was titled *Lipstick in the Basement*. There was also a dedication page that read, "To Judith, the one person wholly responsible for me being who I am today. May you continue to rot in hell you disgusting bitch."

Jolynn was horrified but flipped to the next page and continued reading.

Let me begin by assuring you that what you are about to read is not the rantings of a madman. Instead, what I have tried to do here is bring clarity as to why I committed the murders in the first place. As you will soon learn, these were not simply random killings. More on that later, but for now, how about I just lay out the murders for you?

Chapter One

I rolled the dice and moved the top hat along the perimeter of the game board, landing on the Seattle Space Pin. I drove downtown and within a half hour of scanning the grounds, I saw sweet little Belinda. At first, I only saw her from behind. But then, she turned toward me, and to my surprise, my search was over. She was absolutely gorgeous. Young, vibrant, long, beautiful hair, shimmering skin with light freckles, and she smelled wonderful. More importantly, Belinda had a full set of lips that were heavily drenched in bright red lipstick.

I engaged her in light conversation over drinks, and while things started out slowly, after our second martini, she relaxed. By the third, I knew everything about her including the fact that she was grieving from recently having to have her eight-year-old pug euthanized. Belinda told me her primary source of income was from being an Uber driver but that she also snagged whatever gigs she could from the temp service. After drink number four, not only did I know she wasn't wearing any panties, but that she also worked part time at the Candy Shop.

I asked her how much she made on a typical night and she said she could easily pull in between two- and three-hundred dollars, adding that she didn't even have to have sex with anyone. I reached into my pocket and peeled off five one-hundred-dollar bills and *handed them to her. I told her another five bills were waiting for her at my house in return for a private show with one proviso. I wanted her dressed in one of my ex-wife's sexy nightgowns, which meant the performance would have to take place at my home.*

Without hesitation, Belinda agreed to leave her car in the Space Pin parking lot and hitch a ride with me. Once there, I asked her to make herself comfortable while I made the two of us drinks. Martinis, of course. We spent the next thirty minutes enjoying our cocktails while discussing my ex-wife, who didn't exist. Two hours later, Belinda regained consciousness to find herself naked on a cold cement floor with a canvas hood draped over her head, arms and legs bound, and a metal shackle clamped tightly to her left ankle. The chloroform had worked like a charm.

I carefully explained the rules of the game, making myself crystal clear just to be fair. I told her where she would find all the items she would need in order to survive including food and water, and that for the remainder of her life, her mobility would be limited to the six-foot radius of the metal chain affixed to the shackle. I also told Belinda that she was in total control of how long she lived and that she had my word that, so long as she obeyed, she would stay alive. I mean, who wouldn't want to control their own fate?

The last thing I told her before removing the hood was that once I removed it, she had to ensure her eyes remained shut at all time and that motion-sensing cameras were pointed at her from every angle imaginable and would be rolling around the clock. Unfortunately, she either didn't take what I was saying seriously, or thought she could just sneak a quick peek. In any event, I checked the videotape before turning in for the evening and saw where, no sooner than I left the basement, Belinda started screaming wildly as she pulled hopelessly on the metal chain, eyes wide open, and taking in everything her surroundings had to offer. The damage was done.

Early the next morning, I turned on the local news while enjoying my morning coffee and making a few notes on a subject I thought I'd share with students during our next class. At seven thirty, I went to the basement and saw Belinda on the concrete floor under several burlap sacks she had piled over her naked body. I noticed the sacks moving up and down rapidly, a sure sign that her heart was beating at an accelerated pace.

For whatever reason, watching her pretend to be asleep under the sacks sickened me. I ordered her to stand up, but she didn't move. I walked over to the cabinet and began rambling my hand through the knife drawer, purposely banging the knives against one another, thinking the noise would cause her to end the charade and get to her feet. But that didn't work.

I walked back across the basement and stood next to Belinda, knife in one hand, Mom's photo in the other. Wouldn't be fair to cheat the old bag out of seeing what was about to happen. After all, this was all her doing. I bent over and placed the photo near the metal chain, then grabbed a fistful of Belinda's hair, and yanked her to her feet.

She yelled a lot but, outside of that, didn't offer much resistance. It was obvious she wanted to open her eyes but somehow managed to keep them shut. I wrapped my arm around her head and, in one sweeping motion, pulled the knife from left to right across the front of her neck before stepping back and allowing her body to freefall, where it flopped down hard on the cement floor.

As soon as I wrapped Belinda in plastic, it occurred to me that, once I got rid of her body, nothing would be left to memorialize our time together, so I pulled back the plastic sheathing from over her face, carefully harvested the most perfect little trophies imaginable, then placed them in the meat freezer for safekeeping. I closed my eyes and tried to sense what I felt at that moment, but nothing registered. I didn't feel a thing. I wasn't happy, nor was I sad. Suddenly I felt as if I was floating in a world of nothingness. Taking another person's life was not only easy; it was euphoric. And it was at that moment that I knew I would do it again. In fact, I was already looking forward to it.

Jolynn couldn't believe what she was reading. Even before she relocated to Reese Valley, she'd read about the death of Belinda O'Connell, but this was a firsthand account of the unspeakable murder. This was information no one else had knowledge of. Not even the police. She turned to the next the page and continued reading.

Chapter Two

In furtherance of the game, I rolled the dice, and after moving the top hat around the game board, I landed on the Teddy Lauer space. When I visited the Bellevue store, unlike my experience at the Space Pin, I spotted the ideal woman right away. She was standing in the adjacent aisle, fiddling around with hiking equipment.

Her face seemed a mismatch when compared to the rest of her body. Above the neck, she was no different than any other beautiful woman I had seen around town. Her body from the neck down, however, was nothing short of a living testament to the muscular possibilities of someone pushing themselves beyond insane limits. Muscles were bulging from any- and everywhere her skin was exposed.

Her shopping basket was full of hiking equipment, which, as it turned out, was the perfect conversation starter. I pulled a parka off the rack and walked around to where she was standing, but her cell phone started ringing the moment I stepped into the aisle. She was absolutely gorgeous, with her curly red hair and silky-smooth skin.

She used her hand to shield her mouth as she spoke quietly into her cell phone, doing her level best not to disturb other customers. About a minute later, she was done with her call, and when she lowered her hand, all I saw were those bright red lips. The woman was perfect.

I introduced myself, and she smiled. She said her name was Gretchen, and after we exchanged a few pleasantries, I told her about how I always wanted to conquer something a bit more challenging than the five miles I struggled to complete when I'd hiked the Rattlesnake Ledge Trail near North Bend several years ago, which of course was a lie. Gretchen's eyes lit up immediately, and just like that, I had her attention.

She started telling me about the many hikes she'd completed over the years, each one more challenging than the one before. Wanting to keep the conversation going, I asked her about the items in her basket and what they were used for. Our conversation suddenly kicked into high gear. It was obvious she enjoyed talking about her hiking expeditions as evidenced by the two of us still standing in the middle of the aisle forty-five minutes later. Gretchen made sure I knew that she wasn't in a relationship at the present time.

I suggested we pay for our items and then make our way over to the Habitant in Nordlum for drinks and more conversation, which she seemed more than eager to do. Two drinks later and with our conversation running on fumes, Gretchen stood up, kissed me on the cheek, and began walking toward the parking lot. I followed her out and saw that she pushed the button for the top level of the parking garage, which gave me plenty of time to get to my SUV.

About four minutes after I pulled onto the street just outside the parking garage exit, a white Jeep Wrangler 4x4 drove by. It was Gretchen. I tailed her home and noticed a Volkswagen Beetle parked in the garage, and after a few more days of driving through the neighborhood, I concluded the Beetle belonged to Gretchen's roommate, a mildly attractive female that looked to be in her midtwenties.

The following Saturday, I pulled back onto the street around seven in the morning, just in time to see the roommate tossing her suitcase in the back seat of a black Corvette with the top dropped. She climbed in the passenger seat, and the car sped away while Gretchen stood on the front porch, waving her arms wildly. Seeing all I needed, I pulled off and returned home.

After dark, I returned to Gretchen's house and parked in her driveway. Then got out and walked around back. The bathroom window was open partway, and I immediately heard the sound of shower water accompanied by a woman singing. Or at least, trying to sing.

I turned the knob and found the door to be unlocked, just like more than ninety-five percent of the other doors in Reese Valley. Within seconds, I was standing outside the bathroom door, listening to Gretchen belt out the lyrics to Pharrell Williams's hit song "Happy," totally oblivious to my presence. Abruptly, the water stopped running, and metal rings could be heard scrapping across the shower rod as she pulled the curtain back.

She opened the door, and although the steam from the shower somewhat clouded her vision, she could still see well enough to know I was standing there. Both shocked and terrified, she tried to scream, but before she could make a sound, I grabbed the back of her head and shoved a cloth doused with chloroform hard against her face as I forced her to the hardwood floor.

Once I knew she was unconscious, I pulled zip ties from my pocket and slipped them around her wrists and legs before slinging her over my shoulder and carrying her muscular body outside and into the back seat of my SUV. She woke up several hours later, chained and bound with a canvas hood over her head, but unfortunately for her, Gretchen lasted less than twenty-four hours in the basement before opening her eyes. As a consequence, I murdered her because of her disobedience.

"I can't read this!" Jolynn exclaimed, covering her face with her hands and starting to cry. "This is just horrible!"

She stood up from her desk and paced around the office for a while trying to gather her thoughts. She wanted to stop reading right then and there, but knew she couldn't. The journalist in her wouldn't allow that. Jolynn glanced at the clock on the wall. It was ten-thirty. She took a deep breath and resumed reading, determined not to stop again until she powered through each of the remaining pages.

Chapter Three

The third roll of the dice landed me at a Starrocks on Reese Valley Speedway, where I stumbled upon Amanda and Christina. Although I saw the young women as soon as I stepped foot in the coffee shop, I paid no attention to either of them. After about fifteen minutes of sitting there enjoying my coffee and flipping through the pages of my Psychology Today *magazine, I sensed someone was looking at me.*

I raised my head and immediately locked eyes with the two women who were now smiling hard at me. One of them, who I later learned was Amanda, lifted her coffee cup and said, "Cheers," which I thought was a bit awkward, being that coffee is not the typical drink one would use in making a toast. But rather than enlighten her on toasting etiquette, I chalked it up to a young women just trying her hand at flirting with an older man. After reciprocating smiles, I turned my attention back to my magazine about the same time the two women got up and left.

Five minutes later, there was some shuffling at the booth across from me. The two women were back and had obviously doused themselves with perfume as evidenced by the coffee shop being swiftly overtaken by the sweet smell of honeysuckle. I noticed they were a bit giddy, and like before, both were staring at me. Hard. This time, however, something was different. During their brief absence, both had applied a thick layer of bright red lipstick to their lips. Now, they had my attention.

Amanda was an exceptionally attractive African American, and based on her mannerisms, I could tell she knew it. She was wearing tiny pearl earrings, a colorful silk blouse, and a matching scarf around her head that showcased several thick braids protruding from the top. More than just beauty, she exuded confidence.

Like her friend, the other woman, Christina, was equally gorgeous, and from the very beginning I could tell she was a bit more reserved and totally willing to allow Amanda to lead the charge. Christina was dressed quite nicely, wearing a white blouse and tight-fitting jeans that accentuated her bold curves. Her hair was pulled back in a bun, and I couldn't help but notice her distinctive cheekbones. I also noticed the dainty, colorful butterfly tattoo on her neck just below her left ear.

The two women grabbed their coffee drinks and slid over to my booth and, within seconds, introduced themselves and started telling me about a dare they had made. Actually, it was more of a double dare. They had challenged one another that, before midnight, they would engage an older man in a threesome, and I was the person they had apparently settled on to assist them in fulfilling their sexual fantasy.

After coming to agreement that both hand over their cell phones to ensure nothing ended up on social media, I offered to drive the women to my home, so they didn't have to catch an Uber. To which, they agreed.

Upon arrival, we made ourselves comfortable in my den, where I asked the women if they wouldn't mind having a drink with me and telling me a bit more about how they came about such a dare. Seeing that I wasn't trying to rush things seemed to put both of them at ease. Soon thereafter, I excused myself from the room and, after a while, retuned carrying three glasses of Beringer Private Reserve Cabernet.

It was about eleven o'clock when Amanda awakened to discover that things had gone drastically wrong. The narcotic was starting to wear off. She couldn't see anything, but she knew her clothes had been removed and that her arms and legs were bound. She screamed loudly from behind the hood as she struggled with all her might to break free of the restraints, but to no avail.

Fifteen minutes later, Christina started coming to, and like her friend, she too was terrified to find that her arms and legs were restrained. She squirmed and jerked her body along the cold cement floor, and she tried her best to scream but only managed a long string of heavy moans, apparently still too groggy to vocalize the harrowing thoughts encircling her mind at that moment.

As time passed and I knew both women were alert enough to make sense of what I was saying, I made them aware of my presence and explained the rules of the game we would be playing, before proceeding to remove the zip ties from their arms and legs. Amanda obeyed my instructions to a tee, but Christina started screaming and looking around the moment I removed the hood from over her head. Sixty seconds later, I slit her throat and watched her drop to the basement floor, landing about two feet from where Amanda was standing, who, even with her eyes closed, knew exactly what was happening to her friend. Amanda started screaming and pulling hard on the chain, but didn't open her eyes.

The next morning around five, I reviewed the videotape and saw where Amanda opened her eyes shortly after I left the basement. Apparently knowing Christina's lifeless body was on the floor next to her, coupled with the stickiness beneath her bare feet from her best friend's blood starting to ooze its way into her space became too much of a temptation for her not to look. In any event, after eating my steak and egg breakfast with coffee, and catching up on the morning news, I walked down to the basement and murdered Amanda.

Chapter Four

The next roll of the dice led me over to Benoya Hall in downtown Seattle where I spotted my next victim. Her name was Seoyeon, and she was one of the performers on stage that day. She was wearing a bright yellow dress and her hair was dark, silky-long, and flowing. There was a purple orchid tucked neatly just above her left ear, and while I'm not what you would call a flower person, that had to be one of the most beautiful flowers I'd ever seen in my life. Anyway, she was wearing bright red lipstick that seemed to illuminate the entire stage whenever the lighting hit her lips at just the right angle. According to Seoyeon's bio, her dream was to one day join the ranks of the Seattle Philharmonic Orchestra, and that, along with my influence with the music director, was the ticket.

The performance was over by seven thirty, and after Seoyeon said her goodbyes to her parents and began walking toward her car, I followed her. She was understandably startled when I first approached, but whatever fears she may have had seemed to vanish the moment I introduced myself and said that not only was I a longtime supporter of the arts in and around Seattle, but that I had just come out of Benoya Hall and was thoroughly impressed by her performance, so much so, I planned on putting a good word in for her with the Seattle Phil music director. I also let it "slip" that he and I were personal friends. I told Seoyeon that she was extremely talented and was exactly what the orchestra needed to take them to the next level, words that seemed to cause her to drop her guard, if only slightly. Nonetheless, she smiled.

I started reaching into my pockets one after another, pretending to be looking for business cards I knew weren't there. I told Seoyeon there were more cards in my car and that if she didn't mind driving over to where I was parked, I'd give her my contact information so she could follow up with me on my progress with the director. Obviously excited and perhaps a bit too eager over the possibility of auditioning for a spot on the orchestra, Seoyeon took me up on my offer and began driving slowly behind me as I walked across the street to the parking structure. Once in the garage, I pointed to my SUV, and she pulled into the vacant stall next to my vehicle, which happened to be parked at the far end of the garage.

Seoyeon was driving an older model Toyota Camry, and based on the excessive amount of smoke emitting from the tailpipe, the car was obviously overdue for a trip to the repair shop. The exhaust was nauseating, and in no time, noxious fumes began to settle in the corner of the garage where we were parked. I asked Seoyeon to shut off her engine. And she did.

That was all the time I needed to open the bottle of chloroform and pour a generous portion on the rag. I reached into my glove compartment and pulled the top card from the stack of useless business cards I had collected over time and placed it in my right hand. The chloroform-drenched rag was balled-up in my left palm.

When I turned to face Seoyeon, I held the card in such a way requiring her to stretch her left arm out her side window in order to retrieve it, and when she did, I grabbed hold and pulled her toward me, pinning her body tightly against the inside of her driver-side door. At the same time, I pressed the rag tightly against her nose and mouth. Instinctively, she started pushing down on the car horn with her right hand, which only lasted for about three to four seconds, if that long.

Keeping the wet rag pressed to her face, I yanked Seoyeon out the car window and pulled her to the ground between our two vehicles. Because of where we were parked, there was no chance of anyone seeing what was taking place. I used my weight to hold her down, and within minutes, Seoyeon was unconscious.

The next morning, I walked down to the basement to find Seoyeon lying on the floor. She had rolled herself up so tightly she looked like a little ball. Like the others, she was naked, and a canvas hood was covering her head. The thing is, outside of breathing, she never moved or made a sound. Still, I knew she was well aware of my presence.

Allowing my eyes to slowly pour over the outline of her little body lying motionless on the floor, for a brief moment, I actually felt sorry for Seoyeon, knowing that she was going to die in the not-too-distant future. I wondered about the avalanche of thoughts that had to be streaming through her mind now that things had gotten so far off course. Although she displayed reservations at first, she had gone against her better judgment by allowing a smooth-talking stranger like me to lull her into a state of complacency, and now, her personal well-being had been severely jeopardized.

I bent over and cut the zip ties from around her wrists and ankles before ordering her off the floor. Admittedly, I found it a tad odd that, unlike those abducted before her, rather than shiver and beg for her life, Seoyeon simply got up and stood at attention. She was stiff as a board. As if she had accepted her fate and was simply ready to get on with it.

I gathered my thoughts and went through the ritual of explaining the rules of the game, the last thing being the need for her to never open her eyes again if she wanted to keep living. I asked her if she understood, but Seoyeon maintained her silence, opting instead to continue standing like a soldier in boot camp.

Must be a cultural thing I concluded as I stepped closer. I loosened the hood and pulled it over her head, only to find myself staring into the coldest set of eyes I had ever seen. These were not the eyes of a meek little girl who had spent every waking hour of the past fifteen years honing her skills. Seoyeon's eyes were like those of a shark. Dark, ominous, and devoid of emotion.

Before I knew it, she hit me on the side of my cheek with her left hand, and when I instinctively reached for my face, she performed a leg-sweep, knocking my feet out from under me. I immediately fell to the ground, causing the back of my head to slam hard against the cement floor. Stunned and unsteady, I reached for her, but before I could grab hold, she dropped to the ground and began wrapping her leg around mine until my entire lower body was entangled within the chain. I winced with each twist of the chain as the metal links began to grab and pinch at my skin.

The pounding in my head deepened, and my vision blurred. Still, I remember the exact moment Seoyeon used her right hand to turn my face to the side while at the same time, drew her left arm back and prepared to land a strike. Luckily for me, I dodged the blow as the heel of her hand whiffed by my head and slammed hard into the cement. The two of us tussled on the floor, with me hitting Seoyeon several times in the head with my fist and her landing several hard knee strikes to my midsection, an easy target, complements of the chain still wrapped tightly around my lower body.

About forty-five seconds after the skirmish started, I landed a blow to the side of Seoyeon's face so hard it staggered her. She was visibly dazed, and although she managed to land a few more strikes, no real force was behind them, allowing me just enough time to free myself of the chain. I hastily rolled away from Seoyeon, making sure I had backed out of her reach, all the while glad as hell that her mobility was restricted by the six-foot radius of the chain.

I was disgusted at myself as I watched Seoyeon continue to stare me down through those cold penetrating eyes of hers. Not only had I made the mistake of taking her small stature for granted, for some unknown reason, I was starting to feel sorry for her. Right then and there, I vowed to never empathize with anyone ever again.

While moving to a safe distance away from Seoyeon, I inadvertently backed to within an arm's length of the metal cabinet. I looked over and opened the drawer, removed the stun gun, and while still seated on the floor, I scooted to within two feet of the outstretched metal chain and discharged two electrodes emitting fifty thousand volts of electricity straight into her stomach. She fell to the ground, her body twitching violently as the shock began to overwhelm her nervous system. But she didn't make a sound, nor did her facial expression ever change. It was as if she were immune to pain. Once I was sure she no longer posed a threat, I stepped in and placed my arm around her neck and squeezed with all my might.

The moment she stopped breathing, I got up and walked back over to the metal cabinet. This time I opened the center drawer and removed a knife. There was a moment where I thought Seoyeon was moving her fingers, but I quickly realized I had only imagined it. In any event, after carving out my little trophies and still in disbelief over Seoyeon having the audacity to slap me, I raised her left arm and cut her hand off at the wrist, then snatched that purple orchid from her hair, and shoved it as deep as physically possible down her throat.

Chapter 5

I hadn't killed in over five years, and then one day, it seemed as if the entire weight of the world came crashing down on me. I couldn't see straight, and it felt like my brain was on fire. Like it was about to explode. The thing is, I knew immediately what was happening to me. I had actually expected it. I just didn't know when the day would come.

The sessions with the shrink had become a joke, and the pills were no longer working. Those feelings were back, and killing another woman was the only way to ease the pain. There were no other options.

Early one morning, I walked down to the basement, pulled the dice from the drawer, and wiped the dust off. I gave them a good roll and landed on the Seattle Seafarers Team Store. That's where my sixth victim would come from.

On the day I went there, the Minnesota Triplets were in town to take on the Seafarers, and the store was bulging at the seams with baseball fans trying to snap up everything in sight. Not a fan of the sport myself, nothing in there seemed worth spending my hard-earned money on. It was all junk to me. But I was on a mission, and until I found what I had come there for, I had to hang around at least long enough to see if she was in there.

I started rummaging through a metal bin filled to the rim with an assortment of refrigerator magnets and noticed one shaped like a Major League baseball, complete with red stitching and the word Seafarers, printed across the front. Admittedly, it wasn't bad, that is, as far as magnets go. A timid voice suddenly caught my attention.

Swinging around to see whoever it was approaching, to my surprise, a young man was standing behind me. Chad was his name. My facial expression undoubtedly let on that I thought I would turn to find a young lady standing there. He smiled and said it wasn't a big deal, adding that his voice often caught people off guard.

He asked if I was finding everything all right, and while I really didn't want to buy the magnet, after what had just happened, I felt obligated to at least purchase something. I knew I could always toss it in the trash later. One final look around the team store and still not seeing a woman fitting the bill, I decided to just pay for the magnet and try my luck another day.

I told Chad I'd take the refrigerator magnet, and as I followed him to the cash register, a retail sales associate wearing bright red lipstick emerged from a door behind the counter. She looked familiar, but I didn't immediately recall where I'd seen her. She stepped to the register and greeted me with a warm smile, and then it occurred to me that I'd seen her walking around RVSU.

I finalized my transaction and left the store, figuring I'd just hang around the mall until the young lady got off work, which

I knew was closing time after hearing Chad and her joke about being assigned the late shift so management could attend a social gathering. It was dark outside when she and Chad walked out three hours later. They locked the door, and after a quick friend-level embrace, the two went their separate ways.

Her face was buried in her cell phone when I approached and began clearing my throat to get her attention. She looked up and, just as she had earlier, greeted me with a warm smile. Pretending our running into one another was nothing more than chance, I engaged the young women in small talk where I mentioned I held a professorship in psychology at the university. I also told her that she vaguely resembled a young lady I would periodically see walking around campus.

She laughed loudly, then told me she attended RVSU, and that it was probably her I'd seen walking around, something I knew even without her acknowledgment. She shook my hand and said her name was Sylvia before instantaneously asking to be excused so that she could call for an Uber, adding that her car was out of commission. As she was starting to walk away, Sylvia said she'd make it a point of saying hello if our paths ever crossed on campus.

I told her I could drop her off if she didn't mind riding with a boomer, which made her laugh again. She said she lived in Everett and didn't want to be the cause of me having to go out of my way. I revealed that I lived in Reese Valley and had to drive by Everett on my way home, and just like that, Sylvia and I were headed toward the second level of the parking garage where my SUV was parked.

The game had officially started up again. I found exactly who I was looking for, and there was no chance in hell Sylvia would ever get away, especially after I confided in her that I worked at the university. As was the case with other women I abducted, after I rendered Sylvia unconscious, she woke up shackled to the end of a six-foot chain in my basement. Surprisingly, she lasted longer than any of the others. Three whole days. But true to form, Sylvia eventually opened her eyes, and when she did, I slit her throat and tossed her body in the water behind the lighthouse.

Murdering Sylvia without question satisfied my immediate need, but just like the case with drugs, I knew I would have to up the ante. And that's where RVPD's finest comes in. Detective Braxton Steele. It didn't take long for me to get in his head. Not only did I have him in a couple of my psychology courses over at the university, where I could keep tabs on him, but I would show up at his press conferences and then call him afterward to critique his performance. It couldn't have been more perfect.

Next, I abducted Jennifer and Samantha, murdering them both just like the others. And it felt good. I mean, think about it. I'd kill a woman then pick up the phone and dial the RVPD to discuss the case with the lead detective. It was better than sex!

So here goes. The murders I committed were all connected to a little game I was playing where women who matched simple criteria were selected to play along. It was really that simple. First, they had to be someone who wore red lipstick. Secondly, they had to somehow come in contact with specific locations that appear on the Oligopoly game board. The Seattle edition. That's it. By the way, in case you're wondering why the color red, you can thank Judith for that.

It happened when I was a kid. I pulled a tube of red lipstick from her purse and was goofing around with it. I drew on the bathroom *mirror. On the walls. I also put a little on my lips. She caught me, and for years after that, she'd come home smelling like alcohol and chase me around the house. And on those times she'd catch up with me, she'd pin me to the floor, then take her red lipstick, and smear it all over my face. If I tried to move, she'd slap me until I stopped squirming, and when she was finished, she'd laugh like it was the funniest thing in the world. To this day, I abhor the color red. In any event, anytime I saw a woman wearing red lipstick, I was reminded of Judith to the point that after murdering them, I took the time to cleanse their face of any trace resemblances.*

The next part has to do with Professor Stanley Milgram's obedience theory, which just so happened to underpin my dissertation when I received my PhD in psychology. Dr. Milgram sought to measure the willingness of study participants to obey an authority figure who instructed them to do things that were contrary to their personal conscience, such as cause pain to another person. In a bit of a twist to Dr. Milgram's theory, what I sought to measure in the study I conducted with the women I brought to the basement was whether they would obey my orders to keep their eyes closed forever. But unlike the sterile environment that was used in Dr. Milgram's study, anytime one of my study participants failed to obey my orders, I murdered them.

The last thing I will leave each of you with is the answer to the one question most pressing on your meager minds. Why? Why would someone just murder people with reckless abandon? Well, to be honest, I didn't.

There was a profound method to my, shall we say, madness? That was actually sort of clever, if I do say so myself, and so you know, I'm laughing my ass off as I type this part. Anyway, everything I did was strategic in nature. Carefully planned and executed with the utmost precision. So, no, there was nothing reckless about my actions. But enough about that. Here's your answer. The reason I did what I did was because I could. Nothing more, nothing less.

The End

9 780997 865110